"It's late. I should get going."

"Logan, you haven't been here twenty minutes yet," Maria protested.

"I can't last any longer without doing something, uh, stupid," he said, moving past her to leave her hotel room.

"What if I want you to do something stupid?" she whispered, closing the distance between them until he could smell her light flowery scent. She anchored her hands on his chest, stood on her tiptoes and put her mouth on his.

He didn't try to resist her. He couldn't, even if he'd wanted to. It had been almost a dozen years since they'd kissed, yet she tasted familiar. Their mouths nipped and suckled as though time had never passed.

Dear Reader,

I'm delighted to announce exciting news: beginning in January 2013, Harlequin Superromance books will be longer! That means more romance with more of the characters you love and expect from Harlequin Superromance.

We'll also be unveiling a brand-new look for our covers. These fresh, beautiful covers will showcase the six wonderful contemporary stories we publish each month. Turn to the back of this book for a sneak peek.

So don't miss out on your favorite series—Harlequin Superromance. Look for longer stories and exciting new covers starting December 18, 2012, wherever you buy books.

In the meantime, check out this month's reads:

#1818 THE SPIRIT OF CHRISTMAS
Liz Talley

#1819 THE TIME OF HER LIFE
Jeanie London

#1820 THE LONG WAY HOME
Cathryn Parry

#1821 CROSSING NEVADA
Jeannie Watt

#1822 WISH UPON A CHRISTMAS STAR
Darlene Gardner

#1823 ESPRESSO IN THE MORNING
Dorie Graham

Happy reading!

Wanda Ottewell,

Senior Editor, Harlequin Superromance

Wish Upon a Christmas Star

DARLENE GARDNER

HARLEQUIN®
entertain, enrich, inspire™

Recycling programs
for this product may
not exist in your area.

ISBN-13: 978-0-373-60746-4

WISH UPON A CHRISTMAS STAR

ABOUT THE AUTHOR

While working as a newspaper sportswriter, Darlene Gardner realized she'd rather make up quotes than rely on an athlete to say something interesting. So she quit her job and concentrated on a fiction career that landed her at Harlequin/Silhouette Books, where she wrote for the Temptation, Duets and Intimate Moments lines before finding a home at Harlequin Superromance. Please visit Darlene on the web at www.darlenegardner.com.

Books by Darlene Gardner

HARLEQUIN SUPERROMANCE

*Return to Indigo Springs

Other titles by this author available in ebook format.

To my sister Lynette Revill, the private investigator, for patiently answering my questions and for having such a cool profession.

And to the families of the victims of 9/11, especially the more than 1,000 victims whose remains weren't identified.

CHAPTER ONE

MARIA DIMARCO STARED DOWN at the photo of her once vibrant brother, then back up at the woman who'd broken Mike's heart when he'd been barely eighteen.

"Why would you come here out of the blue and show me this?" Maria asked, a bite to her voice.

The angry question had barely escaped her lips when she caught sight of the glittering gold star on top of the Christmas tree in the corner of her office. In the season of goodwill toward men, she needed to keep better hold of her temper.

"Why wouldn't I come to you?" Caroline Webb asked. "You're a private investigator."

Caroline had been waiting outside her office door at the strip mall on the outskirts of Lexington, Kentucky, when Maria returned from her appointments late that Monday afternoon. At first Maria hadn't been positive she recognized her. In a red coat that matched the stripes in the candy canes on the light poles and high-heeled black leather boots, Caroline looked more like a fashion model than the girl she remembered. Caroline had also lost weight, played down her Kentucky accent and was no longer a brunette but a blonde.

Maria handed back the photo. "Perhaps you'd better explain."

She shrugged out of her black pea coat and hung it on a hook next to the door. Bracing herself to talk about the brother who had died in the 9/11 terrorist attack, she flipped the switch that turned on the tree lights. The festive sight didn't stop the waves of sadness from washing over her.

"Can we sit down?" Caroline indicated the chairs flanking the desk at the back of the room. Perhaps she realized it would be tougher for Maria to get rid of her if she acted as though she'd come here with an appointment.

"After you," Maria said with a sweep of her hand.

Caroline took off her coat, too, revealing a long-sleeved green dress that hugged her slim figure. Above her left breast was a pin of a holly wreath, and she smelled of an expensive perfume. She took her time settling into one of the utilitarian chairs, then passed the photo over once more. Maria's black-haired, blue-eyed brother wasn't the only one in the picture. He had his left arm slung around a much-younger Caroline's shoulder. Mike was smiling. She was not.

"The photo's from senior year, a few days before Mike dropped out of high school and went to New York City." Caroline brushed her newly blond hair back from her face, calling attention to her expertly made-up eyes. "It came in the mail yesterday."

"Who sent it?" Maria asked.

"That's the thing. I don't know. There was no return address, no note." Caroline pulled something from the outside pocket of her leather handbag—Coach, as trendy as it was expensive—and held it out. "There was, however, a second photo."

The teenage Caroline was the only person pictured. It was a side view of her sitting on a bearskin rug beside a fireplace with her knees pulled to her chest, completely nude but with none of her private parts visible.

"Mike promised me he'd destroy that photo," she said, her voice a murmur.

"Obviously, he didn't." Maria couldn't imagine how the person who'd sent the photo had come into possession of it. However, she still didn't understand why Caroline was here. Did she want to hire Maria to make sure no other nude pictures of her surfaced? "Are there more?"

"No, just the one."

"As these kinds of photos go, this one's pretty mild," Maria said. "I suppose I could try to find out who sent it, but I don't see the point."

"I think I know who sent it," Caroline said, her voice steady. "I think it was Mike."

"What?" The word erupted from Maria. Pain lanced through her, strong enough to have felled her if she hadn't been sitting down. "You know that's impossible. Mike died at the World Trade Center."

Her visitor leaned forward in her chair, her gaze pinned to Maria's. "What if he didn't? What if he's still alive?"

Maria had clung tight to that hope after the terrorist attack. Mike had started working as a busboy at the Windows on the World restaurant only a few days before. She'd rationalized that he might not have shown up for work that day. As the days and the weeks and the months went by with no contact from him, however, she'd had to let go of the hope.

With as much calm as she could muster, she handed the two photos back. "I'd like you to leave now."

Caroline made no move to take them. "I

haven't even told you yet why I think they're from Mike."

Maria reached for the other woman's cool hand and pressed the photos into it. "Somebody sent you the pictures as a prank, Caroline. I assure you it wasn't my dead brother."

"It wasn't only the pictures," Caroline said. "Mike called me, too."

Maria shook her head. "You've got a lot of nerve, coming in here and lying to me like this, especially eight days before Christmas."

"It's not a lie!"

"Oh, no? What did Mike do? Leave a message on your voice mail that he wasn't dead, after all?"

"You don't have to be sarcastic," Caroline said.

But she did. Even though eleven years had passed, the pain of losing her brother was still so raw Maria could barely stand it when someone mentioned his name. Of all the DiMarcos, he'd been the most like her, in both looks and temperament. That hadn't always been a good thing.

"What would you have me do?" she asked.

"Hear me out," Caroline said. "Can you at least do that?"

Maria's law enforcement training kicked in. She'd been a dispatcher and a police officer before she'd become a private investigator. She knew not to discount anything, no matter how preposterous, before hearing the entire story. She nodded once.

"Thank you." Caroline took an audible breath. "I got the first call about a week ago on my apartment phone. It was a man. He said in this whispery voice, 'I miss you, Caroline.' I asked who it was. 'How could you forget me?' he said, and hung up."

It sounded like a classic prank, although more insensitive and cruel than most. "What came up on your caller ID?"

"It said Wireless Caller but didn't give a name or number," she said. "I only picked up because Austin was asleep and I didn't want the ringing to wake him."

Maria's eyes dipped to Caroline's ring finger. The overhead light glinted off a pear-shaped diamond that appeared about two carats in size.

"Austin's my fiancé," Caroline explained. "We're getting married on Valentine's Day."

Mike's impassioned voice insisting that Caroline would be his wife someday came to mind, along with her own, telling him he was being a fool. Maria couldn't bring herself to offer congratulations.

"Why did you leap to the conclusion the caller was Mike?" she asked.

"I didn't, not then," Caroline said. "After a

while, I even started to forget about it. But then Saturday, the day the photos arrived, I got another call. I probably shouldn't have picked up, but I couldn't stop myself. It was the same man. Again he told me he missed me."

"Is that all he said?" Maria asked.

Caroline shook her head, her teeth worrying the red lipstick off her bottom lip. "I demanded to know who it was. He said it was Mickey. And that's when I thought it really might be Mike."

"Mickey?" Maria repeated.

"We took a shortcut through an alley once when we were in downtown Lexington. A mouse darted out from behind a Dumpster and Mike screamed," Caroline said. "So I started calling him Mickey. You know, short for Mickey Mouse."

Maria refrained from saying she thought the nickname was mean-spirited. If she tallied up the transgressions Caroline had committed against Mike, that one might not even make the top five. Dumping him in the cafeteria in front of all his friends topped the list.

"I never heard anybody call him Mickey," Maria said.

"Nobody else did, only me, and only when we were alone," she stated. "You know how macho Mike was. He hated the nickname, because he didn't want anyone to know he was afraid of mice."

That sounded like Mike. He'd projected a tough-guy exterior that only those closest to him knew shielded a vulnerable heart. Maria could feel her own heart speeding up, thumping so hard she thought Caroline might hear it. "Are you sure nobody else knew about the nickname?"

"Positive."

Mike's remains had never been found. They'd never spoken to anyone who had seen him go into the World Trade Tower that day. They'd never buried him.

"Did the caller say anything else?" Maria asked.

"No," Caroline said. "He hung up. And Saturday I got the pictures in the mail, just like I told you."

Maria felt almost dizzy. That wouldn't do, not if she was going to get to the bottom of this. She tried to shut off her emotions and think like the private investigator she was. "Do you have the envelope the photos came in?"

"I do." Again Caroline dug into the side pocket of her handbag. "Here it is. And here's a printout of my phone record I got off the internet. I circled the two anonymous calls in red pen."

The envelope was plain and white, with what appeared to be a computer-generated typed address. Handwriting comparison, then, wasn't a possibility. There was no return address. The postmark was from last Wednesday in Key West, Florida.

Think, Maria, she commanded herself before looking back up at her visitor. "Does anyone you and Mike went to high school with live in Key West?"

"I don't think so," Caroline said.

Something to check out, Maria thought.

"How about Mike?" she asked. "Did he ever talk about going there?"

"I don't remember," Caroline said. "But I do remember the warmer the weather, the better he liked it."

That was true. Even during light snowfalls, about the only kind they got in Lexington, Mike had complained as though they were enduring blizzard conditions. The climate in Key West would appeal to him.

If he were alive. Oh, God, could her brother be alive?

Maria was holding Caroline's phone records. That was the place to start. She'd just finished a background check she was running for a client, leaving her free to unravel the mystery. She got up from the chair, went to her desk and picked up a pad and pen.

"After I look into where the phone calls came from, I'll be in touch," she said. "What's a number where I can reach you?"

Caroline crossed one long leg over the other. "I'd rather you didn't call me."

"Excuse me?"

"I'll contact you." She tapped a manicured finger against her lips. "Here's the thing. I don't want my fiancé to know about this. I don't want anything to interfere with the wedding."

"Why would it?"

"Austin's last name is Tolliver," she said. "His father, Samuel, is the former governor."

Caroline could have added that the family was rolling in cash. Maria seemed to remember the Tollivers had amassed their fortune from tobacco and horse racing. She recalled that Samuel Tolliver had provided the bulk of the financing for his campaign for governor.

"Austin's following in his father's footsteps. He's a state senator. This fall he's running for Congress. I can't take the risk the press will pick up on this story." For the third time, Caroline rummaged in her handbag. This time she pulled out a checkbook. "I can pay you."

To find her own brother? Maria's stomach turned over at the thought. "I don't want your money, Caroline." She was surprised her voice was even. "The question is, what do you want?"

"If Mike is alive," she said, her eyes narrowed and her lips pursed, "I just want him to leave me alone."

When Caroline was gone, Maria tried to call up the routine steps she took on missing person cases. She heard blood rushing in her ears. Her heart beat so fast she couldn't concentrate. After all this time, could Mike really be alive?

She got up from her chair and stepped outside, hoping the cool, fresh air would enable her to think more clearly. A chill ran through her and she hugged herself. At five-thirty, and almost the shortest day of year, it was already dark. A thin streak of light slashed through the sky.

A shooting star!

Shooting stars were magical, her mother had claimed when Maria was growing up. If you saw one before Christmas and wished upon it hard enough, she used to say, your wish would come true.

The only other time Maria had spotted a shooting star before the holidays, she'd wished for Rollerblades, and they'd appeared under the tree on Christmas morning.

What could it hurt?

She focused on the streaking light and wished with all her might.

LOGAN COLLIER LAID THE tall, bulky box containing the artificial Christmas tree against the stairs and positioned himself behind it.

"Need any help down there?" his mother called from the top of the steps.

"I've got it," he answered. "I just need you to move out of the way."

He shoved, inching the box a few steps at a time up the stairs until reaching the tile floor of the kitchen. Like the rest of the modest, two-bedroom house where his parents had lived for more than thirty years, the kitchen was big enough but just barely. It would be a tight squeeze to get the box past the table.

"Can you get it to the living room for me?" His mother was a warm, cheerful blonde who got way too into the spirit of the season. On her green sweatshirt, Santa jumped his reindeer-driven sleigh over a snowy rooftop.

Logan pushed, propelling the box across the tile floor, onto the carpeting in the living room and toward the spot where his mother always set up the tree. He'd been surprised not to see it decorated already when he'd come home last night from Manhattan, where he'd lived for the past twelve years since he'd graduated from college.

"Tell me again why we're putting up a tree two days before your trip." Logan wasn't out of breath, but neither was he breathing easy. He needed to take the time from his busy schedule to hit the gym more than just two or three times a week.

"We've got to make the most of what little time we have together, honey." She always called him that. In his early teens, it used to bug Logan until he'd found out she'd had two miscarriages before he was born and one afterward.

He ripped open the duct tape somebody— probably Dad—had used last year to bind the box, then pulled up the cardboard flaps to reveal the tree branches.

"You're trying to make me feel guilty about not spending Christmas with you and Dad, aren't you?" he asked.

"Maybe a little," his mother admitted.

"Not gonna work," Logan said. "Not when you'll both be cruising the Caribbean."

His parents would leave for the trip this Wednesday, six days before Christmas. Logan had made the travel arrangements to coincide with his own return to New York City.

"If you didn't feel guilty, honey, you wouldn't have bought us the tickets." Mom stood back while he set up the base of the tree and got the lower portion in place. "You don't have to keep treating us to trips, you know."

Actually, he did. Because his mother had battled diabetes and other health problems for years, his parents had made do on his father's salary while Logan was growing up. Dad earned enough as a forklift operator in a warehouse to cover necessities but not extras. In recent years Mom had been healthy enough to work part-time as a cashier at a grocery store, but Logan had a sense they still struggled.

"Don't take away my fun, Mom," he said. "I like treating you."

"Then I don't understand why you can't come with us," she retorted.

Logan got down on his knees and started plumping the branches. "I told you why. I have to work."

"You always have to work." She positioned herself beside him and grabbed a limb, shaping one of the flexible plastic branches to achieve maximum fullness.

"Dad's at work right now," he pointed out.

"Today is only December 17," she said. "Your father has Christmas week off like normal people."

"The holidays are a great time to network." Logan had been employed by a financial planning service in New York City ever since he'd moved there. He'd steadily climbed the ranks, in large part because he understood what it took to get ahead. "We've got a lot going on for our clients next week. Parties. Dinners. A suite at the Knicks game. I have to be there."

"I'm glad you have a good job," his mother began. Logan got ready for the "but," certain he already knew what she'd say.

"But don't you think you should spend your money on the woman you're going to marry instead of on me and Dad?" she finished.

He straightened, went to the box and withdrew more of the tree. He got another piece in place before answering. "That woman doesn't exist, Mom. I'm not engaged."

"You're thirty-three years old, honey. That's not so young anymore." She sounded as though she was breaking a difficult truth to him. "Are you at least dating someone?"

"Occasionally." He dated off and on, when he had the time, but rarely went out with a woman for more than two or three dates.

"Anyone special?" She asked the same questions every time he visited Kentucky or he flew her and Dad up to see him in New York. He was used to it by now. He even had a strategy to deflect the inquisition: say as little as possible.

"Nope," he said.

After a few moments of silence, his mother changed the subject. They talked companionably of inconsequential things for the next hour while they decorated the tree with the ornaments and lights Logan brought up from the basement.

After Logan topped the tree with the traditional gilded angel that had been handed down from his grandmother, they stood back and admired their handiwork. With the afternoon sun streaming through the picture windows in the living room, the tree's tiny white lights mimicked flakes of snow. His mother favored an artificial tree because of the risk of fire associated with a real one. Since she'd started putting pine-scented potpourri underneath the tree, he couldn't tell the difference.

"You'll never guess who I ran into the other day," his mother said conversationally, her voice sounding too innocent to be true. "Maria Di-Marco."

Yep. Logan was right. His mother had an agenda.

"Maria looked great. She's such a pretty girl, with that black hair, those blue eyes and the pale skin." His mom paused. When he said nothing, she added, "She's single again, you know."

That wasn't news to Logan. By his estimation, Maria had been divorced for four years and two months.

"Real subtle, Mom," he said wryly.

"But you haven't even brought home a girl to meet me since you and Maria broke up," she said.

"Maria and I were over in high school," he answered. "I haven't seen her in years."

More than eleven years, to be exact. The last time their paths had crossed was at Mike's memorial service. With her then-husband by her side, Maria hadn't said more than a few words to Logan. He hadn't expected her to, not when her brother wouldn't have been at the Windows on the World restaurant at all if it hadn't been for him. He was amazed that her sister, Annalise, still used him as an investment advisor.

"You two used to be so in love," his mother continued as if he hadn't spoken. "What would it hurt to see if the spark is still there?"

"Maria married somebody else," he reminded her.

"Only because she was confused. She wouldn't have even looked at another man if you hadn't—"

"Drop it, Mom," he interrupted, more sharply than he'd intended. It had taken him a long time to get over Maria DiMarco, but get over her he had. "I'm not going to see her."

"Not even though it's almost Christmas?" his mother asked in a small voice.

He knew without saying that she considered it a magical season when anything could happen. No doubt because she was always watching those sappy holiday movies on the Lifetime channel. Real life didn't work that way.

"Not even at Christmas," he said.

THE POUNDING ON THE locked door of her office sounded heavy enough to break the thick, tempered glass. Maria's head jerked up from her computer screen to make sure the closed sign was still in place. Beyond it, her older sister peered in at her.

Maria sucked in a breath through her teeth, not ready to deal with anyone in her family and itching to get back to her work. She'd just run her brother's social security number. Even though she hadn't been able to find any activity on it since 2001, there was more she could do. Using Google to search for his name and variations of his name, for starters. Followed by a thorough social networking investigation. If Maria pretended not to notice her, maybe Annalise would go away.

The pounding got louder.

"Okay, okay, I'm coming." She got up from her chair and crossed the office, deciding not to say anything to Annalise about Mike. Not until she had hard evidence that he was alive. She composed her features and unlocked the door.

Her sister pushed it open, barely giving Maria enough time to back away. A blast of chilled air followed Annalise inside, and she rubbed her bare hands together. She was dressed more for fashion than function, in the black leather jacket she'd gotten from her husband for her birthday a few weeks before.

"I was freezing to death out there." Her teeth were chattering. "For a minute I thought you weren't going to let me in."

"I was caught up in something, is all." Maria maneuvered past her and relocked the door.

"You're ready to go, though, right?" she asked. "I thought we could hit the electronics store before we go to the mall. That way, you can get your presents for Alex and Billy out of the way."

How could Maria have forgotten? Annalise had offered to help her pick out Christmas gifts for her teenage nephews. They'd also planned to search for presents for their parents, their brother Jack and his girlfriend, Tara, before ending the evening at Annalise's favorite restaurant.

Maria glanced back at the computer. Caroline Webb had left only forty-five minutes ago, not nearly enough time to make headway on finding out whether Mike could be alive. "I'm sorry, Annalise. I can't go, after all."

"Oh, no, you don't." She waved her index finger. "You don't get to back out after I went to the trouble of getting a babysitter and dressing up. I even put on makeup!"

Maria's naturally pretty sister always looked nice. She'd gone the extra mile tonight, letting her brown hair down from its usual ponytail and pairing her leather jacket with black dress slacks and heels instead of jeans and sneakers.

"I'm sorry," Maria said. "Something's come up and I need to work."

"This close to Christmas? You said you were taking some time off, like you always do over the holidays."

Maria glanced at the computer again. It seemed to be beckoning to her. Once she finished her searches, regardless of what she found, she intended to make an airline reservation to Florida.

"Things have changed," she said. "I have to go out of town for a few days."

"What? We have tickets tomorrow night to *The Nutcracker,*" Annalise protested. "And you said you'd help me out the rest of the week at the Christmas tree sale."

The yearly sale benefited her youngest son's

baseball league. Annalise was one of the organizers.

"You'll have to find someone else to take my place," Maria told her. "This is important."

"Where are you going?" Annalise demanded. It would have been difficult to tell that Maria was the only one in the room with training in interrogation. Then again, the two sisters were close. They never kept secrets from each other.

"Key West," Maria said.

"Florida? I don't ever remember you going that far for a case before," Annalise said. "You'll be back in time for Christmas, right?"

She hesitated. "I don't know."

Her sister narrowed her eyes, propped her hands on her hips and demanded, "What's going on?"

Maria's instincts told her to remain mum. However, that wasn't realistic. If Annalise was reacting this badly to her possible absence at Christmas, other family members would, too. Maria needed somebody to smooth the waters and support her alibi.

"You'd better sit down," she said.

"I don't want to sit down."

"Then promise you won't freak out."

"You're freaking me out by acting like this," Annalise declared. "Just spit it out."

Maria forced the words through her lips. "I think Mike might still be alive."

Her sister shook her head. "No, he's not. Why would you even say something like that?"

As succinctly as she could, Maria relayed the details of the visit from Caroline Webb. Annalise listened in silence, her expression giving nothing away even though she'd always been the most demonstrative of the four siblings.

"Say something," Maria said when she'd finished.

"I'm thinking about how to phrase it." Annalise scratched her head. "On second thought, to hell with tact. I'll tell you how I really feel. I can't believe you even let Caroline in the front door. Don't you remember how she treated Mike?"

"Caroline's not a high school kid anymore, Annalise," Maria said. "She's almost thirty years old."

"Once a mean girl, always a mean girl," her sister said heatedly. "Mike never would have dropped out of school if she hadn't broken up with him in front of all their friends."

One of the cafeteria workers had later provided their family with the details. Caroline had been cruel, saying she was sick of Mike and adding that he was worthless and stupid. She claimed she already had someone waiting in the wings to take her to the approaching home-coming dance.

Her words had hit the mark. Mike had rushed out of the school building and sped home, side-swiping a parked car on the way. Then he'd had another argument. With Maria.

Afterward, he'd packed a bag and split. Nobody had known where he was until Logan Collier called a few days later from New York City to say Mike was staying at his apartment.

"We don't know that Mike wouldn't have dropped out of school, Annalise," Maria said. "His grades were so bad he barely made it through junior year. Remember how much trouble Mom and Dad had with him?"

"Most of that was because of Caroline," Annalise said. "If I remember correctly, you thought so, too."

Maria couldn't dispute that. Over the years, however, she'd come to realize there were many factors in Mike's disconnect from the family. That included Maria making it crystal clear she'd disapproved of his girlfriend.

"That's water under the bridge," she said. "The important thing now is to find out if Mike's the one who's been in contact with Caroline."

"You said you were doing some online searches

when I got here. You ran Mike's social security number, right? Did anything come up?"

"Well, no," Maria said. "But nothing would show up if he's using an alias."

"An alias?" her sister exclaimed. She shook her head and came forward, laying a hand on Maria's arm. "Listen to me carefully, Maria. Mike's dead. You know as well as I do that nobody in the restaurant survived that day."

The hijacked plane had hit the North Tower a few stories below the Windows on the World complex. The official report was that all the restaurant customers and employees survived the initial attack, only to find the pathways that led below blocked by the impact zone. Everybody died, either of smoke inhalation or in the collapse of the building.

"Mike didn't call any of us after the plane hit," Maria said. "What if that was because he wasn't there?"

"Oh, sweetie. Lots of other reasons make more sense. His phone might have been dead. Or maybe he was looking for a way out and couldn't take the time to call."

"His remains were never identified," Maria reminded her.

"Neither were the remains of more than a thousand other people. That's about forty percent of the victims," Annalise said. "The authorities did the best they could, but it was an impossible task."

"So we can't completely rule out that Mike wasn't at the restaurant that day," Maria said.

"Yes, we can," she insisted. "If he were alive, wouldn't he have contacted us in the last eleven years to let us know?"

"I admit that part doesn't make sense, but Mike was angry at the world when he left for New York. He wasn't getting along with any of us." Maria could tell that her arguments weren't swaying her sister. She tried another tactic. "Don't you want to know what I found out about the phone number?"

"Sure." Annalise didn't sound optimistic.

"The calls came from a prepaid phone, as if whoever made them doesn't want to be found," Maria said. "He must be in Key West, though. That's where the envelope was postmarked."

"I'll admit the entire situation is strange," Annalise said slowly, "but Mike didn't make those calls or send those photos."

"Then who did?" Maria asked. "It seems out of character for Mike to have given that nude photo of Caroline away."

"C'mon, Maria. Someone else might be behind this."

"Maybe," she conceded, "but I think it's worth looking into the possibility it might be Mike."

Annalise held up a finger and got her cell phone out of her purse. She appeared to be scrolling through a list of numbers before she pushed one.

"Hey, this is Annalise," she said after a moment and turned away, walking to the other end of the room so it was harder for Maria to hear her.

That was fine with Maria. She already guessed that her sister had Jack on the line. Their surviving brother had moved to Virginia's Eastern Shore earlier in the year to be with his girlfriend. Maria suspected Annalise was trying to enlist Jack's help in convincing her she was wasting her time. A part of her didn't blame her sister for trying to protect her. If Maria raised her hopes too high and came up with nothing, it would be like losing Mike all over again. But if she found him...

She went back to the computer and entered her brother's name in a search engine. She got quite a few hits, each one of which she'd need to check out. Figuring there was no point to delay in making her airline reservation, she called up another tab and went to a travel site.

"Promise me something." Annalise suddenly stood beside her, looking over her shoulder at the computer screen. Maria hadn't even realized her sister had gotten off the phone. "Promise me you won't make that reservation until you talk to him."

Annalise's eyes looked tortured. She'd lost a brother, too, Maria reminded herself. All three of them had. If Annalise wanted her to talk to Jack before she started her investigation, it was the least she could do.

"I promise," she said. "I won't make the reservation until I talk to Jack."

"Jack?" Annalise shook her head. "That wasn't Jack on the phone. It was Logan Collier."

CHAPTER TWO

Logan spotted Annalise DiMarco the instant he entered the noisy Italian restaurant, which was decorated for the holidays with strung holly and tiny white lights.

He barely had time to breathe in the scents of spicy tomato sauce and baked bread before she sprang to her feet. After pausing to say something to her dining companion, a black-haired woman with her back to the door—who had to be Maria—rushed to his side.

"Hey, Annalise." Logan leaned down to kiss her cheek. He'd barely connected when she grabbed his arm and dragged him off to the side of the hostess stand, nearer the exit and the coat rack.

"Hey, Logan," she said conversationally, as though she hadn't just hijacked him. "Thanks for coming."

Annalise had the dark hair and light eyes common to the DiMarcos, except her hair was brown and her eyes green. The oldest sibling, she was also the only one with children. With

Logan's help, she and her husband had invested wisely enough that they should be able to fulfill their goal of paying for their two sons' college educations.

"For a minute there I thought you were going to push me out the door." He would have gone through it eagerly if Annalise had changed her mind about what she'd asked of him.

"Nothing like that," she said. "I was getting you out of Maria's field of vision. You know, in case she turns around to see if I really went to the restroom."

He groaned. "I thought Maria knew that I was meeting both of you here."

Annalise shook her head. "Not exactly. You know how I called and asked if you needed directions to the restaurant?"

"Yeah." He'd thought that was odd considering Donatelli's had occupied the same location for twenty years.

"I was supposed to tell you not to come. Maria practically ordered me."

"Ordered you? That doesn't sound good."

"It's not good," she confessed. "Her exact words were something like, 'No way in hell am I talking to him.'"

Logan winced. He should have anticipated that. The days were long gone when Maria would jump into his arms and kiss him whenever more than twenty-four hours went by without them seeing each other.

"Don't let it bother you," Annalise said. "Maria doesn't want to talk to me about this, either. She hasn't changed, you know. She's still hardheaded when she makes up her mind about something."

Logan cleared his throat, preparing to ask the question that had been uppermost in his mind since Annalise had phoned him. "Does she really believe Mike's alive?"

His voice broke on Mike's name. Logan hadn't spoken the youngest DiMarco's name aloud in years. He'd thought about him, though, especially when the anniversary of 9/11 rolled around. On those dates, Logan was consumed by memories of Mike DiMarco.

A teenage couple entered the restaurant hand in hand, their eyes locked on each other, the corners of their mouths lifted in smiles. It wasn't only the girl's long, straight black hair that reminded Logan of Maria. It was the way she looked at her boyfriend.

"She's a private investigator," Annalise said. "She has to know there could be another explanation. And the way she was talking, it sounds like she's leaning that way."

He nodded once, fully understanding why Annalise had phoned him. Mike DiMarco was dead. Period. Nothing but pain lay ahead for Maria if she let herself believe otherwise.

"Okay. I'll do my best to convince her she's on the wrong track." He swept a hand to indicate Annalise should precede him into the dining room, where the young couple was following a hostess to a table. "Let's get on with it."

"Oh, I'm not going back in there." Annalise walked past him to the coat rack and rummaged through a number of winter garments before pulling out a black leather one. "I left my jacket over here so I could sneak out."

Everything inside Logan went still. "Maria won't like that."

"Maria hasn't liked anything I've said to her for the past hour," her sister said. "She wouldn't have come to dinner if she hadn't promised to treat me. If I stay, it'll seem like we're ganging up on her."

"If you go," Logan said slowly, "I won't like it, either."

"Thanks for coming to help out," Annalise said, shrugging into her jacket, which looked too thin to keep her warm. She headed for the exit but turned before she reached it. "Almost forgot to tell you, I drove. Maria's car is at her office. You can take her back, right? Thanks!"

She whirled and fled, leaving Logan to gather

his courage for a conversation he should have had in the aftermath of the terrorist attack.

There was something about that day he'd never told anybody, something that had been eating at him ever since.

If the information would help Maria, it was time he got it off his chest, even if it made her dislike him more than she already did.

ANNALISE WAS TAKING AN awfully long time in the restroom. If Maria had insisted on them both driving, she could have jotted down an apology on a napkin and sneaked out.

She regretted coming to dinner at all. She itched to be at the computer, squaring away her flight, or on the phone working the case instead of listening to Annalise tell her not to go to Key West.

At least she'd gotten it through her sister's thick skull that she had no intention of meeting with Logan Collier.

The text tone on her cell phone buzzed. She rummaged through her voluminous leather purse on her lap, annoyed at herself for not putting the phone in the zippered compartment. The text was from Annalise and consisted of one word: Sorry.

"Hello, Maria."

Logan. She jerked her gaze from her sister's

apologetic text to the man she'd once loved with her whole heart. The breath left her, exactly as if she'd been punched in the stomach.

He wasn't quite six feet tall yet seemed taller because of his excellent posture. He was nearly as lean as he'd been as a teenager but more muscular. His thick brown hair was shorter, although it still sprang back from his forehead and the strands at his nape still curled. Age lent his regular features character and added fine lines that bracketed the hazel eyes she'd always thought were so pretty.

Maria had to consciously tell herself to stop staring and start breathing again. "Hello, Logan."

"Mind if I join you?" He nodded to the chair Annalise had vacated after their waitress had cleared away the dinner dishes. Despite the apologetic text, Maria didn't want to believe her sister had cut out on her.

"Annalise is sitting there," she said.

"Was sitting there," he corrected. "She's gone."

"I can't believe it." Maria shook her head as it sank in that her sister had abandoned her. "I told her I didn't want to talk to you."

"For the record, I thought you knew I was coming." He indicated the chair again. "So can I sit down? You might want to say yes, because I'm your ride."

Maria's pulse skittered. It was all her sister's fault. Annalise was going to pay.

"By all means." She worked on composing herself while he took off his black wool car coat. Underneath he wore a burgundy long-sleeved shirt that made him appear vibrant and engaging. He settled across from her.

Before either of them could say a word, their young blonde waitress arrived with two cups of coffee and two slices of chocolate cheesecake. Annalise had remarked earlier in the evening that the girl looked as if she was having a bad day. Not anymore. A smile stretched across her pretty face.

"Well, hello there," she said to Logan. "You must have just arrived. I couldn't have missed you."

"You're right. I just got here." One corner of Logan's mouth lifted in a way that used to make Maria melt when they were teenagers.

The half smile appeared to have the same effect on the waitress. It had been that way in the old days, too. Females found Logan attractive. Maria had always thought it was because he didn't seem to realize exactly how good-looking he was.

"My sister left," Maria announced to get the waitress's attention. "We won't be having dessert and coffee, after all."

"Are you sure?" She tilted her head and chewed her bottom lip. "I'm not certain I can take them back. You did order them."

"Then just leave everything on the table," Logan said. "We'll be here for a little while longer."

"Great!" Her enthusiasm was out of proportion to the situation. "Hope you enjoy!"

"Didn't mean to step on your toes there, but she doesn't seem real experienced," he said when the waitress was gone. "Besides, I can always go for a piece of cheesecake."

He'd always had a sweet tooth. In high school, when they were dating, Maria used to make it a point to have home-baked chocolate chip cookies on hand when they studied together at her house.

"By all means, dig in," she said.

He took a bite of cheesecake, and her eyes arrowed straight to his mouth. With lips that were slightly full for a man's, he had a gorgeous one. She shifted in her seat, feeling decidedly uncomfortable. They hadn't been alone since they'd broken up, senior year of high school. In all that time, she'd seen him only once, at her brother's memorial service. If, that is, she didn't count the time she'd spotted him at the mall and ducked into a children's clothing store to avoid him.

"How long are you home for?" she asked.

"Just a few days." He'd never had much of an accent—most people who lived in the Lexington area didn't—but any trace of Kentucky in his speech was entirely gone. "My parents are leaving for a cruise on Wednesday and I've got to get back to work."

Ah, work. It defined him. If not for his insistence on going out of state to the University of Michigan to get a master's degree in business so he could make the almighty buck, they'd still be together.

She'd wanted him to stick closer to home—and to her—by pursuing his dream of becoming a painter at an art school in Louisville. They could have moved into an apartment together, with Maria getting a job that would have paid the rent.

He'd called her proposal too risky, refusing to consider art school and declaring that he needed to be financially secure before he'd live with anyone.

The fact that he hadn't loved her enough to take a chance on them still stung.

"Are you at the same firm in New York?" She didn't know why she asked when she already knew the answer. The financial giant had hired Logan right out of college, where he'd managed to get both his bachelor's degree and MBA in four years. If he'd changed jobs, Annalise would have mentioned it. She and her husband still used Logan to manage their finances. Since the firm where he worked was such a powerhouse, Maria was sure Logan kept them on as a favor.

"The same one," he answered.

"And still conscientious, I see." Maria couldn't hold back the rest of her thought. "You're rushing to get back to work when most other people are going on holiday."

His shoulders stiffened. "It's a good job."

"I'm happy for you, then." She wanted to know if he was still painting, except that was another volatile topic of discussion. Better to leave it be.

"How are things with you?" he asked.

"Can't complain." She picked up her fork, then put it down. She'd barely been able to choke down dinner. She wouldn't be able to eat the dessert Annalise had talked her into ordering. "I quit the police force four years ago to go into private investigation. I'm a one-woman show, but I like it that way."

"I heard you got divorced," he said.

She was probably imagining the edge to his voice. He hadn't cared enough to hang on to her, so why would her ex-husband be a sensitive subject?

"That was a while back," she said. Before

she'd left the sheriff's office but after she'd made the decision to quit. "We weren't a good match."

Logan nodded, saying nothing, and added two creams and two sugars to his coffee.

"How's the family?" he asked before he took a swig.

She avoided looking at his mouth, determined not to get sidetracked. "Everybody's good. You keep up with Annalise. My parents are still working, and Jack's going back to school to work with developmentally disabled kids. I think he'll be engaged soon."

"Glad to hear it." Logan licked a drop of coffee from his lower lip. He put down the cup and rested his wrists on the table. "Do they know you think Mike might still be alive?"

The conversation and background music that had created a constant hum since she'd arrived at Donatelli's Restaurant seemed to fade. Her ears rang with the question. No way could she avoid the subject any longer.

"No," she stated. "I thought it would be better not to say anything until I know something definite."

"Why's that?"

"It's pretty obvious. Losing Mike was hard enough the first time. I don't want them to have to go through that pain again."

"That's why I agreed to talk to you when Annalise called." Logan leaned forward slightly, pinning her with his gaze. "Mike's dead, Maria."

She dragged her eyes away from the certainty in his. "How much do you know about what's going on?"

"I only know what Annalise told me," he said.

"Then I'll fill you in." Once she shared the details, maybe both Logan and Annalise would leave her alone to conduct her investigation. She relayed the day's events, omitting nothing.

He listened in silence with his arms crossed over his chest. When she was through talking, he released a harsh breath. "Someone's playing a sick joke. But it's not Mike."

"How can you possibly be sure of that?" Maria snapped.

"I already told you," Logan said. "Mike's dead, Maria. He died on 9/11. You've got to accept that."

"Did you personally witness him going inside the World Trade Tower that day?" she asked.

"No, but I talked to him that morning. He was up early because he was working the breakfast shift."

She picked up a thin wooden stick and stirred her coffee, watching the circular pattern as she thought about what Logan had said. Finally, she looked up to find his hazel eyes trained on her.

"What if he didn't go to work that day?" she asked, the idea gaining momentum. "Mike never could stick to anything. He quit a ton of summer jobs for one reason or another."

"Okay, let's go with that," Logan said. "Then why didn't he come back to my apartment and get his things? Why didn't he let anybody know he was alive?"

Very good questions, Maria thought. "That's what I'm going to find out."

"Listen to yourself," Logan argued. "You sound like you've already convinced yourself he's alive."

"I'm a private investigator," she said. "I know enough not to jump to conclusions before I have proof."

"You'll never find proof, Maria. I know you want to believe Mike's out there somewhere. Hell, I'd like to believe it, too. But he died that day." Logan ran a hand over his mouth, a gesture that used to mean he was upset. His brows drew together. "There's something I need to tell you."

She was almost afraid to hear it. This time she was the one who crossed her arms over her chest. "What?"

He pursed his lips and blew a breath out through his nose. "You know I was the one who got Mike the job at Windows on the World?"

Maria nodded. Logan had also given her brother a place to stay in Manhattan. At first she had been angry about that. She'd told her parents that Mike might have come home if Logan hadn't let him sleep on his sofa. Her folks had countered that Mike might just as likely have lived on the streets.

"He didn't much like being a busboy," Logan said. "The morning the towers fell, he talked about quitting."

"I knew it!" Maria cried.

"Hold on." Logan put up a hand. "I hadn't charged him anything up to that point. I told him he needed to help with rent."

"So he was going to quit," Maria said, her mind spinning. This revelation made it more likely that Mike was alive.

"You're not hearing me," Logan said. "He couldn't help with the rent if he was unemployed. I told him he needed to keep the busboy job until he found another one. I talked him into going to work that day."

"You don't know that," Maria retorted. "Mike was bullheaded. If he wanted to quit, he would have."

"I don't think so," Logan said. "Even if that's true, he would have gone in to work and given notice."

"Not if he phoned," Maria said. Something

else occurred to her. "Maybe he didn't feel any loyalty to the people there. Maybe he just didn't show up."

Logan shook his head. "You're grasping at straws. No way would Mike let your family believe he was dead."

"He dropped out of high school and ran away from home, Logan," she said. "He was on the outs with us."

"He wasn't a vindictive kid," Logan said.

"He was a rebellious one," Maria countered. "My parents caught him drinking or skipping school or staying out all night lots of times. He wanted to do his own thing without getting hassled."

"It's one thing to be rebellious," Logan said. "It's another to let your family go through the heartache of believing you're dead."

Logan probably thought he sounded like the voice of reason. It wouldn't do any good to tell him she couldn't rest until she'd eliminated any chance that Mike was alive. Logan was just as closed-minded as always. If he'd been able to open his mind to possibilities, they'd be married right now.

"I hadn't looked at it from that perspective." She pretended to look thoughtful. She had to wrench the next words from her mouth. "Perhaps you're right."

His mouth dropped open. He closed it and let out a heavy breath. "Believe me, that doesn't bring me any happiness."

She nodded.

"What are you going to do now?" he asked.

"What do you think I should do?"

"You should drop it," he said. "It's a cruel trick that isn't worth your time."

Maria tried to look pensive. "You're probably right."

"So you're not going to Key West?"

"What would be the point?" She put her credit card inside the leather billfold the waitress had dropped by their table, and rose. "Would you excuse me for a minute?"

He hesitated only a moment before answering. "Sure."

On the way to the restroom, Maria stopped at the hostess stand and placed a request. Within minutes, she rejoined Logan. Her credit card was on the table, but nothing else.

"Didn't the waitress bring me a receipt?" she asked.

Logan said, "I switched out our credit cards and went ahead and paid the bill."

"Nobody asked you to do that," she said.

"I wanted to."

Because he was flaunting what a success he'd made of himself? Even as the thought came into her head, she knew it wasn't true. Logan had always been generous with what he had, even when he was a broke high school kid.

"Thank you," she managed to say. "We should go. You won't be in town long. I don't want to keep you from your family."

"My parents like you," Logan said. "They won't mind waiting while I drive you back to your office."

"They won't have to wait," Maria said on the way to the coat rack. He helped her on with her coat, brushing against her in the process. A shiver ran the length of her body.

"Oh?" he said. "Why's that?"

She pointed through the glass doors to where a taxi idled at the curb. "I had the hostess call a cab."

He looked wounded. "I would have driven you."

"I know," she said. "Have a nice Christmas, Logan."

"You, too," he said.

She pushed open the doors and hurried to the cab, forcing herself not to turn around for a final glance at him. When she closed the taxi door behind her, she felt as though she were shutting out a past that included Logan. Once upon a time, she never could have fooled him with that guileless act. The fact that she had done so proved they'd become strangers.

She choked back a sob. Now was not the time to let herself get teary over the way she and Logan used to be. She needed to concentrate on finding out whether or not her brother was alive.

EARLY THE NEXT AFTERNOON Maria drove over the Seven Mile Bridge that led to the Lower Keys. Her flight had landed in Miami almost three hours earlier. Flying into the major city had saved her hundreds in plane fare. Even with the cost of the rental car, she was still ahead of the game had she flown into Key West.

She'd expected the hundred-and-fifty-five-mile drive to go more quickly. How was she to know that the scenic route through the Florida Keys would be a two-lane road, with cars clogging traffic whenever they entered or left the highway?

If not for occasional holiday decorations on shops and houses, it wouldn't seem a bit like Christmas. Long stretches of the Overseas Highway were flanked by shimmering blue water on both sides, sometimes dotted with sprawling areas of emerald-green. When she'd stopped for gas, the cashier had told her the green patches marked sea grass beds and shallow reefs.

The Seven Mile Bridge, which spanned a channel linking the Atlantic Ocean and the Gulf of Mexico, was the most beautiful part of the drive yet. Seabirds soared through the clear sky, boats traversed the water and people fished from an old bridge, parallel to the new one, that was missing a piece in the middle.

Lexington and Logan Collier seemed very far away.

Maria was still irked at Annalise for calling Logan. It was crazy, but the old hurts had resurfaced as she'd sat across from him in the restaurant. Never mind that she'd been married and divorced since she'd been with Logan. She still felt like that girl who'd bared her heart and been rejected.

She'd almost convinced herself it would be okay not to inform Annalise that she was going to Key West. Almost, but not quite. After 9/11, the entire DiMarco family, Maria included, kept close tabs on each other.

She'd taken the coward's way out, though, sending a text instead of phoning. Predictably, Annalise had responded by calling her cell. Maria hadn't answered. She had more important uses for her mental energy than arguing with her sister.

She was already operating on a lack of sleep. Last night when she'd gotten home from the restaurant, she'd spent hours on the computer. She hadn't been able to locate the right Mike DiMarco on any social network sites or find mention of him or Key West on the pages of his high school friends.

Every classmate she'd tried had a Facebook page except Billy Tillman, who'd been tight with Mike since grade school. She'd called Billy's mother in an attempt to track him down. As Maria left the bridge for one of the string of islands that made up the Keys, she mentally replayed part of the conversation she'd had with Julia Tillman.

"Key West?" the woman had exclaimed. "Why would Billy be in Key West?"

"That's what I'm asking you, Mrs. Tillman," Maria said. "Has Billy ever talked about Key West?"

"I already told you. Billy's in San Francisco. He moved there a few years ago."

"Did he ever mention if any of his friends lived in Key West or vacationed there?" Maria asked.

"No. Never," she said. "Who did you say you were again?"

"Mike DiMarco's sister."

"Mike? The poor boy who died on 9/11? That Mike?"

Maria had to stop herself from telling the

older woman reports of her brother's death may have been exaggerated. "That Mike."

"Such a tragedy, that was. My Billy was torn up about it."

"We all were, Mrs. Tillman," Maria said and asked for her son's cell phone number. Mrs. Tillman didn't have it handy. Once she promised she'd have Billy call, Maria rang off before Mrs. Tillman could ask any more questions.

Maria didn't want to explain about the phone call and photos Caroline Webb had received. She couldn't listen to anyone else telling her how unlikely it was that her brother was behind them.

If even the ghost of a chance existed that Mike was alive, she needed to investigate. Admittedly, an envelope with a Key West postmark wasn't a lot to go on. But until Maria scoured every inch of Key West and determined that her brother wasn't on the island, she wasn't ready to concede anything.

The task didn't seem terribly daunting. The island was roughly four miles long and two miles wide, with hotels, shops and restaurants packed close together. She should be able to cover a lot of territory in a short amount of time.

Her first inkling that finding someone on the small island might not be that easy came thirty minutes later. She'd booked a hotel on the far side of the island. The traffic en route was bumper to bumper.

A pale pink, two-story building with a circular entranceway flanked by tall palm trees caught her eye while she waited behind a line of cars at a red light. The police station. An excellent place to start her search.

She pulled into the parking lot and minutes later walked into the empty reception area. A burly middle-aged officer with a full head of white hair manned the counter. His name tag read Sergeant Pepper. She did a double take. No, it was Sergeant *Peppler*. He gazed at her expectantly, a bored expression on his face.

"My name's Maria DiMarco," she announced. "Is there somebody I can talk to about a missing person?"

The sergeant perked up. "You can talk to me."

Maria knew how the police worked. He wouldn't hook her up with a detective unless he thought her story had merit. It wouldn't hurt to get him on her side.

"I used to be on the force, too," she said. "In Kentucky. The Fayette County Sheriff's Department."

"Oh, yeah?" He stroked a beard as white as his hair. With his coloring, he could probably get a second job masquerading as Santa. "What do you do now?"

It figured he would focus on the wrong part of her revelation. "I'm a private investigator."

Sergeant Peppler snorted. In Maria's experience, only about fifty percent of the cops she ran across had a full appreciation of the profession she'd chosen. The other half acted as though P.I.s existed to interfere with police investigations.

"So this missing person," Peppler said, eyes narrowed, "it's for a case you're working?"

"Not exactly." She reached into her purse, dug out a computer-generated age progression of her brother and set it on the counter. She'd gotten the image off a generic website that instantly aged people in uploaded photos. "I'm looking for my brother."

The cop raised an eyebrow. "This is an age progression. How long has he been missing?"

She'd rather not tell him but couldn't avoid his direct question. "Eleven years." She fired the next questions. "Does he look familiar? Have you seen him?"

"No." Peppler shoved the paper back at her. "Sorry. Can't help you."

"That's it? You don't want to know why I think my brother is in Key West?"

"Lady, I'm sure you're aware of how police departments operate," he said. "It's the start of the high season for us. That means crowds and

lots and lots of tourists. We don't have the resources to devote to someone who's been missing for eleven years."

"Could you at least see if he's in your database? I think he might have lived here for a
while." Maria had nothing concrete to back up
that theory. It stood to reason, though, that Key
West's remote location made it a good place if
you wanted to fly under the radar.

The tired look came back into Peppler's eyes.
His mouth was set, as though he was about to
refuse. Then he shrugged his broad shoulders.
"If it'll get you out of here, sure. What's his
name?"

"Mike DiMarco." She spelled out the last
name and provided her brother's date of birth
and social security number. Even though she'd
already run Mike's particulars through some
national databases, she couldn't trust that the
information was one hundred percent accurate.
To be thorough, it didn't hurt to check local
channels.

The sergeant held up a finger, went to a
nearby computer and typed in the information.
While he was busy, a woman with a black eye
came into the station and got in line behind
Maria. A minute later, Peppler was back at the
counter.

"I'll be with you in a minute," he told the

woman. To Maria, he said, "Nope. Nothing on anybody named DiMarco."

Just as she had suspected. She'd all but established that he'd have to be using an assumed identity. "He could be going by another name."

"What name?"

She chewed her bottom lip. "I'm not sure."

"Okay, I'll bite." Peppler rested both forearms on the counter. "Why do you think your brother is in Key West under an alias?"

She knew better than to tell him everything. "Mike's ex-girlfriend got an envelope of photos that appeared to be from him. It had a Key West postmark."

"Appeared to be?" Peppler picked up on the operative words.

"I misspoke," Maria said, annoyed at herself for planting the seed of doubt in Peppler's mind. If Mike was in Key West, she'd never find him if she didn't put a positive spin on things. "The photos *were* from Mike."

The woman behind her made an interested noise, not bothering to hide the fact that she was eavesdropping.

A crease appeared between the sergeant's white eyebrows. "Just because he mailed the photos from Key West doesn't mean he's in Key West."

Maria couldn't argue with that conclusion. She'd arrived at the same one a short time ago.

"I'm exploring the possibility," she said. "Perhaps you could direct me to somebody local who knows everybody."

"You're looking at him," he said. "I've lived in Key West all my life and been a cop for twenty-five years. You'll be wasting your time talking to other locals."

"I'm a native, too, and I've never seen him before." The comment came from the lady behind Maria, who was peering over her shoulder.

"He could be a tourist." The sergeant tapped the photo. "Problem is your brother might not look like this. He might have gained weight. He could have a beard. Or long hair. Hell, maybe he even shaved his head."

Earlier in the year Maria had worked on a child abduction case in which an age progression played a key part. Thirty years after the kidnapping, the victim bore a remarkable resemblance to the aged image.

"Or maybe Mike looks just like this." She didn't see any point in prolonging her stay at the police station. Sergeant Peppler wasn't going to provide any information that would help her. She got out a business card and set it on the counter next to the age progression. "Could you keep this and show it around to the other officers? If anyone recognizes him, I'd appreciate a call."

"Don't expect one," the officer said. "People come and go in Key West. Even if that age progression is the spitting image of your brother, he might not look familiar to anybody."

Maria left the police station, spotted a branch of the Key West post office and swung in. She didn't have any better luck there. After checking into a slightly run-down hotel that had appeared a lot nicer on its website, she pounded the pavement in the tourist district, flashing a copy of the age progression at anyone who agreed to take a look. By the time she got back to her hotel at midnight, she was fighting frustration.

Unbidden, Logan's voice filled her head.

"Mike's dead, Maria. He died on 9/11. You've got to accept that."

She'd accepted a lot of disappointment in her life, including Logan's refusal to take a chance on her when they were both eighteen. She'd be damned if she'd accept this.

CHAPTER THREE

THE LOUISVILLE INTERNATIONAL Airport buzzed with activity. Travelers walked quickly along the moving walkway that connected the two concourses, some arriving, others departing, all of them in a hurry. It seemed as if Christmas was hours instead of six days away. A tinny voice over the loudspeaker issued a periodic reminder not to leave bags unattended.

Logan and his parents had gone through the security checkpoint together, since he'd thought to book early morning flights that departed within thirty minutes of each other. The planes didn't leave from the same concourse, though. When the walkway ended, Logan moved off to the side to get out of the way of other passengers. His parents did the same.

"This is where we part," Logan said. "I hope you both have a fantastic time on the cruise."

His mother sniffed, her eyes dewy with unshed tears. In her red coat, black pants and black shoe boots, she was dressed for winter in Lexington instead of in the tropics. "I still wish you were coming with us."

"Boy's gotta work, Celeste." His father slung an arm around her and kissed the side of her head. He was gruff with most people but treated his wife like gold. "Guy I work with, his thirty-five-year-old son lives in the basement."

"Logan's only thirty-three," his mother countered. "And I never said I wanted him to live in our basement."

"Basements aren't for me, anyway," Logan said, attempting to lighten the mood. "We New York types prefer lofts."

"But you're not a New York type," his mother protested. "Not really. You love Kentucky. You've always loved it. Don't you think it's past time you moved home?"

"Celeste, I thought you weren't going to bring this up," his father said.

"I can't help it," she answered. "You tell me not to make waves about it when Logan's home because he's here for such a short time. But it's not the kind of thing to discuss over the phone."

"Whoa," Logan said. "Where's this coming from? I'm happy in New York."

"You wouldn't have moved there in the first place if Maria DiMarco hadn't married someone else," his mother said.

Logan sucked in a breath that felt jagged

going down. His mother was right. When he was in college, he'd fully expected he and Maria would get back together again someday. Finding out she'd gotten married had come as a vicious blow. In that instant, he'd decided to look for a job outside Kentucky.

His father removed his arm from his mother's shoulder and gazed at her with rare disapproval. "Celeste, what are you doing?"

"Saying what I should have said a long time ago." She took Logan's elbow. "I think it's time you and Maria put the past behind you."

"You're way off base about this, Mom," Logan said. "My living in New York has nothing to do with her."

It had nothing to do with Maria *now*, a voice in his head clarified. When he'd graduated from college, the state hadn't been big enough for him to risk running into her and her new husband.

"If you'd seen her when you were home, you could have wiped the slate clean," his mother said. "You'd either have feelings for her or you wouldn't."

Last night Logan had told his parents he was meeting friends for a drink. Now he was glad he hadn't mentioned Maria by name. He wasn't up for a postmortem session discussing his feelings.

"Maria and I were over a long time ago, Mom," Logan insisted.

Then why did he feel as if he was abandoning her? It was ridiculous, considering that in the past Maria had been the one who'd failed to wait for him.

"But—"

"Wish our son a merry Christmas, Celeste," his father interrupted. "You don't want him to stop visiting us, do you?"

"Of course not." She came forward and hugged him tightly, smelling of the familiar light perfume he associated with his childhood. She whispered in his ear, "Forgive a meddling mother for wanting to see her only child happy."

He hugged her back. "You're forgiven."

Then his father was grabbing his hand and pulling him into a hearty hug. He ushered Mom toward the concourse, yet she looked back at Logan three times.

Logan waved, both sad and relieved that it was time for them to part ways. *Sad...* He wondered why that word had popped into his head. And why had the sentence snagged in his throat when he went to tell his mother he was happy?

An image of Maria's face floated in his mind. He shut it out, irked at how potent the power of suggestion could be. He wouldn't dwell on how things might have been. He liked his life in New York just fine, thank you very much.

He started walking toward the opposite concourse from his parents, again moving with the crowd. Though wreaths hung on the walls and Christmas music spilled out of restaurants, he'd seldom felt less holiday spirit.

Logan was halfway to his gate when his cell phone rang. It was Annalise DiMarco. He quickly rolled his carry-on suitcase over to the side, stopped and clicked through to the call.

"Annalise, what's up?" he asked.

"I can barely hear you. Where are you?" Annalise hardly took a breath. "Oh, my gosh, you're already at the airport, aren't you?"

"That doesn't matter," he said. "Just tell me why you called."

"Okay, but you won't believe it. Maria's in Key West. She's been there since yesterday."

"Ah, hell." He'd had an inkling that telling her about his conversation with Mike on the morning of his death had backfired. Maria had heard only that her brother was thinking about quitting his job. "I'm sorry, Annalise. She told me she wasn't going."

"It's not your fault, Logan. She told me the same thing. She didn't want us to know."

"What can I do?"

"Nothing," Annalise said. "I almost didn't call to tell you, but I hadn't thanked you yet."

"For nothing."

"For trying," she insisted.

Had he tried hard enough? Logan wondered after disconnecting the call. He remembered as clearly as though it were yesterday how he'd persuaded Mike to go to work on that fateful morning.

"I can't let you stay here and freeload off me," Logan had said. "You've got to work."

"I know it," Mike had answered. "But I hate being a busboy."

"Then quit after you find another job," Logan had told him. "In the meantime, though, there are a lot of things worse than working at the World Trade Center."

Not on 9/11, there hadn't been.

Logan felt sick to his stomach. It was bad enough carrying around the guilt that he was responsible for Mike being at the restaurant that day. Seeing the false hope in Maria's eyes had been worse.

He couldn't rewind time and take back what he'd said to Mike. He could, however, do something about Maria.

He headed for his gate and got in line at the counter.

"How may I help you?" an airline representative asked when he reached the front of the line.

Logan slapped his boarding pass down on the counter. "I need to make a change. Do you fly to Key West?"

MARIA WOKE UP WEDNESDAY morning thinking about Logan Collier. She turned over on the lumpy mattress, half expecting him to be on the other side of the bed, his chest bare, his face soft in sleep.

He wasn't there.

She sat up, pushing the hair back from her face. Images from her dreams bombarded her consciousness. Of Logan kissing her, stripping off her clothes, making love to her. Of Mike bounding down the stairs, bursting into the basement and covering his eyes with a hand. *"Whoa. Didn't mean to interrupt."*

She groaned aloud. Part of her dream was actually a memory. Mike had been a fan of Logan's, treating him like another big brother. On one memorable occasion, he'd come to the basement to say hello to Logan and had barged in on them necking.

That was all she and Logan had been doing. They'd never gone all the way. Annalise had gotten pregnant when she was a senior in high school, then married quickly. Even though things had worked out great for her sister, Maria had been determined not to repeat that mistake. She'd wanted to wait, and Logan had respected her wishes. If she was having erotic dreams about him, seeing him again must have affected her on a deeper level than she'd imagined.

Maria hugged herself and rubbed her upper arms. She'd been right to get rid of Logan by telling him what he wanted to hear. Her entire focus needed to be on Mike.

Although it was almost nine and she hadn't bothered pulling down the blinds, no sunlight poured into the room. The only window faced a brick wall, which helped explain the relatively low price for a night's stay. Since she wasn't getting paid and didn't know how long the search would take, cost had to be a consideration. She padded to the bathroom over thin carpet and splashed cold water on her face to dispel the cobwebs.

By the time she'd showered and dressed, she was thinking more clearly. She'd been so eager to show around the aged photo of her brother when she got to Key West that she hadn't done all the groundwork she could have.

It seemed a fair bet that Mike wasn't using his birth name, but there were other steps she needed to take before she was certain. Examining the Monroe County property records. Checking listings at the local Clerk of Courts office. Accessing the state of Florida's criminal database.

Maria pulled out her laptop from her bag,

called the front desk for the hotel's wireless access code and tried to log on. After three attempts, she finally connected.

The wireless signal flickered in and out, making what should have taken twenty minutes stretch into two hours. Predictably, she turned up nothing. No property records. No addresses. No vehicles registered to him. No tax liens. The trail simply stopped dead. If Mike were alive, she was even more sure he wasn't using his real name.

The tone on her cell phone signaled she had a text. It was from Annalise. Again.

Worried about you, it read. When will you call?

Not yet, Maria texted back.

She couldn't call until she had information that would convince her sister she wasn't spinning her wheels. Her next step was to visit the Old Town post office, although that was admittedly a long shot. The employees at the branch she'd already checked had been no help.

After that, Maria needed a better strategy. The desk sergeant could be right about Mike not being a local, but she couldn't ignore the possibility. There were undoubtedly people in town besides Sergeant Peppler who had a finger on the pulse of the real Key West.

She sat up straighter, the name of a Key West P.I. popping into her head: Carl Dexter. Key Carl, everybody called him. A large bearded man in his sixties who came to the workshops at the national P.I. conferences dressed in guayabera shirts, shorts and sandals.

With Key Carl's help, she had no doubt she could come up with that better strategy.

INSIDE THE OFFICES OF Dexter Private Investigations later that morning, Kayla Fryburger stood back and admired the beaded white snowflakes she'd strung from monofilament thread in her uncle's office. The dozen or so snowflakes looked elegant, although making them had been a simple matter of adding beads to corsage pins, poking the pins into cork and applying white glitter.

Uncle Carl had nixed her Christmas tree idea so the snowflakes would have to do. Kayla only hoped someone besides herself saw them.

Since Uncle Carl had left with his girlfriend earlier in the week to visit her family in Chicago, nobody had stopped by the office. That was partially due to Uncle Carl spreading the word that he was out of town until after Christmas. Still, a girl could hope for walk-in traffic.

Dexter Investigation's normal office hours were 9:00 a.m. to noon. Even though Uncle Carl had suggested she take some time off this week, Kayla had shown up each day just in case somebody stopped in.

Granted, she wasn't a skilled investigator, but she could make up for in enthusiasm what she lacked in experience.

The past six weeks had been some of the most exciting of her life. Considering her previous line of work had been producing and selling bottle art with her mother, that wasn't saying much.

Kayla had come up with the idea of learning the ropes from her uncle a couple years ago. After much resistance, he'd finally agreed to an eight-week trial, providing she worked for a pittance.

She'd messed up a few times, including on surveillance duty when it didn't occur to her the subject might leave his house via a back window. She was getting better, though.

If a client would walk through the door, she'd get a chance to prove it. Kayla stared at the entrance, willing somebody in need of help to materialize.

Five minutes later, she sank into the orange-and-teal-striped sofa in the waiting area, wondering how to fill the time. In previous days, she'd tidied up the magazines on the coffee table, fluffed the pillows and swept the floor. All that was left to do was clean the baseboards.

Minutes later, with a wet paper towel in hand, she gazed down at the short yellow skirt she'd paired with a white top. Not the best outfit for baseboard cleaning. She balanced on her haunches but almost toppled over on her wedged-heel sandals.

"Forget that." She got down on her knees and went to work.

The swooshing noise was so unexpected it took her a moment to realize the door had swung open. Kayla got to her feet with as much dignity as she could muster and turned to greet the arrival.

Alex Suarez. She fought not to sway. It was Alex Suarez, the object of her unrequited crush. A charming smile split his tan, handsome face. He was wearing sunglasses with silver frames and black lenses. He slid them off slowly and she noticed one of the lenses had a slight scratch. No surprise. She noticed everything about him and had for years.

"Well, hello," he said.

She smoothed her skirt the best she could, terribly afraid the first thing he'd seen upon entering the office was her yellow rear end. This was why people didn't take her seriously. Such things were always happening to her.

"Welcome to Dexter Private Investigations."

Her voice cracked on the name. "How can I help you?"

He walked deeper into the office, the smile still present. With his thick dark hair, high forehead and angular cheekbones, he looked almost exotic. She'd heard his given first name was Alejandro but that he'd started calling himself Alex after he emigrated from Cuba with his parents when he was a child. The name had stuck. An accent hadn't. He sounded quintessentially American.

He studied her. "I know you from somewhere."

She would have been flattered if she hadn't been stopping by his restaurant regularly for nearly a year. The Daybreak Café operated from 7:00 a.m. to 2:00 p.m. daily, serving both American and Cuban specialties for breakfast and lunch.

"I'm a fan of the Cuban sandwiches at your restaurant," she said. "I get one for takeout a few times a month."

He snapped his fingers. "That must be it. I didn't know they let you leave school for lunch, though."

"Excuse me?"

"You go to Key West High, right?" he asked. He thought she was in high school? She felt her face flame. "I graduated from there a long time ago. I'm twenty-five."

"Really?" His eyes widened. They were such a dark brown they were almost black. "I never would have guessed it."

She stood up to her full height of five feet two, taller if you took into account the heels of her chunky sandals. "I look younger."

"You look great," he said, his smile widening.

She hoped she wasn't blushing. "How old are you?"

"Thirty-five."

"Well, then, you look younger, too," she said. "I wouldn't have guessed any older than twenty-nine."

He laughed. "I'm Alex Suarez, by the way."

As if she didn't know.

"Kayla Fryburger." She waited for him to make a crack about her name. Almost everybody did.

"Okay, Kayla," he said, "now that we've established you're out of high school—"

"*Years* out of high school," she interrupted.

"Many, many years out of high school," he said with the smile still in place. "That must mean you're not just helping out over the holidays?"

"I work here," she verified. "I'm Unc— I mean, Mr. Dexter's assistant."

"Is that right?" He nodded. In light-colored slacks and an off-white shirt with the sleeves rolled up, he appeared cool and confident. If he bottled some of that confidence and sold it, she'd be first in line.

"It is." She tried to remember what Uncle Carl said to potential clients. "Tell me what brings you here today."

"I'd like to tell both you and Carl," Alex said. "He's a friend of mine. Is he around?"

It figured Alex knew her uncle. The local business community wasn't terribly extensive. But apparently Key West was big enough that the man she'd been swooning over for years hadn't noticed her. "No, I'm sorry. He's in Chicago until December 27."

Alex grimaced and sucked in a breath. "That's not good news. I need to hire somebody today."

Kayla's heartbeat sped up. "You can hire me."

He looked dubious. "I thought you assisted."

"That's right." Assisting was all she'd ever done. "But I can do more than assist. I can take on a case. That's why I'm here in the office. I'm ready and willful. Uh, I meant ready and willing."

She shut up. She sounded like a total amateur, which she was. It would be best if he didn't know that, though.

Alex scratched his smoothly shaved jaw.

"Perhaps I should tell you why I'm here and we can go from there."

"Sounds good." She tried to contain the excitement coursing through her. "Go ahead."

"Can we sit down?" he asked.

"Sure. Come this way." She led him to her uncle's office and got behind the big desk. Uncle Carl was a large man, more than a foot taller than she was. The desk seemed to swallow her so that she felt like a little girl playing house.

To compensate, she said in her most professional voice, "Please proceed."

"Have you seen this?" He was holding a rolled-up newspaper, which he unfolded and handed to her.

It was a copy of the *Key West Sun*. The headline above the fold read "Baring It All." The story was about a councilman proposing a referendum to allow nude sunbathing along a narrow strip of beach, a move championed by naturists who embraced the anything-goes Key West culture.

"I have seen it and I'm for it." Kayla grimaced as it occurred to her how he could misconstrue her support. "Not that I would sunbathe naked. I mean, I would if nobody was around. It's not like I'm a prude or anything. Although I'm not an exhibitionist. Not that I'm saying these people are."

She had to press her lips together to stop her stream of words. Why couldn't she stop talking?

"Not that story." He leaned across the desk and pointed to a photo below the fold. "That."

She'd seen the life-size fiberglass Santa that was pictured at the intersection of Duval Street and U.S. 1. He held a fistful of money in one hand. In his other was a sign that said "'Tis the Season to Spend in Key West." Someone had painted the statue's face white and added black rings around its eyes and red streaks trickling from its mouth. "Zombie Santa," the caption read.

Kayla giggled, covering her mouth to stop it from becoming an unladylike guffaw.

"That reaction is exactly why I'm here," Alex said. "As a representative of the Key West Merchants Association, I'm authorized to hire a private investigator to save our group from further embarrassment. So far a prankster has dressed Santa like the Grinch and now a zombie."

"Somebody has a sense of humor," she said.

"The Merchants Association doesn't think it's funny," he said. "They're taking this very seriously."

"Then why not just retire the statue?" Kayla asked.

"That was my suggestion," Alex said. "But it's not the way these things work. The group paid a local artist a pretty penny to create that statue. Santa has a lot of fans."

"But it's so…" Kayla's voice trailed off for fear of insulting him.

"Crass?" he supplied.

That was exactly what Kayla had been about to say. By emphasizing materialism, the statue focused on the wrong side of the holiday.

"Don't worry about offending me," he said. "I spoke out against the statue from the beginning. Nothing would make me happier than to get it off the street."

"Then why are you in charge of hiring a private investigator?" she asked.

"Just because I was against the Santa doesn't mean I want to see our group embarrassed," he said. "We need to find out who's doing this. Or at the very least, make sure it doesn't happen again."

"Then you came to the right place." Kayla injected confidence into her voice even though she was already wondering how a one-woman operation would manage twenty-four-hour surveillance on the statue. "Let me tell you our rates."

She had to go to her uncle's file and rummage through a sheaf of papers before finding a listing of costs. The hourly rate seemed high to her. Alex didn't blink.

"That intersection with the Santa is a pretty high-traffic area," she said, referring more to the cars that passed by the spot than the pedestrians. "You said Santa's already been messed with twice. It seems likely somebody saw the prankster in action."

"I'm sure that's something you'll look into."

She planned to do exactly that. She just wasn't sure how to go about it.

"It's settled, then." Alex stood up and reached across the desk, offering his hand.

Kayla took it, the warmth of his grip seeming to travel through every inch of her body. She almost cried out in protest when he let go of her hand.

"Here are my numbers." He took a business card out of his wallet and laid it on the desk. "I'd like to be updated daily and whenever there's a new development."

"Certainly." She hoped she sounded sufficiently professional.

"I'll look forward to hearing from you." He strode toward the exit, pausing to turn around before he reached it. The grin that made him even more handsome was back on his face. "I forgot to tell you. Nice skirt. Yellow never looked so good."

With that, he left. Kayla brought her hands to

her hot cheeks, not sure what disconcerted her more: Alex Suarez or the prospect of conducting a solo investigation.

CHAPTER FOUR

THE PRICKLY SENSATION on the back of Maria's neck started before she'd gotten halfway to her destination.

During her years in law enforcement, she'd learned to trust her intuition. It had served her well on occasions too numerous to count. Such as the time she was chasing a suspect and ducked into an alley just before he turned on her and fired.

Now her sixth sense was telling her someone was following her.

She'd decided to visit the post office before appealing to Key Carl for help. The directions she'd gotten off the internet took her west on Duval Street, a tourist-heavy thoroughfare that cut a swath through the heart of Key West. The farther west she walked, the more numerous the bars, specialty shops, restaurants and pedestrians became. Trolley cars shared space on the road with bicycles, cars and mopeds.

It seemed as if anything was accepted here. She passed a statue of Santa Claus holding a fistful of cash, with the message to spend it in Key West, and a man dressed in the same shade of green as the feathers on the large talking parrot on his shoulder. A woman whose arms and legs were completely covered in colorful tattoos rode by on a scooter. A belly dancer who had a lot to jiggle performed for tips on a street corner.

Yet Maria could still sense that someone was on her tail.

Had word trickled back to Mike that she was looking for him? She'd left her business card with probably two dozen people last night. She'd mentioned the name of the hotel where she was staying to more than a few of them.

Her heartbeat sped up. If Mike had been the one who'd contacted Caroline, he could be thinking about surfacing. He might even be following her right now. This could be her opportunity to solve the mystery of his disappearance once and for all.

She spied an art gallery with paintings displayed in the window. She stopped, pretending to admire them. The sun wasn't yet directly overhead, perfect for her purposes. She repositioned her body and angled her head this way and that, as though examining a painting.

The sun reflected off the window, allowing Maria to see the other side of the street.

A familiar man was stopped in the middle

of the sidewalk, hanging back but not making nearly enough of an effort to conceal himself.

Not Mike. Logan Collier.

She whirled and marched across the street, directly into the path of one of the mopeds that clogged the artery. The driver, a teenage boy, swerved to avoid hitting her. "Hey!" he yelled. "Watch where you're going."

An extra dose of adrenaline surged through Maria, but she didn't break stride.

Logan stood frozen on the sidewalk, his mouth hanging open. "He's right. You could have gotten killed."

Since the moped had missed her, there were more important matters to discuss. "What are you doing here?" she demanded.

He shrugged his broad shoulders. With his short hair and smooth shave, he would have looked out of place in Key West even if he hadn't been wearing dark clothes. His slacks and shoes were black. He'd rolled up the sleeves of his dark gray dress shirt in deference to the heat.

"I was following you," he said.

Never would it have occurred to her that Logan was the one on her tail. How could it? Before Monday, she'd seen him exactly once in eleven years. She would have recognized him anywhere, though. He was even better looking now than he'd been as a teen. His face was a little leaner, his golden-brown hair a little darker, his once-straight nose not quite perfect. Except that didn't make sense. Logan Collier wasn't the type of guy who got his nose broken.

"How did you know I was here?" The answer occurred to her before he could answer. "Annalise. She's the only one I told."

"She's worried about you," he said, not bothering to deny it.

"I didn't tell Annalise where I was staying," Maria said. "What did you do? Call hotels at random and ask to be connected to my room?"

"Not at random, alphabetically," he replied. "I'm lucky you're staying at the Blue Tropics."

If she hadn't been so irked, she would have been impressed.

"I hung up before I got put through to your room," he continued. "I was on my way to the hotel when I saw you leaving."

He sounded matter-of-fact, as though it was perfectly logical that he should be here in Key West following her.

"I don't get it," she said. "Weren't you supposed to go back to New York today? Isn't it vitally important you spend your holidays in the office?"

He stiffened. She wasn't sure why. He'd made

it clear long ago that his job was his number one priority.

"It's only Wednesday," he said. "I can be back by the weekend."

She got close to him to better make her next point. A mistake. Last night's dream was still fresh in her mind and she pictured herself naked in his arms. She breathed in his clean scent, dismayed that it had become familiar again so quickly. Physical attraction. That was all it was. She'd already been down this road with him and he hadn't turned out to be the man she needed him to be. She hardened herself against him.

"You can be back even sooner if you leave today," she snapped.

"Are you going back today?" he asked.

What did that have to do with anything? "No."

"Then neither am I," he said. "I'm going to stay and help you."

"No way." She shook her head. "You think somebody besides Mike contacted Caroline. I've got to conduct the investigation as though it was Mike."

Vertical lines appeared on Logan's forehead. "Why?"

"I haven't been able to connect any of his friends to Key West," Maria said. "Until I rule out Mike, he's the most likely suspect."

"And how can you rule him out?"

"By showing around this age progression." She got a copy out of her purse and handed it to him.

A muscle twitched in his jaw, but otherwise his face revealed nothing. He handed the sheet back to her. "Mike would have been a handsome guy."

Would have been, not turned out to be.

She swallowed back a retort, reminding herself that she couldn't prove Mike was alive. Not yet, anyway.

"So where are we headed?" Logan asked.

"We're not headed anywhere." She started walking and he fell into step beside her. He was only three or four inches taller than her five feet eight, which was always a surprise. He looked bigger than life. "I'm going to the downtown branch of the post office. I hit the other branch yesterday."

She passed a fresh produce store and turned the corner onto Eaton Street, which was far less crowded than Duval. They passed a coffee shop and a retro movie theater that was playing first-run films. Maria slanted a glance at Logan. "You don't listen real well, do you?"

"Think of me as your sidekick," he said. "I gather we're going to see if anybody remembers him mailing the envelope?"

She sighed and gave in to the inevitable. "Nobody will remember that, but they might remember Mike."

The sprawling Old Town post office was in the next block. The line was at least fifteen people deep, a big difference from the post office Maria frequented in Lexington. The lines there had been getting shorter while the number of employees on staff shrank. One of the Lexington tellers blamed the internet.

"Why didn't he email the photos? Why did he mail them?" Maria didn't realize she'd spoken aloud until Logan answered.

"*Whoever* mailed the photos," he said, putting emphasis on the first word, "didn't want someone to track the IP address back to him."

"That makes sense," she said. "I'm getting in line. You don't have to wait with me."

"Sidekick, remember?" He kept by her side, so close she imagined she could feel the heat of his body. Last night's erotic dreams came to mind again. She'd done far too much imagining lately when it came to Logan.

It took more than a half hour to reach the front of the line. An Asian clerk not much taller than the counter she stood behind called out, "Next."

Maria hurried over, the age progression in hand. Logan hung back but only slightly. She got straight to the point, laying the sheet of paper on the counter. "Could you please tell me if you've seen this man."

"You want to mail this?" the woman asked.

"No."

"What do you want to mail?"

"Nothing." Maria attempted a smile. "I'm looking for this man. All I want to know is if you've seen him."

The clerk didn't return her smile. One of her dark brows arched. "What did he do wrong?"

"Nothing. He's my brother." Maria tried not to show her frustration. Some people were tougher nuts to crack than others. "I only want to talk to him."

"How do I know this man wants to talk to you?" the woman asked, her expression hardening. "We're very busy. You need to step aside if you don't have anything to mail."

"But you haven't—"

"I can vouch for my friend." Logan was suddenly at Maria's side, flashing a reassuring smile at the clerk. "She's been worried about her brother since he went missing."

The flint went out of the woman's features. She looked past Maria to Logan. "This man, he's really her brother?"

"He really is," Logan said. "Could you please take a look and see if you recognize him?"

She nodded once, slid the paper closer and examined it for a few seconds. "Never seen him before."

Maria shoved aside her disappointment and tapped the age progression. "Could you hold on to that and show it around?"

"Give me a call if somebody recognizes him." Logan reached into his wallet and handed a business card to the teller. Because he had clearly made a connection with her, Maria suppressed the urge to pull out a card of her own.

"For you, I'll do it," the clerk told him.

Maria didn't speak again until they were outside in the sunshine. Even though she hadn't wanted Logan along, she couldn't discount his help. "I owe you one."

"You don't owe me anything," he said. "I'm here to help any way I can."

Unexpected tears stung the backs of her eyes. She wasn't sure if they were due to the stress of searching for the brother she'd long believed dead or the fact that Logan Collier was being kind to her.

"Where to now?" he asked.

"Let's stop at that coffee shop we passed," she said, nodding back down Eaton Street. "I could use a cup."

"A bottle of cold water sounds good to me."

He wiped his damp brow. "I'm not exactly dressed for warm weather."

There was a line inside the coffee shop, too. *Great,* Maria thought. This would work. "I need to use the restroom. Would you order a cup of regular coffee for me?"

"Sure," he said.

She waited until he was in line and his back was turned before slipping out of the store. Guilt, her constant companion, once again descended. She ignored it.

She could deal with Logan being angry at her. She wasn't at all sure she could deal with his kindness.

MARIA ZIGZAGGED THROUGH the palm-lined Key West streets, walking quickly and taking peeks over her shoulder to make sure Logan wasn't following her. Old Town was a mix of retail shops, business offices, small hotels and private residences housed in wood-frame structures painted in pastel shades. Most of the homes had peaked metal roofs, gingerbread trim, covered porches and wreaths on the doors.

After about a half mile, she stopped watching her back. She continued to work on squashing her guilt over giving Logan the slip when he'd flown a thousand miles to offer his help.

He was a distraction she couldn't afford. If

her brother were alive, she might have only a short window of time to find him before he took off again.

Key Carl could help her focus her efforts.

She spied the other private investigator's office in a pale green, one-story duplex with a real estate office on the other side. A petite young woman with a mass of curly blond hair tied back in a ponytail emerged from Key Carl's place. She checked the door to make sure it was locked before walking in the opposite direction.

"Wait!" Maria called. "You with the blond hair."

A tour bus passed by, drowning out her voice. The woman waited until the bus passed before hurrying across an intersection to a block that appeared mostly residential.

She moved fast for such a small person. Her wedged sandals and snug yellow skirt didn't even slow her down. Maria ran to catch up, crossing the street against the light and slowing only when she got to within a few paces.

"You've gone and done it now, Kayla," she heard the woman say. "You wanted him to notice you. Well, he can't help but notice if you screw up."

The roar of the bus might not be the only reason the woman hadn't heard Maria calling. She was talking to herself.

"Excuse me," Maria said in a voice loud enough to be heard at a rock concert.

The blonde startled, her hand flying to her throat. She whirled, her posture relaxing when she got a look at Maria. "Oh, you scared me!"

"Sorry," Maria said. "I was just trying to get your attention."

"You didn't hear me talking to myself, did you?" She was cute rather than pretty, with a round face and freckles sprinkled across her nose. "You did, didn't you? That is so embarrassing."

"There's nothing to be embarrassed about." Maria had taken an instant liking to the girl. She searched for something reassuring to say. "We're all apprehensive about something."

"It's more of a some*one* than a some*thing*. Alex Suarez just hired me. I've only had a crush on him for, like, two years." She stopped abruptly, shrugging. "You must think I'm some kind of nut job. We're strangers and I'm prattling on like I've known you all my life."

"Don't worry about it." Maria couldn't remember the last time she'd met somebody who was so open and honest. "Sometimes it helps to get another person's perspective."

"You really think so? Because even if it hadn't been Alex who hired me, I'd still have a challenge in front of me. I'm not sure I can…"

She trailed off in midsentence and thumped her forehead. "I'm sorry. TMI. Too much information. I'm just going on and on. I haven't even asked why you stopped me."

"I was on my way to see Carl Dexter," Maria said. "I saw you coming out of his office."

"Oh, no!" She gasped and covered her mouth. "I knew I shouldn't have told you all that. Now you'll never hire us."

Maria smiled despite everything that was on her mind. "I'm not a client. I'm in the same business as you are. I was hoping Carl could give me some advice on a case while I'm in town."

The girl's eyes widened. "You're a private investigator?"

"All the way from the great state of Kentucky," Maria said. "My name's Maria Di-Marco."

"I'm Kayla Fryburger." She made a face. "It's an awful name, isn't it? Kids used to tease me about it, growing up. For a while I was even a vegetarian."

"It's not so bad," Maria said.

"Listen to me. You don't want to hear about my name. You want to know about Uncle Carl. Sorry to tell you this, but he's in Chicago until after Christmas."

Maria felt herself deflate, like a balloon with a slow leak. Now what? She'd been under the impression Carl ran a one-man show like she did, but she should have put two and two together.

"I don't normally tell people I'm Carl's niece..." Kayla paused. "He left me in charge while he's gone. He must have thought I wouldn't have anything to do. Wouldn't you know it? I've got a case."

"Good for you," Maria said.

"It would seem so, right?" Kayla said. "Too bad I'm not real sure how to proceed. I was going to call Uncle Carl for advice, but if I don't find a way to impress him it'll be curtains for me. He took me on for eight weeks on a trial basis. Six of them are already up."

A picture of an inexperienced investigator who was in over her head was starting to crystallize.

"You'll be fine if you use common sense and work on being patient and disciplined," Maria said. "The best trait is being a good listener."

"That's great advice." Kayla touched Maria's upper arm, her eyes shining. "Hey, I've got an idea. Maybe I can help you. In exchange, you can give me some guidance."

Under normal circumstances, Maria would be sympathetic. She couldn't lose sight of her goal, though, and that was finding out whether her brother was in Key West.

"I'm sorry," she said. "I don't see how something like that would work."

Kayla's expressive face fell. "Oh, well. It was worth a shot. I know I'm not real good at being a P.I. yet but I think I can get there. And I'd do just about anything to avoid making bottle art."

"Bottle art," Maria repeated. "What's that?"

"My mom and I recycle glass bottles into various products. Wind chimes. Glassware. Jewelry." A tired look came over her face. "Mom's a Key West institution. I can't remember her not doing it."

"Wait a minute," Maria said, an idea starting to form. "How long have you lived in Key West?"

"All my life." She put up a hand. "Don't say that couldn't have been very long. I know I don't look it, but I'm twenty-five. I've been out of high school for a very long time."

Maria didn't have time to puzzle over why Kayla felt it necessary to mention her high school years were behind her.

"This could work, after all. I think my brother might be living in Key West under an assumed name. I need a list of local hotspots and local contacts who might know people who are trying to keep a low profile."

Kayla clapped her hands and awarded Maria with a toothy grin. "I can help you with that.

And you can give me advice on how to catch whoever's messing with Santa Claus."

Intriguing. Maria's stomach growled, reminding her she'd skipped breakfast. She tried not to think about where Logan Collier would eat his lonely lunch.

"Is there somewhere around here we can grab a bite to eat?" Maria asked. "Seems to me, briefing each other will take a while."

LOGAN HELD HIS CELL PHONE to his ear. Cool liquid from the bottled water he'd bought at the Blue Tropics hotel gift shop slid down his throat as he took heat from his boss.

"What do you mean, you might not be back this weekend? I need you here, Logan." Harvey Stein, office manager for the Pride Financial Group, had a quintessential type A personality. He talked with a staccato beat and walked with quick, light steps. He often said he needed to move fast so the competition wouldn't catch him. "We're having that holiday party on Christmas Eve at the Starlight Roof in the Waldorf Astoria, and you told me you're booked for dinners with clients up until then."

Harvey had all but mandated that his employees go heavy on the wining and dining. He believed money spent splurging on clients over the holidays came back double during the rest of the year.

"Sorry, Harvey," Logan said. "I've got personal business I need to attend to."

Too bad Logan's personal business had ditched him a few hours ago. He'd waited in the coffee shop with their drinks for a good ten minutes before it occurred to him Maria wasn't in the restroom.

Now he was parked in an armchair in the lobby of the Blue Tropics, the better to intercept her when she inevitably returned to the hotel.

"You never miss work because of personal stuff," Harvey said. "What is it? A matter of life or death?"

In a way it was. Maria thought her brother might be alive while Logan was certain Mike was dead.

"It's not like you to let me down," Harvey continued. "Now would be the worst possible time to start disappointing me if you want my job."

Logan had been mulling over how much to tell his boss about what was going on. His mind switched gears. "What do you mean by that? You're not thinking of retiring, are you?"

"I'm considering it. I'm sixty-nine years old, after all. I can't run the show forever."

Three giggling young teens picked the worst

possible moment to walk by, talking so loudly Logan had to strain to hear Harvey.

"Where are you?" his boss asked.

Logan turned the phone away just as one of the girls declared how she really wanted to "you know, like, visit the Hemingway House and then see if we can get served drinks at Sloppy Joe's." Telling Harvey he was in Key West would not be a wise move.

"Sorry," Logan said. "I'm beside a TV."

There was a television in the lobby. At the moment, however, it was switched off.

"As I was saying, you need to be on your toes if you want me to recommend you to take my place," Harvey advised. "You do want to, right?"

It was the next logical step. Logan had moved steadily up the ladder since joining the firm, building the stable career he'd envisioned when he went to college for a business degree.

Maria entered the lobby just then, reminding him that the future he'd pictured had included her. She didn't look her best. Her black hair was starting to fall out of her ponytail and her sundress was wrinkled. Even at her worst, though, Maria was beautiful.

"Logan?" Harvey said. "Why aren't you answering? You do want the job, right?"

"Absolutely," he declared.

"Then get back here ASAP. This weekend at the latest. Can you do that?"

Logan hadn't gotten as far as he had without telling his boss what he wanted to hear. "I can do that."

"Good." Harvey rang off at the same moment Maria spotted Logan. Her shoulders squared and her chin lifted. It didn't look as if she'd be apologizing for ditching Logan.

"Hey, Maria." He indicated the armchair next to him. "Have a seat. Fill me in on what's happened since I last saw you."

She dropped her hands on her hips. They were curvy, the way a woman's hips should be.

"Oh, no," she said. "Don't tell me you're spying for Annalise now."

"Excuse me?"

"That was my sister on the phone, wasn't it?" she demanded.

"Actually, it was my boss," Logan said. "I called to let him know I was delayed."

Her shoulders seemed to relax. "I bet he wasn't happy about that."

"He wasn't."

"So did you tell him you'd be back as soon as you could?" She crossed her arms over her chest, regarding him intently. "You did, didn't you?"

"My job's important to me," he said.

"I know it is." Her words were matter-of-fact; her tone was flippant. "So go back to New York. I won't stop you."

She was as impossible as she'd always been—and as complicated. The hard exterior she presented hid a marshmallow center, a trait she'd shared with her brother Mike. Logan couldn't tell whether she really didn't want him around or if she was using the tough talk as a defense mechanism.

"I'm here at least until tomorrow," Logan said. "Let me help you, Maria."

Her mouth worked but no words emerged. It was as though she wasn't sure what to say, as though she wanted him to stay but couldn't bring herself to say so.

He patted the armchair again. "C'mon. Sit with me awhile."

"I don't owe you anything, Logan," she said. "Yeah, you were a help back at the post office. I'll admit that. But I didn't ask you to come here."

"You'd feel less guilty if you sat down and told me what you've been up to," he said.

She sank into the chair. "What makes you think I feel guilty?"

"I got you to sit down, didn't I?" he asked.

"Okay, so I do feel a little guilty," she admitted, throwing up her hands. "You want to know what I've been up to? I'll tell you. Then you'll understand why you're not needed."

She spent the next ten minutes telling him about a Santa Claus statue that kept getting defaced and her deal to mentor an apprentice private eye in return for information. She had a list of local hangouts, contact information for some longtime Key West residents and a suggestion to go to the nightly sunset celebration at the Mallory Square dock.

"I can usually do a lot of investigative work online but not with this case," she said. "The only way to find out if Mike is in Key West is to physically go out and talk to people."

"All the more reason to keep me around," Logan said. "We can cover more ground if we work together."

"I don't understand," Maria said. "You haven't seen me in years. Why is it so important for you to help me?"

A good question. He wasn't completely sure of his reasons. Guilt had something to do with it, but so did the thought of leaving Maria alone in Key West so close to Christmas.

"Does it matter?" he asked. "Can't you just accept my help?"

"What if I refuse?"

"It won't do any good," Logan said. "I'll follow you around town. I'm better at it now. I got some experience this morning."

"I don't want—"

His phone rang, cutting off what she was about to say. He picked up his cell and looked down at the caller display. "It's a Key West exchange," he told Maria.

"Answer it," she said, scooting forward in her seat. "It could be that woman from the post office."

That was exactly who it was. Logan silently mouthed as much, then, nodding at regular intervals, listened intently to what the postal clerk had to say. He could feel impatience rolling off Maria in waves.

"Well? What did she tell you?" Maria asked the instant he disconnected the call. "Did somebody recognize the photo?"

Logan considered how to answer without getting her hopes up too high. Not for a minute did he believe this lead would pan out. "Possibly."

"What do you mean, possibly?" she retorted. "Somebody either recognized Mike or they didn't."

"Hold on a minute and let me explain." Logan chose his words carefully. "Somebody at the post office thinks the age progression looks like a guy who's a regular at a bar on Duval Street. The guy's there at least a few nights a week."

"Which bar?" Maria asked.

Logan wouldn't normally withhold information to get his way. These, however, were special circumstances.

"I'll tell you tonight," he said, "when we go there together."

CHAPTER FIVE

"I CAN'T BELIEVE YOU still won't tell me the name of the bar," Maria groused.

She and Logan were in the heart of the tourist area. The tiny white lights that decorated many of the businesses were only starting to glow. If Logan hadn't gotten the tip, she would have spent the evening touring the local bars Kayla had told her about.

Late this afternoon she and Logan had stopped by a coffee shop, a barbershop and a diner. Nobody had recognized Mike. They'd intended to go to the sunset celebration but had run out of time.

"I've got a steep learning curve," Logan said. "You gave me the slip once. You might do it again."

"This time you'd know where I was going," she replied.

He slanted her a grin. "Still, I'm not taking any chances."

A quartet of twenty-somethings in shorts and Key West T-shirts passed by, each carrying a plastic cup filled with what was probably alcohol, legal on the island. Behind them a small, elderly man dressed as an elf pushed a shopping cart made up to look like a sleigh.

"Santa's helper coming through," he called in a high, nasal voice.

Logan edged closer to Maria, taking her arm and shielding her from the crush. Even though being on Duval Street was an assault to the senses, she could pick out his clean scent. The hairs on her arm stood at attention. Her stomach tightened.

He kept hold of her, as though it was perfectly natural for him to be touching her.

"You can let me go now," she said.

"Oh, no, I can't," he said. She was summoning the will to wrench her arm away when he added, "Not until that belly dancer goes by."

Sure enough, coming toward them was a woman with a long green skirt hanging low on her hips and a red jewel in her naval. She seemed to be rehearsing her act as she walked.

Logan laughed aloud. "This place is crazy. I like it."

If not for his close shave and expertly cut short hair, he'd almost look like he fit in. He'd exchanged his dark slacks and gray shirt for jeans and a floral print shirt he must have bought earlier today. No way could Maria imagine he'd had that shirt in his suitcase. Or as part of his usual wardrobe.

"It does feel like a different world, doesn't it?" she murmured. "A place somebody would come to get away from it all."

"By somebody, do you mean Mike?"

"Yes," she said. "If he's been trying to lie low, it makes sense that he'd be in Key West."

"I've gotta say this again, Maria," Logan stated. "For Mike to be alive, he'd have to go to great lengths to make sure nobody knew it. Stop and think about that."

Logan let go of her arm. The night was warm, probably still in the low seventies, but it felt as though a chill swept over her. There was no denying she couldn't reconcile that piece of the puzzle.

"I never said I had all the answers," Maria admitted. "Any good investigator knows not everything makes sense until the case is solved."

She expected him to argue with her. Instead, he pointed to one of the indoor-outdoor bars that were popular in Key West. Poised at the edge of its roofline was the likeness of a winged monkey with its teeth bared. "Here we are," he said.

An outdoor seating area filled with café-style plastic tables and chairs led to sliding glass doors that were open wide. Inside, perhaps seventy or eighty customers were gathered around a bar with counter space on three sides.

"The Flying Monkey." Maria read the sign the monkey on the roof was holding. She shuddered. "That thing looks even more menacing than the monkeys in *The Wizard of Oz*."

"That's right," Logan said, a corner of his mouth lifting. "We watched that movie together once. You used to be afraid of them."

"Only because they're terrifying. I'm surprised that monkey doesn't drive away business."

He laughed. "Hardly. The desk clerk at my hotel said this is one of the most popular bars in the city."

Logan was staying a block from the Blue Tropics at a boutique hotel that cost easily twice as much as her room. He claimed it was because her hotel had no vacancy. Maria doubted he would have booked a room at the Blue Tropics even if one were available, though. Not when he could afford better.

"I'm at your disposal," he said. "If you want to hang out here at The Flying Monkey all night, I'm game."

She noticed he didn't say he'd wait with her to see if Mike showed up.

"I'm talking to the owner before I do anything," she said. "Follow my lead, okay? Kayla's staking out that Santa statue tonight. I might ask him about that, too."

"Will you tell the owner you're a private eye?"

"Shh." She placed two fingers against his lips.

He went still, his eyes darkening as they gazed into hers. A jolt seemed to travel from her fingertips throughout the rest of her body.

She broke the eye contact and let her hand fall away. "Sometimes it's smarter not to mention that."

It hadn't been smart to touch him. Her nerve endings still tingled, blurring the boundaries she'd been trying to erect between them.

"Let's go," she said, entering the bar ahead of him.

On the back wall, Maria counted four posters of Ernest Hemingway, the famous author who'd made Key West his home. Interspersed with the posters were numerous photos of a bald man with a thick black beard posing with the customers.

The bearded man in the photos was at the tap, pouring beer into a mug. The monkey that was the bar's namesake decorated his black muscle shirt. The owner, Maria presumed. She asked Logan what he wanted to drink, then ordered a beer and a glass of white wine.

"Coming right up," the man said, filling the

order quickly and efficiently. He set the drinks on the counter in front of them. "Here you go."

"Keep the change." Maria ignored the money Logan was trying to hand her and paid him. "Before you go, do you know where I can find that Santa statue somebody turned into a zombie?"

The bearded man chuckled. One of his front teeth had a gold cap. "Corner of U.S. 1 and Duval. Zombie paint's gone, though. Only the god-awful statue remains."

"You don't like the statue?" Maria had noticed a Key West Merchants Association sticker on one of the bar windows.

"Have you seen that thing?" he asked. "We've got a lot of tacky stuff in Key West. We don't need no more."

"Is that a popular opinion among local businessmen?" she asked.

"Popular enough." He had to raise his voice to be heard above the chatter and the music from the jukebox. "I thought Alex Suarez was about to pop a vein when it went up."

That was the guy who'd hired Kayla, the one the rookie private investigator had a crush on.

"How about Mike DiMarco? What did he say?" Maria didn't expect that the bar owner would recognize the name but watched him carefully for a reaction. Every now and again long shots paid off.

He frowned, his brows knitting together. "Can't say I know anybody by that name."

Maria pulled out the age progression and placed it on the bar. "He's probably going by another name. Do you recognize him?"

The bar owner looked down at the photo, then back at her. "What are you? A reporter?"

This was one of those times Maria wouldn't gain any ground by telling him she was a private investigator. "I'm his older sister."

"The family's lost track of him," Logan interjected. Until now he'd stood silently by, heeding Maria's instructions to follow her lead. "She's worried."

"I hear you." The bearded man addressed Logan. "I've got a big sister, too. She's always checking up on me. Says she can't help it."

Maria pushed the paper toward him. "Somebody told us he might be one of your regulars."

The bar owner studied the image intensely. "This isn't a photo. What is it?"

"An age progression," Maria said. "My brother's been missing for a while."

His mouth twisted. "Kind of looks like Clem."

"Clem?"

"Don't know his last name. He shows up a

couple times a week. Offers to play his guitar
for beer. Sometimes I let him."

Maria's heartbeat quickened. This dovetailed
with the tip Logan had received. Not only that,
Mike had taken up the guitar during the last
year he'd lived at home. Sometimes he'd even
jammed with friends. Once he'd claimed he was
getting good enough to play in a band.

"Does Clem come on any particular night?"
she asked.

"Not Friday or Saturday," he said. "I've already got live music scheduled then. He usually
comes in on Wednesday or Thursday."

Today was Wednesday.

"What time?" Maria could barely contain her
eagerness.

The bar owner thought about it. "Sometimes
early, sometimes late, sometimes not at all."

"Hey, barkeep! Shut your trap and fetch me a
beer," yelled a large, broad-shouldered woman a
few seats away, thumping the bar for emphasis.

"Hold your horses," he yelled back. To Maria
and Logan, he said, "That's my big sister."

He left them to get her a beer, a smile on
his lips. Another time, Maria might have been
amused at their interaction. Not now. Excitement bubbled in her chest. Very soon she could
be face-to-face with the brother she thought

she'd never see again. It was almost too much to process.

"I hope you didn't mind my stepping in like that and backing up what you said."

She should. It was the second time he had done something like that, the first being with the clerk at the post office.

"I didn't mind," she said. "Surprisingly, you've been a big help."

He laughed. "Surprisingly, huh? Well, I'll take the faint praise wherever I can get it."

She felt her lips curl into a smile. Maintaining coolness toward him was too hard when her hopes were so high. "Enjoy it while it lasts. I can't promise praise will keep coming."

"Noted." He tipped back his mug, his throat muscles working as he drank the beer. He set the glass down on the bar. "What now?"

"Now," she said, "we wait."

Two hours later Logan sat across from Maria at one of the outdoor tables adjacent to the street as a waitress from The Flying Monkey served them slices of key lime pie with dollops of whipped cream.

He'd suggested they have dinner while waiting for the guitarist to show up, but Maria had barely touched her cheeseburger and fries. He hoped she'd get something into her stomach, not only to soak up the wine she'd drunk but to fortify herself for the blow that was coming.

He had little doubt that a guy named Clem in Key West resembled the age progression. No way, however, was that guy Mike.

After the waitress left, Maria took a bite of key lime pie. "This is actually good. I was starting to think I could be eating filet mignon and not tasting it."

Her gaze darted from the people walking by on the sidewalk to those entering the bar, as it had since they'd sat down at the table.

Logan chewed a piece of pie and swallowed. "This is fantastic. But then, I've always thought key lime pie was one of life's great pleasures."

"The waiting's still interminable," she said.

A jukebox blared from inside the bar, the tune spilling out the open doors to where they sat, loud but not loud enough to drown out conversation.

"Talk to me," he said. "It'll pass the time."

She popped another piece of pie into her mouth. Good. As long as she was eating, he was happy. But then, maybe it was even less complicated than that. She was dressed as casually as he was, in jeans and an ordinary blue shirt, yet it was hard for him to not stare. He'd forgotten how stunning her combination of black hair and blue eyes was.

No, correct that. He hadn't forgotten. He'd blocked the mental image from his mind.

She flipped her long hair over her shoulder, calling attention to her eyes, small, straight nose and bow-shaped lips. The combination sometimes made her look delicate, when he knew she was anything but.

"What should we talk about?" she asked.

A neutral topic, he thought. One that had nothing to do with the guy she'd married or the brother she was fooling herself into believing was alive.

"Tell me how you became a private investigator," he said. "Back in high school, you weren't sure what you wanted to do."

"Remember my uncle Jim, the cop?" She continued when he nodded. "He told me about an opening to be a police dispatcher. I applied and got the job. I liked it, but after a few years it wasn't enough. I went to the police academy and hooked on with the county sheriff's department."

"Why didn't you stay on the job?"

"Too much red tape." She twirled the stem of her wineglass. "You know me. Sometimes I have a hard time playing by the rules."

"I'm sensing a story."

She lifted her eyes to his. "Not a happy one."

"I'd like to hear it," he said.

For long moments, she said nothing. Then she started to talk. "One night about midnight a woman came into the station, frantic because her twenty-five-year-old daughter hadn't come home and she couldn't reach her on her cell. The woman had already called all her daughter's friends and every hospital in town and come up with nothing. She begged me to search for her."

"Can't you only do that if someone's been missing for twenty-four hours?"

"That was the department's policy. People check out for a day or two for all sorts of reasons, young adults especially. Most of the time they turn up on their own. But there was something about the woman's story that told me this wouldn't be one of those times. If I hadn't been on desk duty, I would have checked into it. But the two patrolmen working that night were sticklers for the rules."

"Was the daughter ever found?" Logan asked.

"Yeah, the next morning." Maria's voice was steeped in sadness. "Her car had crashed through a fence and ended up in a junkyard. Nobody realized the car didn't belong there until the owner was opening up and noticed her slumped over the wheel. The impact might have killed her, but maybe not. Maybe she would have been saved if we'd started looking for her when the mother asked us to."

Maria fell silent while Logan digested the story. It didn't take him long to figure out what the accident victim had to do with her becoming a private eye.

"So now when someone asks you to take a case," he said slowly, "you don't have to check with anyone else."

"Exactly," she said.

He already knew she'd been a private investigator almost as long as she'd been divorced. Logan wondered if the two events were connected. He wouldn't ask, though.

"How about you?" she asked. "What's life like in New York?"

"Busy," he said.

She took another bite of her pie. "I bet you work all the time."

"Not all the time." He managed to run in the park or get to the gym some mornings before his workday started. A few nights a week, he shoehorned drinks with friends or dinner with a revolving cast of women. He wasn't about to tell Maria he went into the office on Saturdays and the occasional Sunday.

"I bet your place is spectacular. Where do you live? A loft in SoHo or Tribeca?" she asked, naming two of the most expensive neighborhoods in the city.

"Neither. I like green space, so it's Central

Park for me." His one-bedroom apartment had a view of the park. The place was both expensive and spectacular, thanks to the interior designer he'd hired.

"I'm sure Central Park is pretty," she said, "but it can't compare to the bluegrass of Kentucky."

"You're right. You can't compare the two places. They're entirely different, each with its positives and negatives."

"Oh, yeah," she said, a challenge in her voice. "You used to love Kentucky. What are its negatives?"

His mother had brought up the same subject at the airport, complete with her theory that Logan wouldn't have left the state if Maria hadn't married someone else.

"You can't make as much in Kentucky as you can in New York." He immediately wished he could take back the words.

As he could have predicted, she pounced. "That's what's most important to you, isn't it? The almighty buck."

He refused to rise to the bait. He'd watched his parents struggle to make ends meet for so many years that there was no shame in wanting something different for himself. "Making a good living is important to me. Not so different from you, when you think about it."

"My job doesn't consume me," she said.

"Neither does mine."

"Oh, no?" She raised her eyebrows. "I remember how much you loved being an artist, how happy it made you. Do you still paint?"

He hadn't picked up a brush since he'd discovered she'd sent some of his paintings to that art school in Louisville and the director had invited him to apply. The only way Logan could get through to her that he'd chosen a more stable career path was to stop painting. He'd never started again.

"No?" she guessed. She shook her head as she studied him. "I didn't think so."

"You can't really want to talk about this," he said.

She tilted her head, her expression closed. "Talk about what?"

"The past and why we broke up," he said. "What purpose would that serve?"

"I don't..." Her voice trailed off, her mouth hanging open, her gaze fixed on a point somewhere beyond his shoulder. "Oh, my God. There he is."

Logan turned around. A man about thirty years old, dressed in worn jeans and a T-shirt, was walking into The Flying Monkey. He had straggly black hair, a sinewy build and a pronounced limp. He was also carrying a guitar.

MARIA'S HEART FELT AS IF it was slamming against her chest. Her palms grew damp and her head felt light.

Was the man with the guitar the brother she'd loved and lost? Was she within moments of finding him again?

He passed through the open doorway and disappeared in the sea of people inside the bar, but she'd seen enough to know why somebody had tipped them off. The guy was the right height, the right age and had the right coloring. The limp didn't fit, but something could have happened to cause it in the years that had passed.

"I'm going inside," she told Logan.

She got up so fast she lost her balance. She swayed, bracing herself with a hand on the table.

"Are you okay?" He rose, too, taking her gently by the elbow.

"I need to see if that's Mike." She headed into the bar, and Logan's hand dropped away from her arm.

If the man was Mike, he'd have no trouble recognizing her. She still wore her hair long and straight. People told her all the time she hadn't changed much since high school. A better question was whether Mike would be pleased to see her.

Her stomach cramped. It seemed more likely he'd still hold their last argument against her.

The Flying Monkey was more crowded than it had been an hour ago. Maria threaded past tall tables and small groups of people trying to converse above the noise of the jukebox.

She looked wildly around for the man with the guitar and spotted him up ahead through the crowd. He was behind some people seated at bar stools, perhaps waiting to ask the owner if he could play a few songs.

Maria made a beeline for him, her heart beating harder with each step she took. Around the bar, the press of people raised the temperature to an uncomfortable level. Suddenly it was hard to breathe.

She kept advancing until she was directly behind him. Drawing in a ragged breath, she lifted her hand and tapped him on the shoulder.

The man turned, an expectant look on his face. His nose was long and straight like Mike's. He even had the square chin that had lent her brother an air of ruggedness.

But it wasn't Mike.

Her knees felt weak as she stared at him. His mouth was wider than her brother's, his lips thinner, his eyes closer together. It was hard to tell in the dim light of the bar, but she was pretty sure his eyes were brown instead of blue like hers.

"Did you want something?" The man's mouth

was different, too. With his overbite, he probably should have worn braces as a child.

"Sorry. I made a mistake." She whirled, took a step and bumped straight into Logan.

"Whoa, there." He took her by the shoulders to steady her. "What happened?"

"It's not Mike," she said.

Logan put a protective arm around her and led her away from the people crowding the bar, not stopping until they had some space.

"It's not Mike," she said again.

"Did you really expect it to be?" he asked gently.

She had, she realized. She'd gotten her hopes ridiculously high, all because some postal worker knew of a man who bore a slight resemblance to her brother. But what if the man she'd accosted wasn't the right one? There were lots of musicians in Key West.

"Maybe it's the wrong guy," Maria said. "Maybe the postal worker meant somebody else."

"It's the right guy," Logan stated. "Did you notice his limp? The postal worker mentioned that."

"Lots of people have limps," she said.

Logan gave her shoulders a gentle squeeze. "Maria, it's a dead end. Maybe it's time to concentrate harder on Mike's friends. He must have given that photo of Caroline to one of them. Somebody has to have a Key West connection."

She felt her back stiffen. She still couldn't imagine Mike passing on a naked photo of Caroline. And why couldn't Logan understand that she had to exhaust the possibility that Mike was on the island before taking the investigation in another direction?

"I'm going to do things my way." She wrenched away from him and walked back through the crowd, heading for the exit.

He caught up to her easily. "Where are you going?"

She might as well tell him. He was getting harder and harder to shake off. "Kayla told me about a local bar that's not far from here. I'm going to show the age progression around."

The bar was on a quiet lane three or four blocks removed from the activity of Duval Street, tucked between a coin Laundromat and an optician's office. Patrons jammed the place, watching basketball games on overhead televisions, playing pool, drinking beer at mismatched tables and chairs that could have been picked up at a yard sale. Christmas decorations were nonexistent. Nobody there knew Mike, either.

"Let's get out of here," Logan said after about an hour. "You look dead on your feet."

"I'm not ready to leave yet," she said.

Coming into the bar was a guy with bleached blond hair and a deep tan, wearing baggy shorts that extended below his knees and a T-shirt decorated with a skull and crossbones. Maria marched straight up to him, the photo in hand, ignoring the up and down glance he gave her and the smell of alcohol that emanated from him.

"Excuse me," she said, "can you tell me if you've ever seen this man?"

He barely glanced at the picture, his bleary gaze focused squarely on her breasts. "Lesh get some beers and discush it."

"I'd like to discuss it now," Maria said, holding her ground. "Have you seen him or not?"

"Don't be that way, shweetheart." He reached for her, his beefy hand clamping on her arm. "Come with me."

"Let me go this instant," she hissed at him, "or you'll regret it."

Before the bleached blond could process her words, Logan came up behind him and yanked his arm so he had to release her. The blond whirled, closing his fist and swinging wildly. His punch connected with Logan's left eye. Logan staggered backward, crashing into a table and knocking over an empty chair. The blond swung again and hit air.

"Stop it!" Maria yelled.

The drunk guy kept advancing. Logan regained his balance and brought up his fists, warding off another blow. He bounced on the balls of his feet like a professional boxer and threw a punch of his own that caught the other man on his jaw. The drunk went down in a heap, moaning and rubbing his face.

"Hey, no fighting in here!" A thickset man at least six feet four barreled up to them, scowling and getting between the two. He pointed to Logan. "You need to leave!"

Logan's hand went to his eye. "He threw the first punch."

"I think he broke my face!" the drunk guy wailed from the floor, where he was writhing in seeming agony.

"Want me to call the cops?" the big man barked, advancing on Logan.

Logan didn't budge. His gaze hardened and he lifted his chin.

"No, we don't," Maria answered. She crossed to his side, captured his hand and tugged. He didn't move. "We're leaving. Aren't we, Logan?"

He glared at the big man, who glowered back. Maria could almost smell the testosterone in the air.

She yanked harder on Logan's hand. He felt like an unmovable object, giving her no choice but to try to be an irresistible force. "Please," she pleaded.

That simple word seemed to finally get through to him. He blinked, meeting her eyes and nodding once. As soon as they were outside in the night air, she dropped his hand.

"Are you okay?" Logan asked, his gaze running over her.

"I'm *fine,*" she retorted. "What was all that about? What were you thinking?"

"I was thinking I wanted him to get his hands off you," Logan said.

She was about to tell him she didn't need him to come to her rescue, that she was trained as a police officer. But then one of the streetlights caught him in its glow. Blood trickled from a cut above his eye, which was already starting to swell.

"You're bleeding," she said.

"Yeah." Logan touched the injured area, then looked down at his hand. "He must have been wearing a ring."

The heat went out of Maria's temper.

"C'mon," she said. "Let's get you back to the hotel so I can do something about that cut."

CHAPTER SIX

LOGAN TRIED NOT TO WINCE as Maria dabbed at the cut above his eye with the antiseptic they'd bought at a twenty-four-hour drugstore. He was sitting on the edge of her hotel-room bed beside the bedside table, where the light was brightest.

She unwrapped one of the bandages she'd had in her toiletry bag, biting her lower lip as she focused on the task. "Hold still."

After smoothing the bandage over his skin with gentle fingers, she stepped back and examined her handiwork. "There. Now for the ice."

She went into the bathroom, where she'd left the ice bucket she'd filled from the dispenser down the hall. Taking some cubes, she wrapped them in a washcloth and seconds later was back at his side, handing him the cold compress.

"The ice will reduce the swelling, but you'll still have a bit of a shiner," she said. "Keep the ice on for twenty minutes and off for twenty and it won't be too bad."

"That means you're stuck with me for the next twenty minutes," he said.

"Only because you insisted on coming here instead of going to your own hotel."

"I didn't want you walking back by yourself," he said.

She crossed her arms over her chest and considered him. "I used to be a cop. I can take care of myself. If you'd remembered that in the bar, you wouldn't have a black eye."

"I did remember it," he said. "It didn't help."

"Do you get into a lot of fights?" She reached out, traced his not-quite-straight nose with a finger and then pulled her arm back. He resisted capturing her hand so they'd still have a physical connection. "It looks like your nose was broken."

"Not in a fight, in a racquetball game. The other guy swung his racket and my face was in the way."

"Ouch," she said.

"Yeah." Logan rubbed his nose, remembering the blast of pain. "My last fight was in high school."

"You mean the time you decked Bobby Jones in the school parking lot?"

"Yep," he said. That had been over Maria, too, although he'd never shared the particulars with her. She thought Bobby had started the fight because he was jealous that Logan had beaten him out as starting shortstop on the baseball team. In reality, Logan had hit Bobby for making a lewd comment about Maria.

She shook her head. "You'll have to come up with a story for when you get back to New York. Telling clients you were in a bar fight won't go over well."

"Don't be so sure about that," he said. "Don't women like their financial planners with a dash of danger?"

"Ha!" she said, smiling. "That's the last thing women look for in their financial advisors."

"How about you?" He met and held her gaze. "What do you look for in a man?"

The mood in the room seemed to change, becoming more charged and reminding him of the lateness of the hour. Once upon a time, she'd told him he was everything she could ever want.

She wet her lips, bringing his gaze to her mouth. "Somebody who knows to duck when a punch is thrown," she said, breaking the invisible thread of tension between them.

He laughed. "Smart aleck."

"Your turn," she said. "What do you look for in a woman?"

"Somebody like you." He hadn't thought before he spoke.

"Yeah, right."

"It's true," he said. For years, his friends had been teasing him that he dated only tall women who wore their dark hair long and straight. "That's probably why none of my relationships last."

"Because the women get on your nerves?" she quipped.

"Because what I feel for them doesn't compare to what I felt for you," he said.

The words hung between them, and just like that the tension was back in the room. She gazed at him, her blue eyes huge in her pale face, her lips slightly parted.

He stood up abruptly, cleared his throat and lowered the washcloth from his eye. "It's late. I should get going."

"It hasn't been twenty minutes yet," she protested.

"I can't last that long without doing something stupid," he said, moving past her to drop the ice in the sink. When he came out of the bathroom, she was facing him.

"What if I want you to do something stupid?" she whispered, closing the distance between them until he could smell her light, flowery scent. She anchored her hands on his chest, stood on her tiptoes and put her mouth on his.

He didn't try to resist her. He couldn't, even if he'd wanted to. It had been almost a dozen years since they'd kissed, yet she tasted familiar. Their lips molded as though they'd never been apart. It didn't take much coaxing for her to open her mouth so he could deepen the kiss. He gathered her close against him as their tongues began a sensual duel. And then they were kissing in earnest.

The old sensations swirled through him, even more powerful than he remembered. He was instantly hard, the same response she'd elicited in him years ago when he'd been a teenager. In the past, he'd always been the one to break off the kiss. If not for the control that almost killed him, he would have taken her virginity long before she was ready to lose it.

She wasn't a virgin now. They were consenting adults who wanted each other as desperately as they had then. Maybe more so. In the years after he'd lost her, he'd dreamed of making love to her, never knowing whether the reality would have been better than his imagination.

He could find out now, but what if making love to her was everything he'd ever thought it would be? What then? He'd still need to be back in Manhattan, and the life he'd made for himself by the weekend.

He lifted his mouth and moved her away from him with gentle hands. Her jaw dropped and the corners of her eyes scrunched up. She didn't understand; that was clear. But if he stayed in her hotel room even as long as it would take to explain, he might still be here in the morning.

With her fingertips, he touched the lips he'd just kissed. Even that contact sent desire shooting through him.

"I'll see you in the morning," he said.

Then he turned and left. He didn't dare glance back.

KAYLA HAD THOUGHT OF almost everything when she'd set out to make sure nobody messed with Santa.

She'd snagged a prime parking spot on Duval Street that provided a view of the intersection where the statue loomed. Then she'd settled into the front passenger seat for the long night ahead, a pair of binoculars and a thermos of coffee at the ready.

She had absolutely no doubt she could stay up all night. What she hadn't counted on was the need to pace herself with the coffee. It wasn't yet 2:00 a.m., the thermos was empty and she was in desperate need of a restroom.

As the hour grew later, she saw fewer cars and people. Across the street from the statue, one of the welcome centers that sold trolley rides of the island sights had closed hours ago. Pedestrians still walked by, though, many of them unsteady on their feet after a night of drinking.

Kayla squeezed her legs together. She'd had too much to drink, too, damn it.

There was a hotel down the block where she could probably talk her way into using the restroom. But what if somebody defaced Santa in the interim? How could she ever convince Uncle Carl she could be a good detective if she couldn't handle a simple surveillance?

Tomorrow night she wouldn't have this problem. She'd taken Maria DiMarco's advice and put a rush order on a wireless security camera that would free her from the front seat of her car. Kayla didn't have that luxury tonight.

She slumped back against the seat, trying not to think about anything involving water, pretty hard when she was parked beside a bathing suit shop.

Drops of rain appeared on the windshield and she gazed skyward through the glass. "Somebody up there hates me."

She trained her binoculars on the lonely statue and then swept them right and left, her vision helped by the businesses and residences that had opted to leave their Christmas lights on all night. Since nobody was coming, she might be able to chance running to the restroom. But, no, off in the distance, heading her way from the direction of Old Town, was a lone figure. A man with his shoulders hunched against the light rain. She'd have to stay put until he was past.

Kayla started to drop the binoculars when something about the man's walk rang a bell. He moved fluidly with a long gait, just like Alex Suarez. She zeroed in on his face. It was Alex!

She grabbed her keys and jumped out of the car, barely remembering to shut the door. She was glad she'd thought to wear tennis shoes instead of her signature high-heeled sandals. They helped her run faster.

"Alex!" she called when he was within earshot. "Can you keep an eye on Santa for five minutes?"

He stopped, his head tilting curiously. "Kayla? What's going on?"

"No time to explain. Catch!" She threw him her keys on the way past, and he snatched them out of the air. "Wait for me in the gray Civic."

Kayla broke speed records getting to the small hotel a half block up the street. She'd noticed it earlier because its exterior and the palm trees flanking its entrance were done up in multicolored Christmas lights. The sleepy employee at the desk tried to tell her the facilities were for guests only.

"I really have to go!" she shouted.

He directed her to the restroom off the lobby, where she finally found relief. After thanking the desk clerk, Kayla jogged up the now-deserted sidewalk through the light rain and past the Santa statue to her Civic.

Alex was leaning against the passenger side, his legs crossed at the ankles, her keys dangling from his fingertips. The rain had turned his shirt a darker shade of red and dampened his hair, calling into prominence his olive skin and chiseled features. Even wet, the man looked fine.

"Now will you tell me what's going on?" he asked.

The skies opened up with fat, drenching drops.

"Let's get in the car!" Kayla called over the pounding rain.

They entered from opposite sides, slamming the doors at the same time.

Kayla's hair felt plastered to her head. She nearly groaned. Here she was, in close confines with Alex Suarez, and she probably looked like a drowned rat.

"I think I've got a beach towel." At least she hoped she did. She'd gone swimming at a friend's pool last week, and tidying up after herself wasn't her strong suit. She reached into the backseat, feeling around for the fluffy towel. "Here it is."

She mopped her face and hair before handing it to Alex.

"Thanks." He wiped himself off, starting with his face and hair, then running the towel over his arms. The sleeves of his shirt were rolled up, revealing the ripple of his forearms. She wondered if he lifted weights.

"So?" he asked.

Yikes. Had he caught her staring? Probably. She doubted she'd been subtle about it. "So, what?" she asked slowly.

He laughed. "So, why did you run past me and throw me your keys?"

"Oh, that." She picked up the empty thermos from the cup holder. "When I started the surveillance, this was full. The coffee ran right through me. I'm starting to wonder if other private investigators bring a jar with them."

"You'll say anything, won't you?" he asked, laughing again.

"Sorry." She felt her face reddening. "I try to think before I speak, but it doesn't usually work."

"I think it's refreshing," he said.

"You're only saying that to be nice," she told him.

"I'm not that nice."

"Yeah, you are," she said. "What about that time at Mallory Square when you helped the old lady who fell down? You stayed with her until the paramedics came."

"You remember that?" he asked. "Wait a minute. How do you even know about that?"

She sucked in a breath. She'd done it again—run off at the mouth before engaging her brain.

The rain was coming down pretty hard, pounding on the roof of the car, so she could possibly get away with pretending she hadn't heard him.

"What about you?" she asked, raising her voice like someone hard of hearing. "What are you doing on Duval Street at two in the morning? Especially since it doesn't seem like you've been drinking."

He opened his mouth, then closed it, as though he hadn't expected the question. No wonder. He must have anticipated she'd answer the question he posed.

"I was practicing for the Christmas dart tournament tomorrow night at Estrada's Pub," he said. "On the walk home, I decided to take a detour and check on you."

"Really?" If Alex had been thinking about her today even half as much as she'd been thinking about him, things were looking up. Her heart beat faster. "How did you know I was here?"

"You hire a private eye to look out for Santa, you figure that's what she'll do," he said. "Have you got an update for me? Noticed anybody strange hanging around the statue?"

Disappointment cut through her. Alex had stopped by not to see her but to get the latest on the case.

"This is Key West," she said. "I noticed lots of strange people but nobody in particular."

"You've got a point there," he admitted. "Getting back to that old woman you mentioned, how did you know I helped her?"

Kayla would have to answer, after all. For once, however, she wouldn't say what popped into her brain: *I've been watching you for years.*

"I've seen you sometimes at the sunset celebrations," she said. "I used to help my mother make and sell bottle art."

If Kayla didn't crack this case, she'd be going back into business with her mom. That wasn't the kind of thing you said to a client, however, even when you did have a big mouth.

"I think I've got one of those bottles," he murmured.

"You do," she said. "A vase. It's hand-painted, yellow with orange-and-red streaks."

"That's right." A nearby streetlamp cast enough light into the car that she could see his brow furrow. "I didn't buy it from you, did I?"

"No, my mother." Kayla had been running late that day, almost six months ago, and had been kicking herself ever since.

"Then how did you know I bought that particular vase?"

"My mother tells me everything," she said.

"About me?"

Kayla cringed inwardly. He was good at picking up on her verbal slips, darn him. She really needed to keep her mouth closed. "Good question," she said vaguely and pointed through the window. "Hey, the rain's letting up."

Not the smoothest transition from one subject to another, but it was the best she could do.

"So it is," Alex said. "I should get going, then."

Without thinking—again—Kayla reached across the seat and grabbed his arm. "You don't have to go."

They stared into each other's eyes. A warm thrill ran through her. Her eyes dipped to his lips. Was he going to kiss her? Should she kiss him? She did nothing, and the moment passed.

"I do have to go," he said. "The restaurant opens in less than five hours."

She let her hand slip away from his arm.

"You need your beauty sleep," she told him, a dumb thing to say.

"Will you be here all night?" he asked.

"All night," she said. "Can't have anything happening to Santa."

He put his hand on the door handle, then turned to her. "Do you play darts?"

"Yes." She'd played once three or four years ago.

"You should stop by Estrada's tomorrow night," he said.

Kayla tamped down her thrill of excitement so she wouldn't scare him. "I just might do that."

"Good night." He smiled at her and got out of the car.

Kayla watched him in her rearview mirror until he'd put enough distance between himself and the car that she could squeal without him hearing.

She'd been cool and told him she might go to Estrada's.

She was definitely going.

"You just might be my ticket to a Christmas romance, Santa," she said aloud, all of her attention once again on the statue.

One hour blended into the next. The rain stopped completely, the sky got incrementally lighter and it became harder and harder to stay awake. At one point Kayla closed her eyes, thinking if she could rest them for a few seconds, she'd make it through the night.

A horn sounded.

Her eyes snapped open. A guy on a moped was at the stop sign, making an obscene gesture to another guy on a bicycle. The sun was up. People walked on the sidewalks. Not tourists. Locals going to work.

She'd fallen asleep.

A small crowd had formed in front of Santa. A woman was gesturing and laughing. Kayla hopped out of the car, her right knee almost collapsing. She was awake but her leg was still asleep.

She shook off the pins and needles and hurried over to the statue. Her stomach fell as though weighed down by a lead balloon. Somebody had given Santa black plastic Groucho glasses and darkened his bushy eyebrows, moustache and beard, as well.

With waterproof marker, she surmised.

A FEW HOURS LATER ON THE second floor of the souvenir shop across the street from the statue, Maria bent over a wireless security camera, with Kayla so close their shoulders brushed. Maria adjusted the lens until she was satisfied with the view of Santa.

"That should do it," she said. "Now you won't have to spend every night watching the statue from your car. You can do it from the comfort of your own home."

Maria straightened and stood back from the small table where she'd set up the camera. The motion made her head throb. Nothing new. Operating on short sleep always gave her a headache. She'd tossed and turned last night after Logan left, then awakened with the sun to get an early start on the day. And to avoid him.

"Are you sure the camera can penetrate glass?" Kayla stood beside her, chewing her lower lip and twisting her hands. The P.I.-in-training had called Maria the instant the camera arrived and begged her to help get it set up.

"Positive," Maria said. "But let's check it out."

They'd already hooked into the store's computer network and assigned the camera a web address that could be accessed wirelessly. The second floor of the shop was being used primarily for storage, so they picked their way past stacked boxes to the computer, breathing in a slight musty smell along the way. Maria quickly navigated to the website with the video stream.

"There he is," she said. "There's Santa."

The picture was so clear they could see the grin on Santa's face, the bills in his hand and the lettering on the 'tis the season to spend in Key West sign. People walked by, some gesturing at the statue and others ignoring it.

"The best part is I don't have to sit in front of the computer," Kayla said. "It's really cool that I'll be able to access the website from my smartphone."

"It has a recorder, too," Maria said. "So if you miss anything, you can rewind and catch whoever's doing this red-handed."

"Are you two done yet?" the salesclerk who'd let them in called from the bottom of the stairs.

"What's this guy's problem?" Kayla asked under her breath. "Did he swallow a couple lemons for breakfast or what?"

The clerk, a painfully thin man in his thirties who was wearing plush, light-up reindeer antlers, had openly scoffed when Kayla told him they were private investigators. Even after a phone call to his boss verified that they had permission to set up the camera, he'd muttered something about privacy laws. Never mind that it was perfectly legal to install a camera that monitored a public area.

"Watch this," Kayla told Maria with a mischievous gleam in her eyes. She raised her voice, calling, "Not finished yet. We're looking for a place to install a second camera to monitor the downstairs of the shop."

"What?" The booming sound of footsteps on the stairs followed his exclamation. He appeared in the doorway of the room, his reindeer antlers incongruous with his pale, gaunt face and pursed lips. "Where is it? Where's the other camera?"

"She was kidding," Maria rushed to assure

him, sending a warning glance at Kayla and hoping she got the message to keep quiet. "We only installed the one camera."

He shook a bony finger at them. "You shouldn't joke about spying on people."

"Who said I was joking?" Kayla retorted.

"She was joking." Maria raised a hand. "I give you my word on that."

A bell sounded below, announcing that a customer was entering the store. With a final glare at Kayla, the clerk pivoted on his heel and descended the steps.

"You shouldn't have teased him, Kayla," Maria said when he was gone. "What if he comes up here and disables the camera?"

She huffed in a breath. "Oh, crap. I hadn't thought of that. It just made me so mad when he refused to believe we were private investigators."

"You have to let stuff like that roll off your back," Maria advised. "The truth is, most P.I.s are men."

"So how will we women ever get respect?"

"By doing a good job," Maria told her. "That includes being nice to the unpleasant man who was ordered to help us."

She sighed aloud. "You're right. That's why you're the pro and I'm the one who falls asleep on surveillance."

Kayla had filled Maria in on what had happened the night before, from Alex Suarez's unexpected visit to her mad dash to use the hotel restroom to falling asleep and waking up to discover somebody had gotten to Santa.

"Don't sell yourself short," Maria said. "It wouldn't have occurred to me to run to the drugstore to buy toothpaste and baking soda."

"I'm lucky I was able to wipe off the marker before more people saw Santa looking like Groucho Marx." Kayla's whole body suddenly seemed to sag. "As soon as we're done here, I need to catch some sleep. You don't think the prankster will strike during the day, do you?"

"No," Maria said. "There are too many people around. Chances are much better he'll use the cover of night."

The video stream of the Santa statue was still playing on the computer screen. Two middle-aged women stood in front of it, their arms crossed identically over their chests, their heads shaking.

"They don't approve," Kayla said. "I don't blame them. That is one tacky statue."

"That's what the owner of The Flying Monkey said last night," Maria said. "He's in the merchants association. He said he spoke out against the statue from the very beginning. Your friend Alex did, too."

"I knew that about Alex. But, hey, maybe the bar owner is the prankster," Kayla said, sounding hopeful.

"I doubt it," Maria replied. "He also said he wished he'd thought of the pranks. If it was him, he'd admit it."

"Yeah. The same with Alex." Kayla shook her head. "What about your investigation? You haven't told me yet whether you're making headway."

"Not much," Maria said. "We had a lead that Mike might be playing his guitar at the Flying Monkey. It didn't pan out. A guy showed up, but he only looked a little like my brother."

"We?" Kayla pounced on her use of the pronoun. "Aren't you in Key West by yourself?"

"N… Yes," Maria said. "It was a slip of the tongue."

"Oh, no, it wasn't." Kayla pointed a finger at her. "I might have a lot to learn, but I can tell you're not being straight with me."

Maria couldn't very well deny Kayla's observation when she was trying to help her become a better detective. "Okay, you're right. My exboyfriend followed me to Key West."

"And the plot thickens." Kayla crossed her arms over her chest and stretched her legs in front of her. "Spill, girl. You better. Especially after I told you all about my crush on Alex."

"There's not much to tell." Maria realized how misleading her statement was, considering she had yet to mention 9/11 to Kayla. She sighed. "Actually, there is. You don't know my whole story."

She proceeded to fill her in on everything that had happened in the past and present. Kayla didn't interrupt, listening intently, the way any good private investigator would. She was silent when Maria finished the story.

Maria didn't blame her. It was a lot to process.

"Logan is sure Mike is dead," Maria added. "He thinks I'm on a wild-goose chase."

"Did he come to Key West to talk you out of looking for Mike?" Kayla asked.

"At first, I think he did," she said. "But I explained that if there was even the slimmest chance Mike was alive, I needed to look for him. Now Logan says he wants to help me."

"He sounds like a good guy," Kayla said.

That was the problem, Maria thought. Logan wasn't only nice to look at, he was honest and decent. She'd been hurt last night when he'd put the brakes on their kiss but only until she'd had a chance to think about it. She hadn't changed very much since her teen years. She still needed to envision a future with a man before she went to bed with him. No matter what his motives, Logan had done her a favor.

"He is a good guy," she said grudgingly. "He always has been."

Yet she'd set her alarm clock for an early hour, dragged herself out of bed and slipped away from the hotel without contacting him.

"So where is Logan now?" Kayla asked.

She was about to say he could be headed back to New York City, for all she knew. Except that wasn't true. Logan wouldn't abandon her like that, not after he'd flown twelve hundred miles to help her.

"I don't know where he is," Maria said. "I've been busy."

"Doing what?"

"Striking out," she said. "I stopped by a couple of those local breakfast spots, and then I went to that hotel in Old Town to talk to the concierge you told me about. Nobody recognized Mike."

"How about the sunset celebration?" Kayla asked. "Have you tried your luck there?"

"Not yet," Maria said. "We meant to go yesterday but got sidetracked."

"Oh, my gosh." Kayla fluttered her hands. "I should have stressed that was the place to go to talk to locals. Almost everybody there—street performers, musicians, artists, vendors—has been around for a while."

"That sounds promising," Maria said.

"Make sure you talk to my mom," Kayla said. "She knows lots of people in Key West. I need to crash, so I won't be there today. I'll let her know you're stopping by, though."

"Thanks," Maria said. "It sounds like there will be a lot of people there to talk to."

"There will be a lot of people, period," Kayla said. "It would help if you had someone with you to lighten the load. Maybe you should think about taking that Logan guy."

Last night, before Logan left her hotel room, he had said he'd see her in the morning. He had neglected to ask for her cell number, though. She'd bet he'd rung her room bright and early to make arrangements to meet, although not early enough.

"I might have burned that bridge," she said.

"Maybe," Kayla answered. "But even if you did, what's to say you can't rebuild it?"

CHAPTER SEVEN

LOGAN PICKED UP HIS smartphone that afternoon, called up an internet browser and clicked through to the website of the airline he'd flown to Key West. Because it was overcast, he didn't even have to duck under one of the poolside umbrellas to protect the display screen against glare. He kept his sunglasses on, though, the better to cover his black eye.

He'd been sitting beside the diamond-shaped pool at his hotel for the past ten minutes, nursing a tall, cool glass of lemonade. The blue water sparkled and soft island music drifted from an outside speaker, yet Logan was the only person here. The other guests either had more interesting things on their agenda or didn't consider a temperature in the low seventies warm enough to sit by the pool.

Logan wouldn't be here, either, if Maria hadn't shaken him for the second day in a row. He'd phoned her hotel room at eight that morning, believing that was plenty early enough to catch her after their late night.

He'd misjudged her again.

She hadn't answered the phone. Kicking himself for not thinking to get her cell number, he'd gone over to the Blue Tropics and knocked on the door. She hadn't answered that summons, either. He'd even hung around the lobby—again—for nearly an hour before he finally gave up waiting for her.

He'd told Maria she needed to accept that Mike was dead. Logan needed to accept that Maria didn't want him in Key West, no matter how willingly she'd kissed him last night.

His body stirred. If he'd thought to buy a swimsuit yesterday, he'd jump in the pool to cool off.

On his smartphone he pulled up tomorrow's schedule, locating a noon flight that would get him into the city in time for dinner with clients on Saturday.

He anticipated having an airline representative on the phone within moments to take his reservation. But before he could punch in the number, he picked up movement out of the corner of his eye. A woman was coming into the pool area. Not just any woman. Maria.

Years ago his heart had sped up whenever he saw her. It still did.

She walked toward him, her shapely legs bare under her casual summer dress. Her silky hair was loose and spilled down her back. A touch of pink tinged her fair complexion, as though she might have gotten too much sun. Sunglasses covered her striking blue eyes.

"I'm glad I found you." She stopped a few steps shy of him, twisting her hands together. She wet her lips. "How's the eye?"

He lowered his sunglasses so she could see for herself. As far as black eyes went, it was mild, but the area under the socket had some discoloration.

She wrinkled her nose. "Does it still hurt?"

"Applying the ice right away was a good idea." He put his sunglasses back in place and held up his cell phone. "We should have exchanged numbers, but that might not have worked for you. Makes it harder to avoid somebody."

She had the decency to look embarrassed. "I deserved that."

"Yeah, you did."

"Give me a chance to explain." She sat down in the pool chair next to him, moving this way and that until she settled into the seat. She still didn't seem comfortable. "I came to apologize for last night."

"Last night?" He frowned. "It wasn't your fault I got punched."

"No, not that." She wrung her hands some

more, barely meeting his eyes. "I kind of threw myself at you."

He wouldn't have put it quite that way. Whatever she was tossing he'd been glad to catch.

"I appreciate how, um, gentlemanly you acted." She must have rolled her eyes, because her brows briefly appeared above her sunglasses. "I should have told you that this morning, but the truth is I was embarrassed."

He cocked an eyebrow, still saying nothing. He was curious as to where she was headed with this.

"With the history between us, I should have known better than to try to start something up. So this morning, well, I couldn't face you."

"You're facing me now," he pointed out.

She rubbed her forehead and gazed out at the pool. She'd never looked more vulnerable.

"I realized I was being a jerk," she said.

"Whoa," he said. "That's taking it too far."

"I don't think so. I mean, you came all this way to help me, even going so far as taking a punch for me, and I keep ditching you."

"When you put it that way," he said slowly, "maybe you have been a jerk."

Laughter erupted from her in a quick, joyful burst. When they were teenagers, her unrestrained laugh was one of the things he'd liked best about her.

"So we're good?" she asked.

"That depends on whether you plan to keep ditching me."

She shook her head. "Nope. I'm taking you up on what you're offering, even if it is for only one more day."

"One more day?" he asked.

"I figured you'd leave tomorrow, so you're back by the weekend," she said, and he thought about the web browser on his smartphone parked at the airline site. "Here's how you can help out today."

She told him about the sunset celebration at Mallory Square, where musicians, street performers, artists and food and drink vendors gathered nightly.

"If you come with me, you can help show the age progression and ask the locals if they recognize Mike." She paused and licked her lips. "You can also keep an eye out for him."

"I can do that," Logan said. "And who knows? We might spot somebody else we recognize."

She tilted her head. "Come again?"

"You're keeping your mind open to the possibility that someone besides Mike contacted Caroline Webb, right?" he asked.

"Of course. But are you keeping yours open to the possibility Mike is alive?" she retorted.

Logan hesitated.

"Listen, I know where you stand," she said. "If you think showing his photo around is a waste of your time, I'll accept that."

"I don't." He decided to be straight with her. "I'll admit I don't believe for a minute that Mike's alive. The longer we go without finding him, however, the closer you'll be to accepting he's dead."

She drew in a quick breath, as though his words had wounded her. "I've been an investigator long enough to know not everything is exactly what it seems, Logan. Not even 9/11."

"Nothing would make me happier than being wrong." He stuck out a hand. "So we're in this together for as long as I'm in Key West, right? No more giving me the slip?"

She slid her hand into his. Like last night, he felt an instant connection. "Deal."

Her cell phone rang. She let go of his hand and reached for the phone, checking the display. "This is a San Francisco area code. It could be Billy Tillman. His mother promised she'd have him call."

Logan recognized the name. Billy had been Mike's best friend growing up. When Logan and Maria were dating, Billy had been a frequent visitor to the DiMarco house.

"Can you put him on speaker?" Logan asked

before she could answer the call. "Then you won't have to repeat what he says."

She nodded. "Hello."

"This is Billy Tillman?" It sounded as if Billy was asking a question. "My mom said you wanted me to call?"

"Thanks, Billy." Maria met Logan's eyes. "She said you moved to San Francisco."

"Is that what you wanted to talk to me about?" he asked. "Are you thinking of coming to California?"

"No," Maria said. "I need to ask you about Mike."

"Your brother Mike?"

"Have you heard from him?" she asked.

There was silence at the other end. "I don't understand."

"I'm exploring the possibility that he wasn't at work the day of the attacks," Maria explained.

"You mean you think he's alive?" Billy exclaimed. "No way. I'd know it if he was."

Logan's contention exactly. Maria cut eye contact with him.

"Maybe not," she said. "Mike could have had a reason for disappearing. Like, maybe he owed money or he'd gotten on the wrong side of somebody."

"I don't know nothin' about anything like that," Billy said.

Maria's chest rose and fell, as though she was taking a deep breath. "I need you to think, Billy. Did Mike have any connection to the Florida Keys? Did he ever talk about coming here? Do you know if any of your friends moved here? Or even visited?"

"No," Billy said. "I don't understand why you're asking me this stuff."

"Caroline Webb thinks she might have heard from him," Maria said.

"That bitch who dumped him in high school?" Vitriol filled Billy's voice. "You can't listen to anything she says."

"Would you do me a favor, Billy?" Maria asked, ignoring his outburst. "Would you call me if you hear anything?"

"What am I gonna hear?"

"Thanks for your help, Billy. Just please call me if you hear anything at all," Maria said and hung up before he could say anything else.

"Well, that was enlightening," Logan said.

"What do you mean? Billy didn't know anything."

"Don't you think he would know if Mike was alive?" Logan said. "Wouldn't Mike confide in his best friend?"

"Interesting questions," Maria said. "Here's one of mine. Since Billy hasn't heard of any of their friends coming to the Keys, doesn't that make it more likely that Mike was the one who contacted Caroline?"

Logan blew out a breath, realizing they were at an impasse. He was afraid she was so emotionally involved that she wasn't thinking clearly. But he knew better than to bring up that theory. At least, not yet.

"There's still a few hours before sunset," he said. "Need help with anything before then?"

"As a matter of fact, I do," she said. "Kayla gave me the names of some valets and concierges who work at the hotels in Old Town. She thought it might be worth showing them Mike's photo."

Maria rose, reached into her pocketbook and pulled out a thin stack of age progressions along with another sheet covered with handwriting. "I took down some names and addresses. I've already talked to the ones that are crossed off. If you take the top half, I can take the bottom."

"Will do," Logan said, getting to his feet.

She laid a hand on his arm, her eyes lifting to his face. "I appreciate your help. Truly I do. Especially after last night."

"I should admit something about last night," he told her, keeping his gaze steady on hers. "It just about killed me to leave you."

"Excuse me?"

He captured a few strands of her hair between

his fingers and slowly rubbed them together. "If I hadn't thought you'd regret it in the morning, you couldn't have pried me away," he whispered.

Her lips parted, but no words escaped. He released her hair, letting her off the hook and leaving her to face an uncomfortable truth.

The attraction that had been so strong when they were teenagers wasn't only still there, it was more potent than ever.

WITH AT LEAST ANOTHER hour remaining before the sun sank below the horizon, the celebration on the Mallory Square dock was in full swing. Knots of people, most of them tourists, surrounded the buskers. The largest crowd gathered around a man with a team of trained house cats that could do everything from walk a tightrope to jump through hoops. No street performer lacked an audience, though.

As far as Maria could tell, her brother was neither a performer nor a spectator. He wasn't hawking wares, selling refreshments or reading tarot cards, either. Worse, not one of the local exhibitors she'd spoken with had recognized him.

She checked the display screen on her cell phone. Time to meet Logan beside the frozen yogurt stand and compare notes. She spotted him immediately, even though there were taller men around him wearing brighter colors. Few of them looked as good in shorts and a T-shirt as Logan did. His legs were long and muscular and his shoulders broad. The slanting sun shone on him, bringing out the golden highlights in his hair and defining the angles of his face.

She raised a hand and waved to get his attention as she walked toward him. His white teeth flashed below the dark sunglasses covering his black eye. In his hands were two containers with spoons protruding. He met her halfway and handed one to her. "I thought you might need fortification."

That didn't sound promising. "I take it you haven't had any luck, either?"

He shook his head. "Nobody thought the age progression looked familiar, and I haven't seen anybody I recognize."

"Thanks for the frozen yogurt." She took a mouthful of the sweet concoction while she planned the next move. "There's still one section of the dock we haven't covered. Maybe we'll get lucky."

"How about we hit that after we take a break?" Logan gestured to where a small crowd was gathering around a middle-aged Hispanic man on a unicycle. He kept upright by pedaling backward, then forward. On top of his head were about a dozen plates, a two-by-four, some books, a couple of VHS tapes and assorted household items. "We can watch the balancing man."

"I don't think so," Maria said.

"How about the comic magician?" Logan asked. "Or the contortionist? When I was walking by earlier, he was folding one of his legs over his head."

"You go on," she said. "I'm going over to that last section now. And I still haven't talked to Kayla's mother."

"Hey, we're in this together," Logan said. "I'll come with you and show Mike's photo to the merchants neither of us have hit yet."

She nodded. Considering she knew he didn't expect to find anybody who recognized her brother, it shouldn't matter what he did. Although with Logan beside her, she didn't feel quite so alone.

She found Helene Fryburger at a stand crammed with bottles of all shapes and sizes. Photo holders, drinking mugs, terrariums and hand-painted bottle vases occupied the table in front of her. Wind chimes made of bottle fragments fluttered above her head in the light breeze.

"Kayla told me you might stop by and see me." Helene was a small woman with long blond hair, big eyes and a way of making you feel you were the only person in the vicinity. "She said you're looking for your brother."

"I am." Maria produced the age progression and showed it to her. "By any chance, does he look familiar?"

Helene studied the photo. The longer she looked at it, the faster Maria's heart beat.

"Something about him reminds me of a guy I see around sometimes," the woman said. "Plays the guitar. Give me a minute and I'll come up with his name."

Maria allowed herself to hope.

"I have it." Helene snapped her fingers. "Clem. His name is Clem."

As quickly as Maria's hopes had risen, they crashed to earth. Clem was the name of the guitarist with the limp from The Flying Monkey. She realized she'd been holding her breath and made herself exhale. "It's not Clem."

"Then, no. Sorry, hon. I don't recognize him." Helene shook her head. "You should ask my brother. He knows everybody in Key West."

"I already did." Maria had emailed the photo to Key Carl, who'd given the same negative response as his sister. "Kayla sent me to you because she said you know a lot of people, too."

"I do, but most everybody I know is here at the sunset celebration," she said. "Have you shown that photo around?"

"Yeah," Maria said. "Nobody knows him."

A woman in a floppy hat and a red sundress decorated with snowflakes approached the booth and picked up one of the vases, turning it this way and that.

Helene held up a finger to Maria. "Can I help you, hon?" she asked the potential customer.

"I can wait until you're finished," the woman said.

"I've taken up enough of your time," Maria told Helene. "Thanks for looking at the photo."

"No, thank *you* for what you're doing for my sweet girl," she replied. "Kayla wears her heart on her sleeve, you know. This job with her uncle Carl means a lot to her. She'll be crushed if it doesn't work out."

"Then I hope my advice helps." Maria liked Helene Fryburger. A lot. The woman obviously had her daughter's best interests at heart. "I'll let you take care of your customer. Nice meeting you."

Maria showed the age progression to a few other merchants who didn't recognize Mike, then went in search of Logan. She found him within minutes, looking through landscape paintings of the Florida Keys at an artist's booth.

"Hey," she called as she approached him. "Any success?"

"None," he said. "How about you? Was Kayla's mom any help?"

"No." Maria indicated the vendors to the left of them, one who sold homemade soap and another peddling straw baskets. "If you hit those booths, we got everybody."

"I did," he said.

She swallowed her frustration and gestured at the paintings he'd been looking through. "See anything you like?"

He flipped to a rendering of a typical Key West house surrounded by lush vegetation, the pastel-blue siding contrasting with the green of the palms and the red flowering trees. "I like the juxtaposition of the colors in this one."

"It's nice." Maria angled her head, taking a closer look at the painting. "You're way more talented than whoever painted it, though."

"A matter of opinion."

She shook her head. "It's a fact. You have a gift. I don't understand how you could have given it up, especially because you were so passionate about painting."

"You wouldn't understand," Logan muttered under his breath.

"What's that supposed to mean?"

"Forget it." He turned away from the booth and began walking through the crowd.

Maria hurried to catch up. "I'd rather not forget it. I'd really like to know what you meant by that."

He slowed and ran a hand over the back of his neck. "C'mon, Maria. Today couldn't have been easy on you. We don't need to talk about this. There's no point."

"Why not?" She knew she was belaboring the point but couldn't stop herself. "I only stated the obvious. I can't understand how you could love something so much and just give it up."

A muscle worked in his jaw. It occurred to her that her words had a double meaning. Once upon a time, back in the days when she'd believed in happily ever after, Logan had claimed to love her, too.

"You really don't get it, do you?" His voice was tight. "I only gave up on painting. You gave up on me."

Before Maria could form a reply, cries of delight split the air. All around them people pointed at the horizon, where the sun was dipping in a sky that glowed red, yellow and orange. Camera shutters whirred, street performers suspended their acts and people jostled for better positions. Two girls about nine or ten years old held hands, jumping up and down in delight.

"The show's on," Logan said.

He walked to a less crowded area, staking

out a spot with an unobstructed view. Maria stared after him, dumbfounded by what he'd said, as the crowd oohed and aahed at the sun's fiery descent.

Questions filled her head, paramount among them how Logan could have such a skewed view of the past. She wouldn't ask any of them, though. Logan had been right.

There was no point in discussing it. What was done was done.

KAYLA CHECKED THE VIDEO stream on her smartphone and assured herself Santa was untouched before filling her lungs with jasmine-scented air.

Giving silent thanks for the technology that rescued her from doing surveillance work sitting in a car, she smoothed down her flirty red skirt and tried not to notice that her hands were shaking.

Since she could check in on Santa every ten or fifteen minutes, she hadn't allowed her big case to wreck this long-awaited chance with Alex. She wouldn't let her nerves derail her, either. Instead of acting like the schoolgirl he'd initially thought she was, she'd be adult and sophisticated.

Holding her chin high and lifting her lips in

a smile she hoped was serene, she glided into Estrada's Pub.

A young man at the door thrust out a Santa Claus hat similar to the one he was wearing. "You can't get in tonight without one of these."

Kayla's hand flew to the hair she'd spent thirty minutes styling so it fell just so. "You're kidding me. I really have to put that on?"

The bouncer picked up a white bit of fluff that looked like it was made from cotton balls. "It's either the hat or the clip-on beard."

Kayla put on the hat and stepped into the bar. Paralysis hit her hard. People in Santa hats and beards laughed, talked and hoisted mugs of beer and assorted drinks. Dartboards lined a wall in the back. Strung above them was a banner that read First Annual Christmas Mixed Doubles Dart Tournament. Multicolored Christmas lights twinkled from every fixture, adding to the assault on the senses.

She ventured forward on her high-heeled sandals.

"Kayla!" Alex beckoned to her, breaking away from a knot of people and meeting her halfway. He wore a grin and a Santa hat similar to hers yet still looked so handsome she had a hard time catching her breath. "Glad you could make it."

He touched her arm, making her think of the

other places she'd like him to touch. She almost groaned at the thought. *Think adult and sophisticated,* she warned herself.

"My pleasure," she said.

Ugh! Had she really said that? With that snooty intonation?

"No, it's mine." Alex raised his voice a little to be heard over a jukebox that was playing a corny Christmas song with barking dogs. "Something came up and my partner couldn't make it. Can you fill in?"

Uh-oh. She shouldn't have told him she knew how to play darts.

"Is that allowed?" she hedged. "Don't tournaments make you preregister or something?"

"This tournament's for fun," he said. "Nobody will mind if you step in. Come on."

The hope on his face decided her. That, and the chance to spend time with him. After all, how hard could darts be?

"I'm in," she said.

"Terrific." He took her hand and led her to a group of men and women roughly his age. She didn't know any of them. "Everybody, this is Kayla, my new partner."

"Alex always picks quality partners." The comment came from an exotic-looking woman with slanted cheekbones, short dark hair and a willowy build. "She must be a ringer."

A ringer? Kayla would be lucky if she could hit any of the rings on the dartboard.

"You can keep up with her, *querida*." A handsome man with dark hair, olive skin and a Spanish accent slung an arm around the woman. To the group, he said, "Nalani looked great in warm-ups."

"Do I get some practice throws?" Kayla asked Alex.

"'fraid not." He indicated the area with the adjacent dartboards. Two couples had already started squaring off against each other. "We're starting. It's 501, by the way, not cricket."

The only cricket Kayla knew of was the English game played with bats and balls. She had a better handle on 501.

"That's the game where the first team to reach 501 points wins, right?" she asked.

"Not quite," he said slowly. "The objective is to count down from 501 points to zero."

Kayla thumped her forehead. "Of course. The principle's the same, though. Aim for the 20s and the 19s."

"And the triple line," Alex added.

There was a triple line?

"We're up next, against Jorge and Nalani," he said, "but I've got time to get you a drink. What would you like?"

"Tonic water, please," Kayla said. "With lime."

"Not gin?"

"I don't drink," she said. "I'm silly enough as it is."

He laughed. While he was gone, Kayla moved away from his friends to a quiet corner where she could check her smartphone. As expected, Santa was unscathed. Somebody would have to be awfully bold to pull off another prank at this relatively early hour of the night when lots of people were in the street.

She slipped the phone back into the deep pocket of her skirt and watched the side-by-side games. The teams took turns, with each contestant throwing three darts per visit at the board. She couldn't figure out all the rules, though. She sidled up to Nalani. "I hope you don't mind if I ask you a question."

"Not at all," Nalani said with a friendly smile. Her speech had a musical quality.

"What does going bust mean?"

"The last dart you throw needs to hit the bull's-eye or a double segment," she said. "If it doesn't, or if you don't end on a double, it's a bust."

"Duh! Of course!" Kayla said. "Thanks for the refresher."

Nalani smiled. "I haven't seen you around before."

"Bars aren't really my scene."

"So Vanessa doesn't have anything to worry about?" Nalani asked.

Kayla thought the name sounded elegant, as if it belonged to a woman of great beauty and poise. "Who's Vanessa?"

"Alex's regular partner." It seemed to Kayla that Nalani put extra emphasis on the word *partner.* Did that mean Vanessa was also Alex's girlfriend?

He returned with her drink a few moments later and stood beside her as the other teams finished up their games. And then it was their turn at the dartboard. Alex and Jorge squared off to determine which team would start, with Alex's bull's-eye beating Jorge's throw.

"Ladies first," Alex told her, sweeping his hand out with a flourish.

Kayla fought the urge to wipe her damp palms on her skirt. Drawing in a deep breath, she gathered the three darts in her left hand and stepped up to the line. Now what? One of the previous competitors had flicked her wrist back and forth four or five times before letting the dart fly. That seemed like a good idea.

Kayla went into the motion and sent the dart airborne. It hit the outer portion of the board. A four. Kayla forced herself to smile and looked at Alex over her shoulder.

"Just warming up," she told him.

Her next toss landed on a two. The third throw missed the board entirely. Nothing was left to do but take the walk of shame back to Alex's side while Nalani started her turn.

"Now you know I'm a fraud," Kayla said. "I can't play at all."

"Sure you can play," he said. "You hit the board twice."

"I only got six points!"

"Better than zero." He winked at her and waited for his turn, where he racked up ninety-nine points. He didn't strut when he rejoined Kayla, probably because a high score was nothing unusual for him.

"You're really good at this, huh?" she asked.

Nalani turned around and called, "He's really good at it."

"Now I feel worse," Kayla admitted.

"Then cut it out," he said. "I like to win as much as the next guy, but the fun is in playing. If not for you, I wouldn't have a partner."

"Because your girlfriend, Vanessa, couldn't make it?"

One of his eyebrows lifted. "My girlfriend? Vanessa and I only hook up at darts."

"Oh," Kayla said. Now she had something else to feel embarrassed over.

"You're up next, Kayla," Jorge called.

"My partner's a bit inexperienced," Alex told his friends. "Mind if I give her a few pointers?"

"We would if we were losing," Jorge said. "But since we're up, go right ahead."

They approached the dartboard together, with Alex standing close enough behind her that she could feel his breath. Her heart drummed, her legs felt rubbery and she thought she might hyperventilate. He took gentle hold of her forearm.

"Align your shoulder, elbow and hand to point at the board in a straight line," he said, his mouth close to her ear. "Yeah, that's right. Now keep the dart level and throw it with the same motion you would a hammer. Got it?"

She didn't trust herself to speak, so she nodded. The instant she did, he released her. She felt strangely bereft.

"Now let that dart fly," he said.

She concentrated on what he'd told her, this time hitting the ten, the twelve and the fourteen. Her contribution wasn't nearly enough even though Alex was the best player in their foursome. Jorge and Nalani prevailed and advanced to the next round.

Alex snagged a table for two near the action, pulling out a chair for Kayla. She couldn't remember the last time a man had done that.

She sat down. Across from her, Alex looked

darkly handsome. "I'm sorry I wrecked your chances to do well in the tournament."

"Forget about that," he said. "I'm glad you could come at all. I thought you might be tied up on surveillance."

"I have to leave at ten o'clock," she said. "I'm pulling another all-nighter."

"I might stop by later tonight to say hello, then."

"Oh, I won't be in my car," Kayla said. "I'll be watching Santa from the comfort of my own home."

His nose scrunched up. "How will you do that?"

"I'll show you." She reached into her skirt pocket, pulled out her smartphone and went to the video stream of Santa. "It's really cool. We installed a wireless security camera in the souvenir shop across the street from the statue."

"We? I thought you were a solo operator."

"I've got a—" Kayla hesitated, thinking about how to word it "—a consultant who knows about these things. Once we connected the camera to a router, we could access the feed. Voilà! Twenty-four-hour surveillance."

"That's why you keep looking at your phone," he said.

She nodded. "I check Santa every ten or fifteen minutes. It seems pretty unlikely anything will happen while the night's still young, though."

"What if it does?" he asked. "Won't you miss it?"

"I'm staying up all night, but the camera has a recorder and a rewind button. Even if I don't see the guy in the act, I'll have him on tape."

Alex took a long pull of beer. "As long as the newspaper doesn't get any more embarrassing photos, sounds good to me."

"About that." Kayla took a deep breath. "There's something I should tell you. The *Sun* almost got a shot like that this morning."

She told him about waking up to find that somebody had marked up Santa and how she'd rushed to a nearby drugstore for toothpaste and baking soda and wiped Santa clean. As she was walking away, she'd noticed a photographer wearing a *Key West Sun* T-shirt approaching the statue. She hadn't stuck around to talk to him.

"That was lucky," Alex said.

"You're telling me. The thing is, it was really early in the morning. Before seven. Who'd expect a photographer to be on the scene so fast?"

"Maybe the photographers make a habit of driving by Santa just in case they can get another good photo," Alex suggested.

"Possibly. But not that early in the morning. I think somebody tipped him off." Kayla wondered why this line of thought hadn't occurred to her before. "That could be how he got the photo of Zombie Santa, too."

"Could be," Alex said.

Kayla didn't agree. She thought it was likely. She'd even go so far as to say it was probable. She'd find out tomorrow when she paid the *Sun* photo department a visit.

CHAPTER EIGHT

L<small>OGAN STRAIGHTENED FROM</small> the wall where he'd been leaning, watching Maria leave the latest in a seemingly endless stream of bar managers who booked live talent. She headed Logan's way, weaving through the crowd.

She met his gaze and gave a quick shake of her head. This guy had never seen Mike before, either.

Unlike most of the other women in the bar, she wore neither red nor green. In a pale blue summer dress and with her long hair swaying slightly, she was the picture of tired elegance. Her shoulders sloped, the corners of her mouth sagged and putting one foot in front of the other seemed to be a chore.

Enough was enough, Logan thought. He closed the gap between them and took her gently by the arm.

"Let's get out of here," he suggested.

He expected an argument, but she nodded and let him guide her from the bar. After leaving the sunset celebration, they'd spent the evening walking from one establishment to the next, operating on her theory that Mike might be making some money playing the guitar.

They hadn't found him, of course. Nor had any of the bar managers who booked live talent recognized the photo.

"Disappointing night." Logan stated the obvious once they were outside the bar at the renovated historic seaport, better known as the Key West Bight. During the day, the Bight was the place to arrange a day on the water or to peruse the shops and galleries. At night, visitors frequented restaurants and bars that stayed open into the wee hours.

"I might be on the wrong track with the guitar," she said. "Just because Mike was into playing as a teenager doesn't mean he still is."

Logan was silent, letting her talk.

"I still need to check out some local bars on the other side of the island," she said, lines furrowing her forehead. "And Kayla gave me the names of some more valets and concierges I haven't talked to yet. She thought they might know of businesses that pay their employees under the table, just in case Mike is flying under the radar."

"Sounds like a plan," Logan said. "For tomorrow."

"But…" Her voice trailed off and her chest

heaved. "You're right. I've had about all the frustration I can stand for one night."

"Let's take the scenic route back," he said. "It won't take any longer if we walk along the water for a few blocks. That way, we can enjoy the Bight before Christmas."

"The what?"

"That's what they call the holiday celebration that's going on down here at the harbor," he said. "The Harbor Walk of Lights is the main attraction. So far, I'm impressed."

"I haven't paid much attention." She looked around now. Nearest them, tiny white lights covered the trunks of palm trees, with strings of green lights fanning out to the swaying fronds. The effect was festive and tropical all at once.

"Wow, that's pretty," she said. "I think I would like walking along the water."

Holiday lights twinkled all around them, even under the water. Logan knew that the city had hosted a boat parade earlier in the month. Most of the vessels docked at the Bight were still decorated, with their lights shining even though it was after midnight. Lights snaked up masts, encircled railings and formed familiar shapes, wreaths, sleighs, angels, elves and trees among them. Along the shore, some shops and restaurants had gone with an all-white theme.

Other lights glowed red, orange, green, yellow and blue.

"This is nice," Maria said. "Different from the Southern Lights in Lexington but just as beautiful."

Logan hadn't thought of the Southern Lights in years, a light display that stretched for miles through the Kentucky Horse Park, celebrating both the holiday season and the Kentucky horse culture.

"Do you still go?" he asked.

"Every year with Annalise and the boys," Maria answered. "When they were younger, they liked it so much they went twice, once with Annalise's husband and once with me. I haven't gotten them out of the car yet, though."

Most people toured the display by car, although some elected to stroll through it. There was yet another way to see them.

"Remember when we jogged through the display?" He chuckled. "That wasn't the best way to appreciate the lights, especially when you challenged me to a race the last mile."

He'd let her take the lead because he enjoyed watching her run. He'd liked watching her, period. He still did.

Maria was smiling. He didn't know whether that was because of the memories or the super-size garland that was draped around the ferry terminal.

"You only won because you distracted me with those loud kissing noises," she said.

"Really?" He grinned. "I thought you lost on purpose so you could give me my prize."

He no longer remembered what he'd bet, only that he had every intention of winning after she'd wagered a kiss. He'd collected it beside a lit-up display of Santa riding a Thoroughbred. They hadn't stopped kissing until a young father with a bunch of kids in the car had laid on his horn. Then they'd had an attack of laughter.

"We had some good times," she said.

They approached a trio of live Christmas trees gracing a plaza. Logan breathed in the scent of evergreens, enjoying himself more than he had since arriving in Key West. "We're still having them."

"Not for long," she said. "You're leaving soon. It'll probably be another eleven years until we see each other again."

He stopped dead. Even though the hour was late, couples and small groups of people walked the harbor, their voices and laughter carrying on the sea breeze.

"You really believe I'll go to New York and forget about you?" he asked.

"Why not? You've done it before."

That was so far from the truth it was laughable. Maria had been already married by the time Logan was a junior in college, but that didn't stop him from comparing every coed he met to her. All of them came up short. So did the women he'd dated since graduating and moving to the city.

"I wasn't the one who married someone else." He hadn't expected his words to sound so accusing.

"Only because you jilted me," she retorted.

He'd repeatedly resisted discussing the past with her, but he couldn't let that comment pass.

"That's not how I remember it," he challenged. "I wanted to keep dating you while I was in college. You were the one who broke up with me."

"Yeah, because you didn't care enough to take a chance on us."

"I didn't care enough?" He heard the volume of his voice rising and tried to tone it down. "How long did it take you to find another guy? Six months?"

"At least Jerry loved me."

"I loved you!"

She shook her head. "Not as much as Jerry. He had a single red rose delivered to me every day for two weeks until I agreed to go to dinner with him. On our first date, he said he knew I was the one."

"So you married him when you were only twenty years old."

"What did you think I'd do? Sit around pining for you?"

"I thought you'd eventually realize that by getting an education I was making an investment in our future," Logan said. "I thought we'd get back together."

"We never would have parted if you'd loved me enough."

"How about Jerry?" Logan had believed he'd come to terms with Maria's marriage long ago, yet every time he said the other man's name a shudder ran through him. "If he loved you so much, why aren't you still together?"

She looked away, out toward the rippling water and the luminated boats. "It's complicated. There were things about him I wasn't aware of when we got married."

No surprise there. She couldn't have known the guy very well when they'd taken the plunge. Logan felt his hand ball into a fist. If Jerry had mistreated her, he'd hunt him down and hurt him. "What things?"

She shrugged as though it wasn't a big deal, yet he didn't buy that for a second. "He was... controlling. I wasn't about to let him know where I was every minute of every day, no matter how much he loved me."

"Sounds more like obsession than love," Logan said.

She seemed about to say more, then closed her mouth and shook her head. "What's the use of talking about this? What does it matter now?"

It mattered. He wasn't sure why, just that it did. Now wasn't the time to discuss it, though, not when she was dead on her feet. He shouldn't have let himself get drawn into the conversation. She didn't need any more stress tonight.

"Okay," he said. "But for the record, I'm sorry."

She tilted her head, her expression unutterably sad. "Sorry about what?"

"Sorry I didn't fight harder for you," Logan said. "No matter how much you think Jerry loved you, it wasn't as much as I did."

COULD IT BE POSSIBLE that Maria had been wrong about Logan not loving her enough? Not once in all the years since they'd been apart had she second-guessed herself about the breakup. Until tonight.

He had sounded so sincere when he'd gazed into her eyes and spoke of love.

A half dozen times since they'd left the harbor and started walking back through the tourist area, she'd started to ask him why he hadn't tried harder to make her understand. She'd equated him not wanting to move in with her while he went to art school in Louisville with not loving her enough. What if she'd been wrong?

She continued to keep her thoughts to herself as they walked side by side down Duval Street, because what she'd said at the dock still applied.

They couldn't turn back the clock. So what did it matter now, eleven years after the fact?

A fair number of bars were still open, and most of the restaurants and shops that were closed for the night had left on their holiday lights. The moon and the stars shone in the clear night sky, adding natural beauty to the evening.

A streak of light slashed across the darkness above.

"Oh, my gosh!" Maria stopped dead and pointed overhead. "Is that another shooting star?"

"That's a shooting star, all right." Logan gazed upward, too. "What do you mean by another one?"

"I saw one that night in Lexington when you showed up at the restaurant to talk me out of coming to Key West," she said.

"Hmm. I don't think I've seen more than a handful of shooting stars in my entire life."

Could the star be a sign?

"My mother says if you see a shooting star before Christmas and make a wish, it'll come true." Maria wasn't sure why she told him that unless it was to give her mom's claim validity. Because, oh, she wanted desperately to believe.

"I never figured you for the fanciful type," he said, "but I guess it can't hurt to make a wish."

Maria's thoughts, exactly. She shut her eyes tight and mentally repeated the wish she'd made that night in Lexington. She wouldn't tell Logan what it was, though. Her mother said the same rule applied to shooting stars and the candles on a birthday cake. If you spoke your wish aloud, you'd jinx it.

She'd barely finished wishing when she caught the faint strains of what sounded like guitar music. She strained her ears, trying to determine whether it was her imagination. No. Somebody was playing a ballad on the guitar. Not just any ballad, but one she'd heard Mike practicing in the basement.

"Sweet Caroline," the Neil Diamond song with the catchy chorus. Mike had been determined to perfect the song after he'd started dating Caroline Webb, although nobody else in the DiMarco family would have labeled her as sweet.

Maria laid a hand on Logan's arm. "Can you tell where that guitar music is coming from?"

"Sounds like the next block," he said. "Probably a street performer hoping for some change."

"I think it might be Mike." She gripped his arm. Her chest felt so tight with anticipation she could hardly breathe. "That's one of his favorite songs."

"Let's check it out, then." Logan didn't hesitate, taking her hand and crossing the street, heading toward the music. It was probably because of what he'd told her earlier, that the less successful she was in tracking down her brother the more open she'd be that someone else was behind the photos and phone calls. At the moment, she didn't care about Logan's motivation. She held on to him, glad he was guiding the way, while other thoughts whirled through her mind.

She hadn't heard the song "Sweet Caroline" in years. It was too much of a coincidence that a random street performer would choose to sing it after she'd seen the shooting star, wasn't it? In case wishes weren't enough, she said a silent prayer that her quest was coming to an end.

"There's a guitarist on the corner in the next block," Logan said, increasing his pace. She lengthened her steps to keep up with him, her heart hammering harder with every one.

"Sweet Caroline" was still playing, its cheerful melody louder now. Could it be that she was a few notes away from a reunion with her brother?

A knot of people clogged the sidewalk ahead. Maria tried but couldn't see around them. Logan was not only taller, he had a better angle.

"Can you see the guitarist?" she asked breathlessly. "Is it Mike?"

Logan craned his neck. Then he came to a standstill, tugging on her hand to slow her down.

"It's not Mike, Maria," he said.

She started shaking her head even before he finished the statement. "You can't know that yet. Not from this distance."

She pulled her hand free from his and broke into a jog, weaving through the other people until nothing but sidewalk was between her and the guitarist.

She skidded to a stop.

He was a heavyset black man.

"What's your hurry, sweetheart?" One of the young men she'd brushed by called to her as he passed. "Things move slower here in Key West."

"Like a sea turtle," one of his friends added. The entire group laughed.

Maria didn't acknowledge their comments. She couldn't. Her throat seemed to close up. Tears welled in her eyes. She blinked them back.

Logan's arm came around her, gathering

her close. "I'm sorry you keep getting disappointed."

She nodded. No matter how certain he was that Mike was dead, she didn't doubt Logan was sorry.

"Let's get out of here," he said, repeating his words from earlier in the evening.

Maria walked beside him back to the hotel on autopilot, her mind trying to think through the puzzle. On an island as compact as Key West, somebody should have recognized her brother's picture by now. Maybe Sergeant Peppler had been right about Mike not being a local. If he was a tourist who happened to be in Key West when he'd mailed the letter, he could be living anywhere, maybe even on one of the other keys in the island chain. Or maybe he'd gotten wind that Maria was searching for him and had gone underground again.

"What are you thinking?" Logan asked. They were in the hotel elevator, with his hand resting against her back.

"Lots of things," she said. "Mostly I'm trying to come up with reasons we can't pick up Mike's trail."

Logan appeared about to say something. She held up a palm. "Don't say anything about 9/11. I don't think I can bear to hear any of your negativity right now."

"I wasn't going to," he said. "Believe me, I don't like to think about that day any more than you do."

She remembered what he'd told her at the restaurant in Lexington, about talking Mike into going to his job that day. At the time, all Maria could hear was verification that Mike had been thinking about quitting, giving her hope that he'd ignored Logan's advice. Now, however, she identified the guilt in Logan's voice.

"You couldn't have known what would happen," she said. "Nobody could."

"Yeah, but I did know Mike was an unhappy high school dropout a thousand miles from home," he said. "I could have talked him into going back."

"He wouldn't have come," she said. "Not after I drove him away."

"What are you talking about?" Logan asked.

Maria dug into her purse, removing a large key chain imprinted with the hotel's name. She inserted the old-fashioned key in the lock and pushed open the door to her room. "Perhaps you'd better come in. I have a story you need to hear."

AFTER MUSTERING UP the resolve to leave Maria's hotel room the night before, Logan had vowed not to put himself in the same position again.

Yet here he was for the second time, alone with her late at night.

The attraction that still simmered between them, however, was taking a backseat to what she had to tell him. Whatever it was had her on edge. He was surprised to see that her room had a minibar, since the hotel was short on frills. She hadn't had alcohol all night but went straight there now and removed a small bottle of whiskey.

"I make a mean whiskey and water," she said. Even her joke sounded strained. "Want to share?"

"Sure," he said, not so much because he was craving a drink but because he didn't want her to drink alone.

She poured a glass for him and one for herself before settling in the armchair at a corner of the room. He'd chosen the chair at the desk. He was anxious to hear what she had to say, but didn't prompt her, figuring she'd tell him at her own pace.

Maria swallowed some whiskey and made a face, telling him she wasn't used to it. He heard her sigh.

"You shouldn't blame yourself for anything involving Mike," she said at last. Lines of strain bracketed her pretty mouth. He'd switched on the lamp at the desk and the light picked up the pain in her blue eyes. "If not for me, he wouldn't have been in New York in the first place."

Logan balanced his elbows on his thighs and leaned forward, his mind on the past and what Mike DiMarco had told him about his reasons for leaving Kentucky. "I had the impression Mike dropped out of school because of Caroline Webb."

"Caroline's not blameless, that's for sure," Maria said. "Did you know she was Mike's first girlfriend? He was shy growing up, without a lot of female friends. I'm certain she made the first move."

"Mike always seemed sure of himself to me."

"He was only fourteen when you and I were going out. As he got older, being the brother of a star athlete was hard on him." She was referring to her other brother, Jack, who pitched briefly in the major leagues before he was sidelined by an injury. "Mike couldn't keep up with Jack in either sports or schoolwork. After a while, he stopped trying."

"I'm sure Mike had other things going for him," Logan said.

"Oh, he did. He was a really good guitar player and he could fix anything," she said. "But his self-esteem was already low by the time he started dating Caroline. Then it got lower."

"Getting a girlfriend usually has the opposite effect," Logan remarked.

"Caroline was a pretty terrible girlfriend. She was always bossing Mike around to get her way. She'd get him to do stuff like skip school to stand in line for concert tickets. Or blow off studying to take her to the movies. That kind of nonsense. His grades started to suffer and he'd have these blowout arguments with our parents. It was like living in a war zone."

Logan thought that was a strange statement. He'd heard that Maria had moved into an apartment in downtown Lexington with her husband as soon as they married. "But you didn't live there, right?"

She looked confused for a moment before she nodded. "Oh, right. But you know how close my family is. We know each other's business. And, well, Caroline reminded me of Jerry."

"Because Jerry tried to boss you around, too?"

"Exactly."

"It doesn't sound like Mike resented that as much as you did."

"Caroline's one of those women who use sex as a weapon," Maria said. "Mike was obsessed with her and did whatever she told him to. She even got him into pot. She wasn't hooked on it like Mike was, but when I caught him smoking, he told me he tried it the first time because she wanted to experiment."

"So far all I've heard is that Mike got mixed up with the wrong girl," Logan said. "I still don't see how you were to blame for him turning up in New York."

"I haven't told you everything yet." Maria started to take another drink of her whiskey and water and seemed surprised that she'd already finished it. "I couldn't stand the way Caroline treated Mike. She'd blow him off, then he'd hear she'd been out with friends. When I found out she wanted him to wear a pink tux to homecoming, I lost it."

"I don't get it," Logan said. "Why would you care about something like that?"

"It seems silly now, but in high school those things matter," she said. "Mike was afraid the other kids would laugh at him. He wouldn't tell Caroline how he felt, though. He never did. Not until I shamed him into sticking up for himself."

Logan sensed they were getting to the crux of the story. "I take it things didn't go well?"

"They couldn't have gone worse. Mike confronted her about the pink tux in the cafeteria," Maria said. "I heard later that Caroline erupted, calling him a loser and an embarrassment. She said she was sick of him, anyway, and there was another guy who'd take her to homecoming."

"Pretty tough stuff for a teenager in love to hear."

"Mike was so upset he ran out of the cafeteria and drove home. He sideswiped a car on the way," she said. "I didn't know about that when he came through the door, but I was surprised to see him home. I asked what was going on."

Logan was starting to get the impression that Maria had spent more time at her parents' house than her own apartment. Maybe her marriage had been more troubled than she'd admitted.

"Mike started shouting at me. He told me Caroline had broken up with him. He said it was my fault, that things were going fine before I butted in. I tried to tell him he was better off without her, but he wouldn't listen. He stormed to his room, packed some things and drove off." Maria wiped at her eyes and he noticed they were watery. "That was the last time I saw him."

Understanding dawned. Logan reached across the space between them and took her hand. It was cold to the touch. "Now I understand why it's so hard for you to accept that Mike is dead."

"I want so badly for a second chance," she said in a broken voice. "I need him to know I'm sorry and that I love him."

"I know you do." Logan squeezed her hand gently. "But you're a private investigator, Maria.

You operate on facts, and you haven't turned up any evidence that points to Mike being alive. You've got to put aside your emotions and listen to what your investigation is telling you."

She wiped at her eyes a second time. "I know."

"You have to go back to Lexington, Maria. Annalise can make excuses for you only for so long," he continued. "You don't want your mom and dad to get their hopes up that Mike might be alive, too, do you?"

"I wanted to bring Mike home to them for the holidays," she said. "That would be the best present I could give them."

"Your family's gotten used to holidays without Mike, but they need to have you there with them," Logan said. "Let me book a flight back to Lexington for you. I'll even pay for it."

"No, thank you," she said with a touch of her characteristic spirit. "I can book and pay for my own flight."

"Okay. But in the morning, we'll drive to the airport together."

"I'll probably be flying out of Miami."

"Then I'll drive up there with you."

"No." She blinked a few times, drying her eyes. "Not only do you need to get back to New York but I've never been good at goodbyes."

"Me, neither." He thought about the terrible

day she'd finally realized he had no intention of going to art school and moving in with her. No matter what he'd said, she wouldn't let go of her pie-in-the-sky notion that all they needed was love.

"Then this is goodbye," she'd told him.

She swallowed now. "It would be easier if we said our goodbyes right here."

"Tonight?" he asked. "Don't you at least want to get together for breakfast tomorrow morning?"

She shook her head.

He felt moisture in his own eyes. Dropping her hand, he raised his fingers to her cheek and lightly traced her soft skin. He didn't need to memorize her face. It was already burned into his brain.

"Maria DiMarco," he whispered, "I'm going to miss you."

Thinking this might be the last chance he'd ever have to kiss her, he pulled her to her feet and lowered his head. Slowly, so she'd have a chance to back away. Instead, she strained toward him, clasping his shoulders and accepting his kiss.

Her lips clung to his. One of her hands snaked around his nape and she buried her fingers in the hair. She used to do that when they were teenagers. She'd make soft noises in the back of her throat, too, the way she was now.

Logan didn't need to coax her mouth open. She touched her tongue to the tip of his, then deepened the kiss herself. And then they were kissing in earnest, her body pressed so close to his that he could feel the soft outline of her breasts against his chest.

He felt himself grow hard, not surprised that he was getting so turned on merely by a kiss. He'd experienced the same lightning-quick reaction years ago whenever he took her in his arms. It had happened the other night, too. Her tongue teased his and he slanted his mouth to kiss her even more thoroughly. She rubbed against his erection, and he groaned.

Soon kisses wouldn't be enough. He'd had the willpower to put a halt to things the night before. He tried to stop now, lifting his mouth from hers, but she trailed kisses from the side of his mouth down his neck. He shivered.

"I…can't stop. Not tonight." He could barely choke out the words. "You…have to."

She gazed up at him, her clear blue eyes steady on his. "I don't want to stop. I want to make love to you."

Maria ran her hands over his back, keeping her body anchored to his. She sounded far more in control than he was.

"Are you sure?" he rasped.

"Very sure. I don't want to keep wondering what it would be like to make love with you."

If he wasn't having problems formulating sentences, he would have told her she wasn't the only one who wondered. He'd been fantasizing about her for years.

"I ask only one thing," she said.

His head was already lowering again, his mouth hovering above hers. He wanted to kiss her so badly he could barely restrain himself. "Name it."

"You can't be here in the morning."

His knee-jerk reaction was to refuse, but was it really such an unreasonable request? Tomorrow they'd go their separate ways. Tonight was for satisfying their curiosity about what it would be like to spend a night in each other's arms. Once they had, they could put the past behind them once and for all and get on with their separate futures.

"Okay," he said and closed his mouth over hers.

CHAPTER NINE

MAKING LOVE TO LOGAN wasn't like Maria had thought it would be. It was infinitely better.

He unbuttoned her blouse and unhooked her bra, his eyes darkening when her breasts spilled free. She felt her nipples harden even though he wasn't touching her. She reached for the waistband of her skirt and shimmied out of the garment, reveling in the way his eyes seemed to drink in the sight of her.

"You're even lovelier than I thought you'd be," he breathed.

"I want to see you, too." She stepped toward him and reached for the bottom of his shirt, helping him to pull it over his head. He looked different than he had as a teenager, his musculature more defined, but of course he was almost fifteen years older. She felt her lashes grow damp. So many years had passed.

"Are you okay?" he asked gently, brushing a tear from beneath her eye.

She nodded, swallowing back the emotion. "I'm more than okay."

She gently traced the discolored skin under his left eye, where he'd taken a punch for her. Then she lifted her mouth and kissed him, enjoying the feel of her bare breasts against the hair-sprinkled skin of his chest. It seemed as though she'd been waiting forever to be in his arms like this. No matter how deeply she kissed him, it wasn't enough. She was plastered against him but longed to be closer.

The feel of the mattress against the back of her legs came as a surprise. She hadn't been aware he was moving them toward the bed. He lowered her gingerly, kissing her the entire time, until they were stretched out beside each other.

She drew back slightly and undid the top button of his shorts. He lifted his hips and she helped him get rid of them and his underwear. He gathered her against him and her heart stuttered, then galloped.

How had they been able to resist this when they were teenagers? Maria had been ultraconscious of teen pregnancy because of Annalise, but she also remembered thinking there was no rush, that she and Logan had all the time in the world. She never would have imagined she wouldn't make love to him until she was thirty-two.

She ran a hand from his broad shoulder to his hip, pulling him toward her, getting lost in his kiss. His hands seemed to be everywhere, stroking her breasts, smoothing over her stomach, tracing the outline of her hips and her bottom. His kisses went on and on, as though they really did have all the time in the world. Yet she'd waited fifteen years. She couldn't wait any longer.

"Now," she said, reaching down and stroking him, guiding him toward her. "I want you now."

"We've got time," he said, strain evident in his voice. "I want to make it good for you."

The other men she'd been with had been much more concerned with satisfying themselves than with gratifying her. She groaned.

"Logan Collier," she said, "if you don't make love to me right now, I'll have to hurt you."

He was laughing slightly when he slid inside her. She was wet and ready even though she couldn't remember the last time she'd made love. Being with Logan drove thoughts of everybody but him from her mind. She marveled at how perfectly they fit together, how they seemed to anticipate each other's needs as though they were longtime lovers.

Far too soon, her inner contractions started. She closed her eyes, desperately wanting to prolong the experience, wanting for them to climax together. "It's already happening."

"Not yet," he said.

He slowed down, instinctively knowing exactly how to prolong the pleasure. She opened her eyes, watching the strain on his face, knowing he was holding back because of her.

"We can go faster," she whispered against his mouth.

"Oh, no." He kept up his slow, sensual assault. "We only have one first time."

Tears pricked her eyes again, but now there was no sadness, only joy. He rolled onto his back and pulled her over so she was on top of him, changing the angle, then starting again, all in an effort to make the pleasure last. She lost all sense of time as he continued to prolong the delight, barely able to form any thoughts except that nothing had ever felt so right.

"Please," she finally said against his mouth, hardly knowing whether she was pleading for their lovemaking to continue or for her release.

He picked up the rhythm and she matched his pace, clinging to him and breathing his name as sensations burst inside her. She saw colors reminiscent of those that had appeared in the Key West sky at sunset. Wave after wave of pleasure rolled through her, the aftershocks even more powerful than the initial release.

"Maria," he groaned, his climax following hers, sending more ripples through her body. When it was finally over, his arms tightened around her with their bodies still joined. Neither of them made a move.

"I never imagined it would be like that," she said, snuggling against him.

"I did," he said, and kissed her again.

They made love one more time in the middle of the night. The lovemaking was as passionate but the tempo more frantic, as though they both realized time was running out on them. Maria fell into a deep, exhausted sleep with Logan's arms still around her.

She dreamed of shooting stars and Rollerblades under the Christmas tree and her brother Mike throwing back his head and laughing the way he used to when they were young. She woke up with the images imprinted on her brain. No, not images. Signs.

She'd made the decision to leave Key West last night, when things had seemed darkest. Light spilled over her now, clarifying her thoughts and highlighting the folly of ignoring signs. If she didn't reach for the sky, how could she expect a miracle?

She couldn't leave Key West. Not yet. Not when she hadn't exhausted all her resources.

She turned over to tell Logan of her decision, but his side of the bed was empty. She inhaled sharply before remembering the promise she'd extracted from him, to not be there in the morning.

Disappointment sliced through her, as sharp as any knife. She fortified herself against it. Of course it was for the best that Logan was gone. They'd said their goodbyes last night. Not only did his absence save her from another wrenching parting but she might make better progress on the case now that she didn't have to deal with his skepticism. So why didn't she feel glad?

She pushed the hair from her face and stretched out on the sheets, feeling the slight soreness in her muscles. She could still feel the imprint of his body on hers. When she turned her head, she could smell his heady scent lingering on the pillows.

She ran her hand over the side of the bed where he'd slept, finding the sheets cool to the touch. She sighed. If Logan hadn't listened to her, they could be making love right now.

Sitting up abruptly, she swung her legs off the bed and rose. She'd gone way too long without a man if a single night had her thinking like this.

Annalise was right. Maria needed to date more. When she got back to Lexington, she could let her sister fix her up with that guy from church she was always telling her about.

Everything inside Maria rebelled at the thought and she knew that she wouldn't carry through, that no other man could be a replacement for Logan.

On the way to the bathroom, she passed the spot where he had kissed her the night before. Before she could fully relive the moment, she crossed to the sink, turned on the faucet and deliberately splashed cold water on her face.

She couldn't think about Logan now. She needed to figure out the next step in her quest to find Mike.

She hadn't come up with anything by the time she got out of the shower. Her cell phone pealed when she'd barely dried off.

"Logan," she breathed.

Wrapping herself in a towel, she rushed to the bedside table where she'd left the phone and picked it up.

Not him. The number, which looked vaguely familiar, had a Lexington area code. Maria shook her head, dismayed at herself for hoping it was Logan.

She pressed the key that answered the call. "Maria DiMarco here."

"Maria, it's Caroline Webb. I need to know what you've found out about your brother."

Maria bristled at the other woman's demanding tone. She'd managed to be civil toward her during their first encounter but it had taken an effort.

"Really?" She sat down on the unmade bed. "If my memory serves me correctly, you weren't particularly interested in what I found out as long as Mike left you alone."

"That's the problem," Carolina said in a clipped voice. "He isn't leaving me alone. He contacted me again."

"What?" Maria's heart raced. Adrenaline shot through her. She'd been right all along. Mike was alive. "Did he call you again? What did he say?"

"He didn't call. I got another envelope. It must have come yesterday, but I forgot to check my mail slot until this morning."

"What was in the envelope?"

There was silence at the other end of the line. It stretched for so long that Maria stared down at her phone, afraid her cell service had dropped the call.

"Caroline?" she said. "Are you still there?"

More silence, then she answered, "I'm still here. I'd rather not say what was in the envelope."

"What? How do you expect me to find Mike if you won't give me all the details?"

"Then you haven't been able to track him down? I thought you were going to Key West."

"I'm here right now," Maria said. "I'm not sure Mike is."

"He must be," Caroline said. "This second envelope was postmarked Tuesday from there."

Tuesday, three days ago. The day Maria had arrived in Florida.

"For whatever reason, it seems Mike doesn't want to be found," Maria said. "Caroline, you have to tell me what was inside the envelope. I need to know everything so I can figure out where to look for him."

She hesitated again. "My fiancé can't find out. Neither can anyone else."

"I'm not following you," Maria said, her frustration spilling over into her voice.

"It was a note." Caroline cleared her throat. "And some more photos."

The photo in the first envelope had been of Caroline strategically positioned on a bearskin rug. She'd said it was the only one Mike had ever taken of her in the nude.

"You mean more *naked* photos?" Maria asked.

"Yes. These are a little more…explicit."

That explained why Caroline hadn't told her about them. She was obviously reluctant to share additional details.

"Was anything else in the envelope besides the photos?" Maria pressed.

"There was a note, as I said." Caroline cleared her throat. "I'll read it to you."

Maria heard the rustling of paper, then Caroline's shaky voice.

"'I came close to dying that day,'" she read. "'You'll pay or these go public. Instructions to come.'"

LOGAN WAITED FOR THE elevator in the lobby of Maria's hotel, breathing in the scent of pastries and coffee wafting up from the white take-out bag he carried.

It wasn't yet 8:00 a.m., which meant that theoretically he had time to catch the noon flight to New York City and fulfill his obligations that night. He'd need to get to the airport with plenty of time to spare, because extra security measures were a reality of life since 9/11. As long as he didn't linger with Maria, he should be fine.

He would deliver the breakfast, explain that he couldn't take off without a word after the night they'd spent together, and say a proper goodbye.

If she gave him a hard time, he'd argue that he'd honored her wishes to be gone from her bed before morning. He was simply coming back.

He pressed the button for the elevator, wondering why it was taking so long. He should have used the stairs. He would have if they'd been beside the elevator. He was debating going in search of them when the elevator doors slid open.

Maria rushed out, nearly plowing into him. Her eyes flew to his face and grew round in surprise. He got ready to be chastised for not listening to her.

"Logan! I'm so glad you haven't left yet," she exclaimed, laying a hand on his arm. He felt the connection that had been between them last night bloom to life.

He held up the bag. "I brought you breakfast. Cuban roast coffee, pain au chocolat and an apricot croissant." He'd chosen the foods carefully, thinking that it would be harder for her to be angry with him if her mouth was watering.

"I don't have time to eat right now," she said. "Caroline Webb just called me. Mike contacted her again!"

With her long hair tied back in a sloppy ponytail and wrinkles creasing the cargo shorts she wore with a short-sleeved tee, she should have looked far from her best. Hope and excitement practically vibrated from her, however, infusing her complexion with color and making her blue eyes shine.

"Caroline talked to Mike?" Logan asked, hearing the skepticism in his voice.

"Well, no," she said. "But he sent her another envelope. He mailed it from Key West on Tuesday, Logan. That was only three days ago! And to think that just last night I was ready to give up looking for him."

"Slow down," he said. "What was inside the envelope?"

She checked her watch. "I don't have time to get into it right now. I'm meeting Kayla at the *Key West Sun*. She's going to ask some photographer about the Santa statue, but it's an opportunity to see if anybody at the newspaper knows anything about Mike."

That wasn't a bad idea. Journalists had their fingers on the pulse of the community.

"I'll come with you," he said. "You can fill me in along the way."

A few minutes later, he was in the passenger seat of Maria's rental car as she drove through the narrow streets of Key West to the less touristy side of the island. He listened without interrupting while she relayed her conversation with Caroline and the other woman's fear that the nude photos could hurt her fiancé's chances of becoming a congressman.

"I remember when Samuel Tolliver was governor, but I don't know anything about his son," Logan said.

"Austin Tolliver has a squeaky-clean image," Maria said. "He's running on a family values platform."

"That explains why Caroline is panicking,"

Logan said. "If those photos get out, it could wreck Tolliver's campaign."

"Exactly." Maria braked for a red light, turning to look at him. "But the important thing is that the envelopes Caroline received were postmarked almost a week apart. Even if Mike doesn't live in Key West, there's a very good chance he's still around."

"I don't know, Maria," Logan said, shaking his head. "I'm not convinced Mike sent the envelopes."

Her eyes narrowed. "Caroline said he took those nude photos. Who else could have sent them?"

"Mike could have given the photos to somebody before he left for New York," Logan argued.

"I can't see him doing that."

"It doesn't make sense that he had the photos with him that morning," Logan said.

"Sure it does," Maria countered. "He always carried a backpack. The photos could have been inside."

Logan couldn't remember what Mike had taken with him that morning when he left for work, but it was possible he'd had a backpack. Logan had shipped Mike's other belongings to his parents' house after the tragedy.

A horn sounded from a car behind them. The

light was green. Maria refocused on the road and stepped on the gas. She traveled half a block before she spoke again.

"Let's say you're right and Mike did give those photos to somebody," she said. "Why would this person contact Caroline pretending he was Mike?"

"He's a blackmailer, Maria. There could be lots of reasons to remain anonymous."

"Not all blackmailers care if you know who they are," she said. "Some of them just want what they want."

She kept her eyes on the road. Appropriate, he thought. She had tunnel vision where this subject was concerned.

"We're talking about your little brother, Maria," he said. "Do you really think Mike would have it in him to blackmail somebody?"

"Not Mike the teenager, no," Maria said. "But who knows what he's been through in the last eleven years or what his life is like?"

Logan crossed his arms over his chest. "Sorry. I don't buy it."

"That's because you can't open your mind to possibilities," she said, restating a familiar refrain. "I told you how Caroline broke up with Mike. If he was going to blackmail someone, it would be her."

"Does Caroline have a lot of money?" Logan asked.

"She says no," Maria said, "but her fiancé is loaded."

"If she wants to keep Tolliver in the dark about the nude photos, she won't ask him for money."

"She won't have to ask anybody. Once I find Mike, I'll convince him Caroline's not worth getting into trouble over. If he needs money, I can give him some. I know our parents would be glad to help, too."

She was talking as though any doubt in her mind about Mike not having survived 9/11 was gone.

She pulled into the parking lot in front of the nondescript two-story building that housed the newspaper office and switched off the ignition.

"Hey." She turned and gave him a sharp look. "Shouldn't you be on your way to the airport?"

"I'm not leaving today," he said, realizing he'd made the decision the moment he'd stepped into the car.

"But I thought you had dinners with clients lined up," she said.

"I'll cancel them." Logan would need to figure out something to tell his boss that wouldn't jeopardize his possible promotion. "If you're not leaving Key West today, then neither am I."

Wasn't that the real reason he hadn't checked out of his hotel this morning or purchased the return plane ticket? Hadn't he known deep down that Maria would remain on the island and continue to search for her brother?

She stared at him, pressing her lips together as if trying to decide something. "Why are you staying? Is it because you want to sleep with me again?"

"I told you why," he said. "I don't like thinking of you in Key West all by yourself so close to Christmas."

"Then it's okay with you if we forget what happened last night?"

His body already craved her again. "Why would we forget something so amazing?"

"Circumstances have changed," she said. "I wouldn't have slept with you if I knew you were staying. I'm not getting involved with you, Logan. If we keep sleeping together, I'll just get hurt."

"I wouldn't hurt you," he protested.

"Not deliberately," she said, "but we don't fit. Maybe we never did. I'd hate New York and you'll never move back to Kentucky."

"You don't know that."

"Really? So if you get that promotion, you'll pass it up?"

He'd been working toward the promotion for

years, putting in untold extra hours, never complaining because he knew the payoff was coming that would solidify a secure future. "No," he admitted. "I wouldn't."

"Now that we understand each other, let's go." She got out of the car, as though that was the final word on the subject.

It wasn't, not by a long shot. At the moment, however, Logan couldn't come up with an argument to counter what she'd said.

THE PHOTOGRAPHER WHO HAD arranged to meet her at the newspaper office this morning was late.

Kayla blinked her gritty eyes and took another hit of the coffee that had helped her stay awake all night.

When morning dawned and she'd survived another night without the Santa statue being defaced, she probably should have gotten some shut-eye. Instead, she'd called the newspaper to get a contact number for James Smith, the photographer who'd taken the photo of Zombie Santa. She figured he was the same guy she'd seen at a distance the other morning. Smith happened to be in the office. He'd been preoccupied but a coworker relayed the message that he could meet her as soon as she got there.

So here she was, slumped in a tiny reception

area at the *Key West Sun,* waiting on him. James Smith had left word with the security guard that he needed to step out of the office. He hadn't said when he'd return.

Kayla had elected to wait for James instead of going into the newsroom with Maria and her ex-boyfriend. A metro reporter had agreed to look at the age progression photo of Mike Di-Marco and answer Maria's questions. After giving them visitor badges, about fifteen minutes ago the security guard had admitted them to the newsroom.

The door to the inner offices opened and Maria and her ex emerged. Logan Collier, that was his name. Aside from Alex Suarez, Logan was the most appealing man Kayla had seen in a long time. He had thick brown hair shot through with gold, and pretty hazel eyes that lingered on Maria. He stood closer to her than he would have if they were merely acquaintances.

Whatever had once been between them, Kayla thought, wasn't over.

"Was the reporter helpful?" she asked.

Maria gave a quick negative shake of her head. "Neither were the other employees he introduced us to. I should have tried later, when more people are in."

"You can come back," Kayla said.

"I intend to."

Kayla directed her attention to Logan. "It's great Maria has you helping her. Have you done this kind of thing before?"

"Hardly," he said. "I'm a financial advisor, but I've got a vested interest in her case. Mike was staying at my place before the towers fell."

"Such a terrible, tragic day." The memory was so vivid in Kayla's mind, it was as though it had happened yesterday. She'd been in English class at her high school. After the news hit, students had huddled around televisions, tears streaming down their faces. "To think that Mike could still be feeling the aftershocks."

"I don't understand what you mean," Logan said.

"Maria told me what a good kid her brother was. Troubled, but a good kid," Kayla said. "It makes you wonder what happened in his life that he might be resorting to blackmail."

"I'm not convinced he is," Logan said. "It seems out of character for Mike."

"That's my point. Is it out of character?" Kayla asked. "Think about how it would mess with your mind if you were supposed to be at the World Trade Tower that day. Who knows how that would change you?"

"I'd never thought of it that way," Logan said.

"That's why they pay us private investigators the big bucks," Kayla quipped, wishing it were so. Not so much the compensation part, although big bucks would be nice. She longed to be a full-fledged investigator and not a girl on a tryout.

"Are you making any progress on the Santa case?" Maria asked.

"Not much. I'm hoping this photographer will know something. He's the one who got the photo of Zombie Santa," Kayla said. "How about you? What's your next step?"

"More of the same, I guess," Maria said. "We've pretty much exhausted the search in the tourist area. I thought we'd concentrate on the quieter part of the island."

"Did my mom have any suggestions?"

"Only that I talk to your uncle," Maria answered. "She said he knows everybody on the island."

"Oh, my gosh, he does," Kayla said. "Why didn't I think of that?"

"Don't worry about it," Maria said. "I already faxed Mike's picture to your uncle Carl. He didn't recognize him."

"Uncle Carl does know a lot of people, but I think my mom was talking about Uncle Frank. He's retired now, but he delivered mail on the island for forty years."

Maria's face brightened. "I didn't know you had two uncles. Where can I find Frank?"

Kayla gave her the information and sensed Maria's eagerness to check out the new lead as soon as possible.

"Why don't you give me one of those age progressions of Mike to show to the photographer?" Kayla offered. "That way, you and Logan can get out of here. Uncle Frank's a creature of habit. He'll be exactly where I told you."

Maria and Logan took her suggestion, and moments later Kayla was alone again, the age-enhanced photo clutched in her hand. She tilted her head back and let her eyes close.

"Kayla Fryburger, it sure is good to see you."

Kayla's eyes snapped open at the pronouncement. She must have fallen asleep. Standing in front of her was a man about her age who looked familiar. He resembled a surfer in long baggy shorts, a Hawaiian shirt and flip-flops. His sandy-blond hair was tied at his nape and a few days' growth of beard offset features that were almost pretty, especially his long-lashed green eyes.

"James Smith." He tapped his chest and gazed at her expectantly. She squinted, trying to think how she knew him.

"You're hurting my feelings here," he said with a lopsided smile. "You might remember me as Jimbo."

"Jimbo Smith?" Kayla's mouth dropped open.

They'd gone to high school together. He'd even sat beside her in a number of classes. "How much weight have you lost?"

She covered her mouth with her fingers and grimaced. "Forget I said that. It's none of my business."

"No, I don't mind." He waved a hand. Slung over one of his arms was a digital camera. "Eighty-five pounds."

Jimbo—no, James—was way taller than Kayla but probably no more than five feet eight. Subtract eighty-five pounds from a man of that size and no wonder she hadn't recognized him.

"You look great." She ran her eyes down the length of him, taking in his tan, toned limbs. He was just right, neither too fat nor too thin.

"You do, too," he said. "But then you've always looked fantastic."

"Thanks," Kayla said, surprised by the effusiveness behind the compliment. "I don't think I've seen you since high school. You'd think we would have run into each other before now."

"I only moved back to Key West a few months ago, when I got the job at the *Sun*," James said. "I jumped at the chance. I never forgave my parents for moving when I was a junior in high school."

He hadn't graduated from high school with her? Why didn't she remember that?

"It's nice to have you back." She injected enthusiasm into her voice to make up for not noticing he'd left town.

"Sorry I wasn't here earlier," he said. "A motorboat crashed into the dock and another ship last night. I needed to get the photo before somebody cleaned up the damage."

"Perfectly understandable," Kayla said. "I'm thankful you could meet with me at all."

"For you, anything," he said with a wide grin. "You want to get a cup of coffee?"

She picked up her cup from the table beside her and held it out. "I'm good on coffee. What I need is information."

"Cool," he said. "Nobody will be in Photography. We can talk there."

Aside from the blown-up photos lining the walls, the photography department looked as bland as the rest of the place. Beige carpet, beige walls, desks nestled inside cubicles beside photography equipment.

James rolled out a desk chair for her, waited until she sat down and hoisted himself up on the edge of the desk. His calves were nicely toned, she noticed.

"What can I do for you?" he asked.

"Two things, actually."

First she asked if he recognized Mike Di-Marco and discovered Maria had beaten her to the punch. She and Logan had run into the photographer when they were leaving the newspaper office. James was already in possession of an age-progression image Maria had asked him to show around the office.

Then Kayla got down to the real reason she was there, explaining how the merchants association had hired her to save the group from additional embarrassment.

"Wow! So you're a private eye now." James grinned at her. He'd been doing a lot of that. "I'm impressed!"

"Don't be. If I don't crack this case, my uncle will can me. And then it's back to making bottle art." Now why had she told him that? Until now, she'd shared that information only with her mother and Maria.

"I've got faith in you," he said. "You'll kick the case's ass."

She giggled. "I'm trying, which brings me to my question. Did somebody tip you off Thursday morning that Santa had been defaced with Magic Marker?"

"Yeah. I got a text," he said. "It was the second one about that statue. That's how I got the photo of Santa looking like a zombie."

She was right! But he'd gotten a text and not a call. That was interesting.

"Who was the text from?" Kayla asked.

"I didn't recognize the number."

"Wouldn't it have to come from someone you know?"

"Not necessarily. I give my cell number out to lots of people."

"Why text you, though? Why not call the newspaper?"

"It was seven in the morning. Usually nobody's around the newspaper that early," he said. "Whoever it was must have really wanted me to get the photo."

"Do you still have the texts?"

"Nah," James said. "I get so many, I delete 'em after a few days."

"Can you check your bill and give me the number?"

"Sure thing." He hopped down from the desk, logged on to the computer and a few minutes later handed her a piece of paper with the number written on it. "Here you go."

"Thanks," she said and got up to leave. "You've been a big help."

"Let me walk you to your car," he said.

"Um, okay." She hid her surprise at the offer. Maybe he was leaving the office, too.

He was strangely silent on the way to the parking lot. Kayla was never quiet. She filled him in on what some of their former high school classmates were up to. In no time, they were at her car.

She hit the remote and went to open the driver's-side door. James got there first and opened it for her.

"Thank you," she said and started to duck inside the car.

"Would you like to go out sometime?" James blurted, the first thing he'd said in minutes.

Kayla paused in the act of getting into the car. If she'd seen this coming, she'd be better prepared to handle it. But maybe she was reading the situation wrong.

"You mean, like, on a date?" she asked.

"Yeah." He rolled his eyes when she continued to say nothing. "C'mon, Kayla. I'm dying here. I've wanted to ask you out since high school."

Her jaw dropped.

"Wow. What a question," she said, stalling for time. The last thing she wanted was to hurt his feelings. "Not a bad question, don't get me wrong. A very good question."

He shifted from foot to foot. "What's the answer?"

"The thing is, I can't. I'd like to," she said quickly, trying to soften the blow, "but, well, I'm sort of seeing somebody."

"Sort of?"

"Yes." She couldn't explain without going into great detail about the subtle signals Alex had been giving her at the bar last night. "It's in the beginning stages."

"No problem," James said, backing away, not doing a very good job of hiding his disappointment. "Good seeing you again."

He was across the parking lot and back in the newspaper building before Kayla gathered herself to get in the car.

James hadn't expected her to say yes, she realized. He probably had insecurities dating back to before he'd lost the weight, although the inside of a person had always been more important to Kayla than the outside.

The next time she saw James, she'd make sure he knew her refusal had nothing to do with him. Why, if he'd asked her out in high school, when he was eighty-five pounds heavier, she might have said yes.

She thought again of the wounded look that had entered his eyes when she'd refused him and suppressed the urge to run after him and tell him that now.

CHAPTER TEN

Kayla's Uncle Frank was exactly where she said he would be, with three of his cronies on the covered back deck of a houseboat moored at the Key West City Marina. *Cronies* was his word, not Maria's. She had expected Frank Knowles to be around the same age as Kayla's mother, but he was easily twenty years older. Maria put Frank and his friends in their mid to late seventies.

"Me and my cronies play poker out here every Friday. Beats sitting in a dark smoky room." Frank gestured to the glistening blue water of the Gulf of Mexico, which contrasted with the white masts of sailboats. Seabirds soared overhead and the smell of salt water filled the air.

Maria, however, was most aware of Logan's hand resting gently on her back.

He'd turned into a distraction—no surprise, considering how great the sex had been between them. Her mind should be one hundred percent on finding Mike and not on how her skin tingled whenever Logan touched her. She should have told him to go back to New York. He'd developed a stubborn streak, though. There was no guarantee he would listen to her.

"It's a great setting," Logan said, "but I guess that's what you get when you live on a houseboat."

"This is a floating home," Frank said. "Unlike a houseboat, it's stationary. I can't take it out on the water, but I've got a million-dollar view without the price tag."

The floating home was also surprisingly spacious, with rooms on two levels leading to the double-decker patio with the killer views.

"We used to play poker at night before Arturo started falling asleep on us," a thin man with a craggy voice said. He was one of three men sitting at a fold-up table, drinking what appeared to be iced tea. All were deeply tanned with varying amounts of white hair and wrinkles.

"I need my beauty sleep," retorted a man in a Miami Marlins baseball hat who looked to be of Hispanic descent. He must be Arturo.

Everybody laughed, with Frank guffawing the loudest. If Maria had overheard Kayla's uncle from an adjacent room, she would have guessed he was a big, stocky man like his brother, Key Carl. In reality, Frank was probably five feet four and about one hundred thirty pounds. His last name was different than his brother's, though, indicating they didn't have the same father.

"You two want to join us?" the guy with the craggy voice asked.

"They're not here to play poker. They're here to ask questions. This is Maria DiMarco and that's Logan Collier," Frank said in his earsplitting voice and completed the introductions. The man in the baseball hat was indeed Arturo. The craggy-voiced man was Pete. The quiet guy was also named Pete, but his friends had nicknamed him Repeat. "You all know my niece Kayla. She sent Maria and Logan over. They're private eyes."

"Maria's the private eye," Logan corrected, still with his hand on the small of her back. Maria supposed she could move away. She stayed put.

"What kind of questions? What case? Anything we can help you with?" Arturo shot the inquiries at her.

"Let the girl speak!" Frank bellowed. "Geez. Anyone would think you were the private eye."

"I'd be good private eye," Arturo retorted.

Maria figured she better cut in before the men got even more off track. "I appreciate that you want to help. The more people who look at the image, the better." She dug the age progression out of her slouchy bag and set it on the table. "This is an approximation of what my brother Mike would look like today. He's been missing eleven years."

Pete whistled loud and low. "That's a long damn time."

"I'd appreciate if you'd pass it around and take a good look," Maria said. "I have reason to believe my brother is in Key West, probably under an assumed name."

"Let Frank look first," Pete said. "He knows everybody who lives here year-round."

"Almost everybody," Frank amended. "People come and go around here."

Maria held her breath while he considered the image. Logan moved closer to her, putting a hand on her shoulder. Again, she thought she should move away. Again, she didn't.

"Nope, sorry," Frank said. "At first I thought it might be Clem. Chin's different, though."

"We've got that before," Logan said. "It's not Clem."

Frank walked over to the table and handed the photo to Arturo, who shook his head and passed it to Pete. He put on a pair of reading glasses and took his time, but ultimately the result was the same. Repeat was the last to look. He didn't recognize her brother, either.

"That's a pretty good approximation, but he

might have gained weight or grown a beard."
Maria repeated what Sergeant Peppler had said
when she'd stopped by the police station.

Logan glanced at her and she imagined she
could read his mind. He thought she was grasping at straws.

"Maybe it would help if you told us why you
believe your brother's here," Frank said.

"He mailed some envelopes that were postmarked from Key West to an ex-girlfriend,"
Maria said.

"What was in the envelopes?" Arturo asked.

Why not tell them? Maria thought. It wasn't
as though she was breaking a confidence. Even
if she mentioned that Mike's ex-girlfriend was
engaged to Austin Tolliver, it was the longest of
long shots they'd recognize he was a state senator from Kentucky.

"Nude photos," she said. "The last one came
with what could be considered a blackmail
note."

"Wait a minute." Repeat lifted his index finger. "I remember hearing something about
naked pictures."

Maria tried not to get too excited. Caroline
Webb wasn't the first woman who'd posed in
the altogether for a man. "From who?"

"Not somebody I knew. Somebody I overheard. Now where was that?" Repeat screwed

up his forehead. After a moment, he snapped his fingers. "I know. It was a couple weeks ago at the Daybreak Café, that Cuban-American place on Duval. Frank, you were there."

"I was?" He sounded doubtful. "I don't remember anything about naked pictures."

"It was before you arrived," Repeat said. "You were late, like always."

"Why didn't you mention it?" Frank demanded.

"My hearing's not so good anymore," his friend said. "I thought I might have it wrong. I didn't catch much, anyway. Just that this guy had naked pictures of some woman."

It was a tenuous connection at best. However, at the moment it was all Maria had. She wasn't about to discount the information. "What did the guy look like?"

"I didn't see him real good. Couldn't even tell you if he was with a man or a woman."

"You didn't turn around when you heard the word *naked?*" Pete asked.

"'Course I did," Repeat said. "But the guy was in the booth behind me. All I could see was part of his arm."

"Fat lot of good you'll do Maria," Pete said. "You can't identify a person from an arm."

"Shows what you know," he retorted. "This guy had a tattoo."

Maria's breath caught in her throat as a scene from her past replayed in her mind. Mike coming home with a tattoo on his forearm when he was seventeen. Her parents hitting the roof, especially because minors were supposed to get parental permission.

How had the fact that her brother sported a tattoo slipped her mind? If she'd thought of it before now, she could have mentioned it as an identifying mark when she was showing around the age progression photo.

"What kind of a tattoo?" she asked.

If Mike's had been in a less visible place, her parents might not have been so hard on him. They hadn't understood how her brother could permanently etch a serpent on his forearm. They didn't care that it was the logo of his favorite alternative rock band.

"I saw it pretty good," Repeat said. "It was a snake."

A FEW HOURS LATER MARIA sat with Logan at an outdoor table at the Daybreak Café, the restaurant where Repeat had spotted the man with the serpent tattoo. She was peripherally aware of the steady stream of tourists passing by.

Logan had pointed out two young women who'd paired their Santa hats with red micro shorts and sleeveless shirts trimmed in white fur. A middle-aged couple with their arms linked belted out a jaunty Christmas tune as though they were performing on stage.

The constant distractions made it hard for Maria to think. Logan provided another one, although he seemed to accept that things between them couldn't progress any further. Why that annoyed her she didn't care to analyze.

"This place closes at two, right?" Logan asked. "It's almost that now. Alex Suarez might not make the time to talk to you."

When they'd arrived at the café more than an hour ago, they'd been told Suarez was occupied with restaurant business. Maria said they'd wait around until the owner was free. In the meantime, they'd finished off a lunch of Cuban-style sandwiches and fried plantains while Maria flagged down servers and busboys. None of them recognized Mike as a customer.

"I'm not leaving until he makes time." Maria picked up her water glass, only to find it empty. Their waitress had cleared their lunch dishes away about fifteen minutes ago. She hadn't come by since to refill their glasses, a strong hint that it was time for them to leave. The restaurant was closing. It was already a few minutes past 2:00. "You heard that waitress. She said Suarez goes from table to table, making sure the customers are happy. He's the man to talk to."

"Just keep in mind that a tattoo of a snake isn't that unusual, Maria," Logan said. "Lots of people have them."

A prickly sensation skittered up her spine. "What are you trying to say, Logan?"

He was wearing sunglasses, so she couldn't see his eyes. His mouth, however, turned down at the corners. "I don't want you to get your hopes up, okay?"

"You don't think a guy with a tattoo of a snake talking about naked photos is worth getting excited about?"

"Look, none of the people who work here recognized Mike," Logan pointed out. "I'm just saying Suarez probably won't, either."

She picked up the water glass again, found it empty again and set it down. She crossed one leg over the other, although she felt anything but relaxed. "What's it like to be so pessimistic?"

"I'm not a pessimist," he insisted. "I'm a realist. And look who's talking. If anybody's a cynic, it's you."

"Me?" She uncrossed her legs and pointed at her chest. Nobody had ever called her a cynic in her life before now. "I believe Mike is alive!"

"I'm not talking about Mike," Logan said.

"I'm talking about what's between you and me. You're the one who thinks it can't work out."

He sounded grumpy. Good.

"Because it can't." Only three little words, but they were so difficult for Maria to say it felt as if they were wrapped in sandpaper. "I live in Kentucky and you live in New York."

"Why should we let distance stop us?" He reached across the table and took her hand, sincerity practically pouring off him. Awareness skittered through her, the way it did any time he touched her. "Don't try to deny there's something between us. I know you feel it, too."

If she tugged her hand away, she'd only prove his contention. She almost laughed aloud at the thought that she was attempting to hide her feelings from him. After last night, he already knew how much his touch affected her.

"We're attracted to each other," she admitted slowly. "That's nothing new, though. We've always been attracted to each other."

"It's more than that." Logan gave her hand a gentle squeeze. "It would have fizzled out years ago if it was that simple. We can't just ignore what's between us."

"Oh, I see." She pulled her hand from his. Her voice was heavy with sarcasm. "Since you'll be here another night, you're trying to talk your way back into my bed."

"No." He actually sounded offended. "That's not it."

"You don't want a repeat of last night?" She felt hurt at the prospect. What was wrong with her?

"Of course I do," he snapped.

"Aha," she said, her mood lightening. "I knew it!"

"That's not all I want." He blew out a breath. "I think we should give a long-distance relationship a try."

Something bright flashed inside Maria before her brain processed the operative word. "A *try?*"

"Yeah, a try," he said. "I couldn't get to Kentucky more than one weekend a month, but you could visit me in New York, too. You wouldn't have to worry about the expense. I'll pay for the tickets."

Of course. He made a lot more money than she did. Wasn't that part of the reason he lived in Manhattan?

"You really think that would work?" Maria asked.

"Lots of couples make it work. Why not us?" he asked. "We could see how it goes."

Her heart dropped like a boulder rolled off a cliff. "You haven't changed at all."

He leaned closer to her. "I don't know what you mean by that."

"Of course you don't," she retorted.

He waited a few beats in silence. "Are you going to explain it to me?"

"Let me put it this way." She crossed her arms, inwardly scolding herself for sleeping with him. It had taken her years to get over Logan, and now she'd made herself vulnerable to him again. A stupid move. He'd done nothing to indicate he'd changed. "You're a look-before-you-leap kind of guy."

His brows knotted. "And?"

She was formulating a reply about the importance of taking chances when a tall man with dramatic dark coloring strode up to their table. "I heard you two were waiting on me. I'm Alex Suarez, owner of the Daybreak Café."

"The same Alex Suarez who hired Kayla Fryburger?" Maria asked.

"Yes." Alex's teeth flashed. He oozed charm and a certain Latin mystique even though Maria didn't detect an accent. No wonder Kayla was taken with him. "How do you know about that?"

"She's consulting with me on the case," Maria replied. "I'm Maria DiMarco and this is Logan Collier."

Alex shook hands with them in turn, then directed his attention to Logan. "I heard that you tried the pork sandwich. Our chef is ex-

perimenting with a new marinade. What did
you think?"

"Delicious," Logan said.

"Muy bien." Alex smiled at Logan. He was
an equal-opportunity charmer, Maria thought.
He nodded at a vacant chair at their table. "Mind
if I sit down?"

"Not at all." Maria had been about to propose it herself.

"I'll answer whatever questions you have, but
I doubt I'll be much help," he said. "I've already
told Kayla everything I know."

"We're not here about the Santa Claus statue,"
Maria said, surprised by his assumption. "I'm
in Key West looking for my brother." She produced the age progression and handed it to Alex.
"I think he was in your restaurant last week. Do
you recognize him?"

He lifted his eyes from the likeness. "This
isn't an actual photo of him, is it?"

"He's been missing for eleven years," Maria
said. "This is what we think he may look like
today."

"If he's alive," Logan added. The caveat
shouldn't have irked Maria, but it did.

"Do you recognize him?" Maria asked Alex.

He studied the paper once more, then handed
it back to her. "Can't say that I do, but we get

a lot of traffic. I can't get around to talk to everybody who comes in."

"Mike has a tattoo of a serpent on his left forearm," Maria said.

"Sorry," Alex said. "That doesn't ring any bells."

"He was here last Tuesday right around noon." Maria decided to try a shot in the dark. "Maybe you could pull the receipts from that day and I could look at them?"

Alex shook his head. "You know I can't do that. Besides, this isn't an expensive restaurant. Most people pay in cash."

Maria swallowed the disappointment that seemed to have become her constant companion. "You're sure you don't recognize him?"

"Like I said, a lot of people come through here." He shrugged, making the gesture seem elegant. "I'm sorry I can't help you."

"Why don't you give him your business card?" Logan suggested. "That way, he can get in touch if he thinks of anything."

"Yes, please." Maria got one out and extended it to Alex. She felt her phone vibrate but ignored the call. She'd check voice mail after she finished the conversation.

Alex spent a few moments examining the card before pocketing it. "How long have you been in the P.I. business?"

"Going on five years," she said.

"Maria was a cop before that," Logan said. "A good one."

"Impressive," Alex said. "You must be a great help to Kayla. What exactly is your role in her case?"

"Like I said, I'm a consultant," she said.

"So you're the one who advised her to set up the surveillance camera?"

"Yes, I am," Maria said.

"Do you have any notion of how the case is going?" Alex asked. "I'm due to send another email update to the merchants association."

"Another?" Maria sucked in a breath. "You didn't email the group about the camera, did you?"

"I sure did," he said. "Everyone is eager for an update."

Maria frowned. She'd rather it wasn't widespread knowledge that there was a camera pointed at the statue. It probably never occured to Kayla that Alex would spread the word.

"So what do you think?" Alex pressed. "Can I expect her to get results?"

He didn't sound as though he had much confidence in Kayla. "You can expect her to make sure the prankster doesn't bring more embarrassment to your organization."

"Yes," he said, "but is she close to finding out who the prankster is?"

"You should ask Kayla. It's her case," Maria said. "But I was under the impression that catching the culprit wasn't the main objective."

"Doesn't mean it wouldn't be nice." Alex stood up and made a sweeping gesture that encompassed the empty tables on the patio. The only customers left were Maria and Logan. "As you can see, we're getting ready to close."

It was a dismissal if Maria ever heard one.

They said their goodbyes and she and Logan joined the crowd on the street. She waited until they'd walked half a block before asking, "What did you think of Alex Suarez?"

"I thought he was a bit…practiced," Logan said. "Yeah, that's the word. Practiced."

"Blunt, too," Maria said. In fact, Maria thought Kayla was headed for heartbreak. Alex seemed like a man who had no compunction about going after what he wanted. If he hadn't made his interest in Kayla clear by now, he wasn't interested.

"Where to now?" Logan asked.

"I'm not sure." Maria wished she had a strategy, but her mind was blank. Her phone vibrated again. Whoever had called earlier had probably left a voice mail that had just come through. She dug out her phone and checked the number on the display. It was from a Key West exchange. "Let me see if this is important."

She called in and tried to listen to the message over the sound of blood rushing in her ears. The quiet voice was familiar but it didn't belong to Mike. Only then did she realize how much she'd been hoping it was her brother.

"It's from Repeat," she told Logan.

She listened carefully, taking mental notes, trying to bank her excitement.

"Well?" Logan asked when she hung up.

"Repeat remembered something else he overheard the guy with the serpent tattoo say," she told him. "We've got somewhere to be tonight."

TOURISTS FLOCKED TO THE corner of South and Whitehurst Streets even though neither of the claims printed on the concrete buoy were true. The concierge at Logan's hotel had told him that the buoy was ninety-four miles from Cuba, not ninety. Neither did it mark the southernmost point in the continental U.S.A. That distinction belonged to Ballast Key, a privately owned island southwest of Key West.

None of that mattered to the throng of people gathered at the tourist attraction to listen to an up-and-coming soul singer belt out some Christmas tunes. Her stage name was Amaryllis. A Key West native, she'd recently been signed to a major record deal after appearing on one of those televised singing talent shows.

"I'm surprised at how many people are here." Logan kept hold of Maria's arm, a necessity so they wouldn't lose each other in the crush. Otherwise, she probably wouldn't let him touch her.

She'd reacted negatively to his suggestion that they try a long-distance relationship, but he wasn't ready to give up on the idea. He was smart enough to bide his time, though.

"I'd never heard of Amaryllis until Repeat mentioned he'd overheard the guy with the serpent tattoo say he wanted to see her sing." Maria spoke close to Logan's ear so he could pick up what she was saying. "Supposedly there's been a rumor floating around for weeks that she was planning a free concert."

Half the people on the island must have heard about it. Maria and Logan had walked the few blocks from their hotels to the Southernmost Point—a good thing, for they'd never have found a parking spot. Maria had gotten rid of her rental car, anyway, since most places on the island were accessible by foot.

"People turn out when something's free," Logan said.

Amaryllis was already showing off her impressive set of lungs with a soulful rendition of "Silver Bells." The arrangement was unaccompanied, her strong, clear voice the only instrument that was necessary.

"Her tone is amazing," Maria said. "She's gorgeous, too."

The tall, willowy singer had beautiful mocha skin and hair cut daringly short. She wore a flirty red dress and pranced around on stiletto heels between the concrete buoy and a Christmas tree. A spotlight shone on her, but elsewhere the lighting was poor.

Logan craned his neck to get a better view of the people in the crowd but mostly saw the backs of heads. "It's too dark and crowded to see whether Mike's here."

"Don't tell me you're willing to concede he might be?" Maria sounded skeptical.

"I'm trying to keep at open mind," Logan said. It wasn't easy. Signs might point to Mike being alive, but Logan still had serious doubts. "Things aren't adding up, though."

"What things?"

"The blackmail note, for one," Logan said. "If the blackmailer's serious about making Caroline Webb pay, why hasn't he made a ransom demand?"

"Just because he hasn't made a demand doesn't mean he won't. Now how should we go about this?" Maria surveyed the crowd, her change of subject signaling that the original topic was closed. Logan thought it warranted further discussion, but they were already getting dirty looks for talking while Amaryllis sang.

He bent down so his mouth was close to Maria's ear again. "It'd be hard to find someone in this throng even if you knew for certain he was here."

She turned her head to answer him and her mouth brushed his cheek. Her eyes flew to his, awareness in their depths. *That's why we should give a long-distance relationship a shot,* he wanted to say.

"We have to try." She checked her cell phone. "It's eight-thirty. Let's meet back at this spot at nine o'clock. I'll take the right side and you get the left."

She took off without waiting for a response. Just as well. Logan might have asked if she had any night-vision goggles handy. Doubtless she wouldn't appreciate that.

He circled behind the audience, searching for men near his own height, as Mike had been on the morning of the terrorist strike. But then Mike had been only eighteen, an age when a lot of boys had more growing to do. Had he lived, Mike might be well over six feet.

The task was all but impossible. The spectators fanned out from the singer, with people standing shoulder to shoulder. Amaryllis had such a powerful voice that even the angels on high might hear her singing.

Logan caught a clear view of her through a break in the crowd. The night was mild, but this close to the ocean there always seemed to be a breeze. Amaryllis raised her arms, and a gust of wind plastered the material of the red dress against her shapely body.

Somebody was taking photographs. It was James Smith, the *Key West Sun* photographer. Logan and Maria had introduced themselves to him that morning in the parking lot when they were leaving the newspaper. It hadn't been difficult to figure out James was the photographer Kayla was meeting. Then, like now, he was toting photography equipment.

He was starting to pack up. Logan didn't blame him. The photographer wouldn't get a better shot than the one of the singer with her arms uplifted and her dress hugging her curves.

Logan started walking toward James, intending to ask if he'd had a chance to show the age progression to his coworkers.

Their paths were about to intersect when James stopped and with a half hug greeted a tall, dark-haired man. Something about the way the guy carried himself seemed familiar. Logan squinted, making out the long, distinctive nose of Alex Suarez. He was with a woman, a busty brunette with an hourglass figure. Alex had his hand on the small of her back, and he laughed at something she said to James.

The photographer slapped Alex on the arm, nodded at the woman and continued on his original path. Logan intercepted him.

"Hey, James," he said. "It's Logan Collier."

"From this morning in the parking lot," James said, nodding. He shifted the photography equipment on his shoulder. "I remember you. What can I do for you?"

"I wondered if you got a chance to show any of your coworkers that image of Maria's brother," Logan said.

"Yeah, I did show it around. Nobody knew him. Sorry, man."

"Thanks for checking." Logan refrained from telling him the results didn't surprise him. "I'll pass the information on to Maria."

"Sure thing." James raised a hand. "See you around."

Logan verified on his cell phone that it was nearly nine o'clock and went to meet Maria. He could tell by her expression that she hadn't made any progress on the case. He shook his head to let her know he hadn't, either.

"Let's stay until the end of the concert," she suggested. "People are packed pretty tight. We might spot something when they start leaving."

Amaryllis had been singing for a good forty-five minutes. Logan didn't imagine the impromptu event would last much longer, especially because the wind was picking up. The singer no longer lifted her arms. They were down at her sides, holding on to her skirt. Fifteen minutes later, the concert was over.

Maria and Logan stood their ground as people streamed toward them and around them. Logan dutifully kept an eye out for Mike but also watched Maria in his peripheral vision. He heard her gasp over the ambient crowd noise.

"Mike," she said. Without another word, she gave chase after a man about the right height and weight, who was headed away from them. Logan followed.

She caught up to the guy in a few running steps and grabbed him by the arm. He spun around, his stance aggressive. Just as quickly, he relaxed. Maria staggered backward. Logan was still a few yards away, but he could tell from her body language that the man wasn't Mike.

Logan lengthened his stride to eat up the ground between them. With a broad forehead and thick features, the man looked nothing like her brother. He was also about ten years older than Mike would have been.

"Hey, pretty lady." The man's grin was lascivious. "You want some of this?"

"Leave her alone," Logan all but growled, drawing even with Maria.

The other man put up his hands in a sign of surrender. "Hey, I didn't know she was with somebody. I don't want no trouble."

And then he was gone, melting into the crowd.

"Are you okay?" Logan asked Maria, his heart aching for her. The scenario he'd witnessed kept repeating. Maria kept mistaking other men for her brother, only to have her hopes dashed.

She blinked a few times—to dry tears of disappointment? But then she raised her chin and balanced her hands on her hips. "It sounded like you were fixing for another fight."

"That's not true," Logan said, willing to go along with her change of subject. If she found it too difficult to talk about Mike, he could roll with that. "But I would have thrown another punch if I had to."

"Your black eye from the first fight isn't even healed," she said, gaining steam. "And did you forget again that I used to be a cop?"

"Can't say that I did," Logan said.

"So you understand I can take care of myself?" she challenged.

"Yep," he said and figured he might as well lay it on the line. "But that doesn't seem to matter."

She was about to say something else, then shook her head and grabbed his hand. They were only five or six blocks from their hotels. They covered the distance in silence. Logan knew she had to be fighting disappointment over another lead that hadn't panned out. He didn't say that, though. It would have felt too much like rubbing salt in an open wound.

"The temperature's dropping. Mind if I grab a jacket in my hotel room?" he asked. The night was relatively young. He fully expected that she'd suggest they show the age progression at another bar or restaurant.

"I'll come up with you," Maria said.

The silence between them continued, lasting until Logan opened the hotel room door to admit them both and turned on the light. His jacket hung from a hook in the narrow closet. He started to reach for it.

"You won't be needing that," Maria said.

Logan's hand paused in midair. "Why not?"

"There's not much else we can do until there's a ransom demand." Her statement surprised him, even though he'd been thinking along the same lines. Then again, he didn't quite believe there would be a demand.

"Then what should we do?" he asked.

She anchored a hand on his shoulder and kissed him. The heat was instantaneous, chasing away the slight chill of the night. She tasted of the salt air and her own unique scent. He could get drunk on her, he thought. She swept her tongue inside his mouth, taking the kiss from sweet to passionate in a millisecond. Even as his body reacted, his mind rebelled. He couldn't let this go any further, not until he got an answer. He drew back, keeping her in his arms.

"I don't understand," he said. "I thought we weren't going to repeat what happened last night."

"I changed my mind," she said and kissed him again.

After that, he didn't question his good fortune. He wasn't sure what had caused Maria's change of heart. For now, it didn't matter. Especially because having her back in his arms verified what he'd begun to suspect last night.

He'd fallen back in love with her.

MARIA LAY NEXT TO LOGAN in his hotel room bed, listening to him breathe. Her eyes had been open long enough to adjust to the blackness. The dim glow from the night-light in the bathroom was the only illumination.

She was skin to skin with Logan, her entire left side flush against his. Even while contentment filled her, she knew she shouldn't be here, not after telling him they had no future. She be-

lieved that. She couldn't open herself to heartache by agreeing to a long-distance relationship
with a man who wasn't willing to take a chance
on them. They'd been interrupted before she
could explain that the kind of arrangement he
was proposing wasn't a real commitment. If
things didn't work out, he wouldn't have lost
anything. He'd go on his merry way, she, on the
other hand, would be devastated.

The operative question was what was she
doing here? She'd made the first move, not
Logan. Part of it, of course, was fallout from
the frustration of not finding her brother. For a
little while, at least, she'd been able to lose herself in Logan's arms.

If she was honest with herself, she'd admit
that wasn't the entire reason. It was illogical,
but back at the Southernmost Point, when Logan
had made yet another totally unnecessary attempt to protect her, tenderness had risen up in
her like the ocean at high tide.

Nestled against him as she was, she found
the tenderness hadn't ebbed. That was why she
needed to get out of bed. Right. Now.

Logan's arm was around her even in sleep.
Very carefully, so as not to awaken him, she
started to edge away. She hadn't gotten more
than a few inches when his arm tightened
around her, drawing her close.

"Going somewhere?" he asked, his voice heavy with sleep.

She was tempted to say she needed to use the bathroom, then wait until he fell back asleep before she dressed and slipped out of the room. But she'd never been a coward.

"I was going back to my hotel," she said.

He didn't tighten his hold or stroke any of the places he'd learned would make her sigh with pleasure. He kissed her softly on the lips, the contact brief and sweet.

"Don't go," he breathed against her mouth.

Maria's will to get out of bed evaporated.

She swallowed the lump in her throat, because the time for them to part ways was getting inexorably closer. "Okay," she whispered.

His mouth found hers once again in the darkness. Her body melted against his and she kissed him with everything she had, because she didn't know what tomorrow would bring.

For now, however, they had tonight.

CHAPTER ELEVEN

KAYLA DRIFTED IN AND OUT of consciousness. Every time she felt herself start to surrender to sleep, worry reared its ugly head, pulling her back to awareness.

Her continuing strategy was to stay awake all night and attempt to sleep during the day, operating on the assumption that the prankster wouldn't strike in broad daylight.

The snag was that she couldn't be one hundred percent sure of that.

She flopped over in bed, only to get a blast of sunlight in the face. One of the slats in the window blind was askew. Groaning, she sat up and reached for her smartphone. The bedside clock showed that it was half past ten, meaning she'd been trying to sleep for only a few hours.

She'd gorged on caffeine and scary movies last night, the better to help her stay awake. She'd gotten a jolt of pure adrenaline early in the evening when Alex called. After the dart tournament, she'd been full of hope that he'd ask her on a real date. All he'd wanted, however, was a report on the investigation. She'd told him about the anonymous texts James Smith had received, her attempt to call the number from which the texts had originated and her conclusion that the sender had used a prepaid phone.

Maybe Alex was waiting for her to make the next move. Yeah, that must be it. He'd invited her to stop by the dart tournament. Now it was her turn to reciprocate.

Feeling better, she pressed the keys that pulled up the website she was using to monitor Santa. Once she checked on the statue, she'd go back to sleep for a few hours and then call Alex. She could invite him to dinner and make the chicken marsala her friends raved about. Except it seemed she had something to do tonight… That's right. Her mother was having a holiday gathering at her house. Would it be too forward to invite Alex to come along?

Kayla stared down at the phone, wondering why it was taking the website so long to respond. With every moment that passed, she was becoming more fully awake. She'd be a mess tonight if she didn't get more sleep.

The screen remained completely black.

Kayla hit the refresh button. The website responded instantly, as it always did. The result was the same. The screen was black.

Frowning, she brought the phone closer to

her face for a better look. The blackness wasn't uniform; a sliver of the screen was darker than the rest. It looked almost like a crease.

The cobwebs of sleep completely disappeared, leaving her with a crystal-clear thought: Was it possible somebody had draped a dark cloth over the security camera?

The bottom fell out of Kayla's stomach. She was almost sure that was what had happened.

She swung her legs off the mattress and got up, so quickly she saw stars. Steadying herself on the bedpost, she searched for shoes. She spied a pair of orange clogs peeking from under the bed and pulled them on. She'd fallen asleep in a T-shirt and black spandex capris. No need to change clothes when time was of the essence.

She rushed out of the house and hit the sidewalk running. The soles of her clogs slapped against the pavement. She had a moment's thought that she could have made a better shoe choice, then it was gone.

It was vital that she get to the statue as soon as possible. Even if she was right about the prankster striking again, she might be able to minimize the damage. The merchants association didn't have to find out. Neither did Uncle Carl.

"Hey, Kayla!" The UPS driver who'd had the same route for the two years Kayla had lived in the neighborhood raised a hand from beside his truck. "Where you headed in such a hurry?"

"To Santa," she answered as she zoomed by.

"He's not making the rounds till tomorrow night," the man called after her.

Kayla couldn't slow down to explain. Every minute was crucial. She kept running, past pastel-colored houses decorated with Christmas wreaths and holly and palm trees with giant red bows tied to their trunks.

The corner where the statue was located finally came into view. Across the street was a marketplace called Truval Village and a welcome center for the Conch Train, a popular attraction that took tourists on a ride past the Key West sites. The main embarkation point for the tour was near Mallory Square but Truval Village was one of the train's regular stops.

A double-decker tour bus from a different sightseeing company was waiting at the intersection for the light to turn green, blocking Kayla's view of the statue. The crosswalk was up ahead. She hesitated only a moment before crossing the street in the middle of the block and weaving around the stopped cars. She stepped onto the curb, finally with an unobstructed view of the statue.

Somebody had dressed Santa in a Hawaiian shirt and perched sunglasses on his plaster nose.

Considering this was the tropics, that wasn't so bad. But the devil horns were.

Only a few people paid Santa any attention. One of them, however, was a good-looking young guy holding a camera. Kayla did a double take. It wasn't just any guy. It was James Smith, the *Key West Sun* photographer.

"Don't take that photo!" she shouted.

James turned toward her voice, giving her the opportunity she needed. She swooped in and knocked the devil horns off the statue. They were made of black rubber with red tips and attached with an elastic band.

Feeling pleased with her quick thinking and more than a little relieved, she walked up to James. He was dressed in khakis and a cream shirt with the sleeves rolled up, looking far different from the surfer boy she'd met with at the newspaper office the day before.

"You look good!" she said.

A corner of his mouth quirked. "You seem surprised."

"No, I just didn't expect..." She stopped. That didn't sound right. "I mean, with the hair and the tan, I didn't think..." She let her voice trail off again. "Help me out here, would you?"

"My six-year-old cousin was in a Christmas play at the church," he said. "He's been talking about it for weeks."

For the first time since she left the house, she became aware of her appearance. Her hand flew to her hair. It felt tangled and frizzy. No wonder. She hadn't taken the time to run a brush through it.

"I must look a fright," Kayla said.

He smiled at her. "I think you look kind of cute."

He did? She still felt compelled to explain.

"I woke up and couldn't see Santa." She told him about the video stream from the security camera. "I needed to get over here fast, before somebody took an embarrassing photo."

"Are you talking about me?"

"Yes." She heaved a sigh. "But it's okay. I got here in time."

His smile disappeared. "Sorry to break this to you, but I took a bunch of photos before you arrived."

The air left her lungs, deflating her spirits. Her short-lived career as a P.I. passed before her eyes, probably over before it had barely begun. "I don't suppose you'll sell them to me?"

He scratched the side of his nose, looking uncomfortable. "Are you trying to bribe me?"

"No. Yes. I don't know." She rubbed a hand over her face. "No. The answer's no. You're doing your job. I'm the one who messed up."

"It can't be as bad as all that."

"It is," she said. "This was my one shot to be a private investigator. Uncle Carl won't keep me on after this."

"Hey, you don't know that." James looked genuinely distressed.

"Yeah, I do," she said. "He wouldn't have taken me on in the first place if I wasn't his niece."

James lifted his camera and snapped another photo of the ceramic Santa. "I think the Hawaiian shirt and the sunglasses look cool."

Kayla removed the items all the same. She didn't mind the tropical look, either. How the statue was dressed, however, wasn't up to her. She'd been hired to make sure nobody changed its appearance.

"How did you find out about the statue this time?" she asked. "Another text?"

"Yeah," he said and produced his phone. The message was from the same number he'd given her, the one she'd determined came from a prepaid phone that was untraceable to a specific user. The text was direct and to the point: Check out Santa.

"Thanks for showing me the text," Kayla said.

"Will it help you catch the guy?"

"I don't think so."

"Can you narrow it down to the people you told about the camera?"

Kayla pressed her lips together. Maria had phoned her yesterday to let her know the surveillance details were common knowledge. If only Kayla had thought to mention to Alex Suarez to keep news of the camera under wraps. It was no consolation that Maria claimed even a veteran P.I. could have made the oversight. "An email went out about the camera to the merchants association. Word could have spread."

"Ouch," James said.

She pasted on a smile she hoped looked brave. "Don't worry about it. I'll be fine."

"You sure?"

"Positive," she lied. "See you around. I need to check out what went wrong with the security camera."

"Good luck with that," he said, as though he really meant it. She felt a little better knowing he was on her side.

A half dozen or so customers milled about the gift shop. The same rail-thin clerk who'd been on duty when Kayla and Maria installed the security camera was helping one decide which T-shirt to buy. He wore elf ears today instead of reindeer antlers.

Kayla decided against informing the clerk she was headed upstairs. She hurried up the steps and found the door to the storage room open.

Just as she expected, the camera lens was covered with a dark cloth.

She whipped it off, feeling the rush of blood through her veins. That salesclerk downstairs had probably put it there. She'd give him a piece of her mind.

She was halfway across the room when a thought stopped her.

The second floor should be off-limits to everybody except employees, but the clerk had been so preoccupied he hadn't seen her come upstairs.

Kayla wasn't ready to rule him out as the culprit, but the fact remained that anybody could have sneaked up and tampered with the camera.

THE THEME SONG FROM THE old *Pink Panther* cartoon played as Maria was getting out of the shower. Her cell phone ring tone. She swore, grabbing for a towel and wrapping herself in it before heading out of the bathroom.

Her phone kept ringing at the most inopportune moments. At about eight this morning, when Logan was in the process of awakening her in the most pleasurable way imaginable, Annalise had called.

Of course, Maria hadn't known who was phoning until later. She hadn't asked Logan to stop. That would have been insanity. For his part, Logan hadn't given any indication he'd heard the phone until much later. He'd told her about an off-Broadway play that was a takeoff of the old cartoon, which featured a bumbling French police detective. He could get them tickets to see it, he'd said. As though they were already in that long-distance relationship she'd refused to enter into.

She would set him straight soon, maybe even when she met him downstairs in the lobby in ten minutes. After their morning lovemaking, she'd come back to her hotel to shower and dress. The conversation she needed to have now, however, was with whoever was on the phone.

She picked it up from her bedside table and checked the display. Not Annalise calling back to ask why Maria hadn't returned the earlier summons. Kayla.

Maria dialed her friend. "Kayla. What's up?"

"Are you busy this morning?" she asked.

Maria had intended to suggest to Logan that they revisit some of the local hangouts, hoping somebody might recognize Mike if she mentioned he had a tattoo of a serpent on his arm.

"Nothing that can't wait," she said. "Why?"

"Somebody tampered with the security camera," Kayla announced. "If you could come down to the gift shop, I'd love a second opinion."

"I can be there in twenty minutes," Maria promised.

She and Logan made it to the gift shop in fifteen, with Maria telling him what little she knew about the events of that morning along the way. The first person she saw upon entering the shop was the disagreeable clerk who'd been there the other day.

"Well, well, well." The man propped his hands on his narrow hips. "If it isn't Mammary P.I."

"Excuse me." Logan stepped forward. "What did you say?"

The clerk seemed to grow smaller in front of their eyes. "I said here's the other half of *Magnum P.I.* It's an old television show. With Tom Selleck."

"That better be what you'd said or you owe the lady an apology."

"Oh, it is," the clerk lied. To Maria, he said, "Your friend is upstairs."

Maria waited until they were halfway up the steps before she turned to Logan. "This chivalry thing you're doing isn't necessary. I told you last night I can take care of myself."

"And I told you I can't seem to help myself from defending your honor," he said. "It doesn't matter that you're tougher than me."

"Says the man who got a shiner in a bar

fight," she quipped. The yellow-and-green blur under his eye was already fading.

"We make quite the pair," he said, as though they actually were a couple. It reminded her that she'd have to clarify her position on that very soon. Not now, though. Kayla had already spotted them through the open door of the storage room.

"Maria! Logan!" she called, leaping to her feet from the chair where she'd been sitting. "I'm so glad you're here."

"Did you find out anything?" Maria asked.

"Nothing helpful," she said. "At first I thought whoever put the cloth over the camera had to work here. But the shop was so busy when I arrived that I walked right upstairs. Nobody saw me."

"Did you question the salesclerk?"

"He claims he had no reason to do it," Kayla said. "He got so indignant I actually believed him."

"Let's think about this," Maria said. "You went to sleep at about eight this morning and woke up to check the website at ten-thirty or so, right?"

"Right," Kayla said.

"The gift shop doesn't open until ten, so the incident had to have happened between ten and ten-thirty," Maria added.

"Unless the clerk is lying," Logan pointed out. "He could have tampered with the camera when he arrived to open the shop."

"How can we be sure he's telling the truth?" Kayla asked.

"Let me go downstairs and talk to him," Logan offered. "I think we've established a rapport." He winked.

"Good idea," Maria said. "While you're down there, ask him who came in the shop when it opened."

"Will do." Logan headed down the stairs.

"This is a disaster." Kayla hugged herself and rocked back and forth. "Even if we find out who the culprit is, my P.I. career is doomed. I messed up big-time."

"We're in the tropics, Kayla," Maria pointed out. "Santa probably should have been wearing a Hawaiian shirt and sunglasses in the first place."

"But not devil horns," Kayla wailed. "It made him look demonic and cheerful all at once. You'll see when the photo's in the newspaper tomorrow."

"I feel your pain," Maria said. "But if you find out who's doing this, the photo might not be as damaging as you think."

"You're right." Kayla's chest expanded and she seemed to grow a few inches. "If I want to make private investigation a career, I need to act like a detective. There are a couple of things I can check out. It's a busy intersection. It seems likely that somebody saw something."

"You can talk to employees who work at the other businesses within view of the statue," she suggested.

"Exactly what I was thinking. I'll get right on it." Kayla started to pick up a wildly colored print shirt from the back of a chair, then let it drop. "I guess I can leave this here."

"Is that the shirt Santa was wearing?" Maria asked, reaching for it to get a better look.

"Yeah. Why?"

"I think I saw this same shirt in a shop yesterday. If you want, I'll check it out for you."

"Oh, thank you." Kayla pressed her hands together and gave a little bow on her way past. "I'll call you later and we can compare notes."

That was exactly what Maria and Logan did after they left the gift shop. He reported that the clerk insisted he hadn't tampered with the camera. Minutes after the shop opened, about a dozen people from a cruise ship had come in to buy souvenirs, the man had claimed. They'd kept him so busy that any one of them could have sneaked upstairs. So, too, could a stray customer who hadn't been part of the group.

"In other words," Maria said as they walked, "the clerk was no help at all."

"Bingo," Logan said. Although he didn't put his arm around her or enfold her hand in his, he was so close their shoulders almost touched. So close passersby would think they were a couple. "Are you going to tell me where you saw the shirt for sale?"

"I'll show you," Maria said.

She took the same route she had the day before, passing by the table at the Daybreak Café where she and Logan had eaten lunch and going straight to the small gift shop adjacent to the restaurant. It sold all things Cuban. Maria went directly to a stack of shirts. Sure enough, the one on display featured gold flowers, green palm trees and colorful parrots on an aqua background.

"I knew I'd seen this shirt before," Maria said. "At first glance, it seems like Hawaiian, but it's actually a guayabera."

"What's the difference?" Logan asked.

"Mostly the large front pockets and the stitching pattern." She showed him the two vertical rows of tiny pleats running along the front and back. "Somebody I talked to about Mike a few days ago was wearing one, although the pattern wasn't nearly as tropical as this one. I think most guayabera shirts are pretty plain."

"Do you think the prankster bought the shirt here?" Logan asked.

"Not necessarily," Maria said slowly, as her thoughts formulated. "I don't think he needed to pay for it."

"Alex Suarez?" Logan's eyebrows drew together. "Why would he be doing this? He's the one who hired Kayla."

"That could have been misdirection," Maria said. "Haven't you noticed how all roads seem to lead back to Suarez? Remember the owner of The Flying Monkey telling us Suarez was opposed to the statue? What better way to throw suspicion off yourself than by offering to hire someone to catch the culprit? When he found out about the camera, he could have sent that mass email to cover his tracks."

Logan grinned at her. "You really are a good private investigator, aren't you?"

"I have my moments," she said, wishing those moments translated to her brother's case. She felt glad that she could help Kayla, but not for a second had she forgotten why she was in Key West.

"What now?" he asked. "Will you confront Suarez?"

"I'm going to run my theory by Kayla," Maria said. "It's her case. I just hope she'll consider it. She has a pretty big crush on him."

"Too bad for her," Logan said.

"What do you mean?" Maria asked, although she'd had the same thought.

"I saw him last night at the concert, getting cozy with a tall, busty brunette," he said.

The physical opposite of Kayla. "Ouch," Maria said. "But if Suarez is behind the shenanigans with Santa, Kayla is better off without him."

A harried-looking waitress stuck her head into the small shop. "If you want to buy something, you can take it up to the cash register in the restaurant."

That was their cue to leave. Maria didn't see Alex Suarez anywhere in the place, which was just as well.

"Didn't you get the impression yesterday that Suarez was a pretty smart guy?" Logan asked when they were outside again.

"Yeah, I did," Maria agreed. "Why do you ask?"

"Why would a smart guy pull a dumb move like using a shirt from his own shop?"

While Maria was mulling over the answer, she caught sight of something aqua in her peripheral vision. She stopped dead, grabbing Logan's hand so he had to stop, too.

"Oh, rats," she said.

"Rats?"

She pointed to a store window display that included the same guayabera shirt they'd seen at the shop attached to Alex Suarez's restaurant.

"I have a feeling," Logan said slowly, "that you can buy that shirt all over Key West."

THE INSTRUMENTAL VERSION of "White Christmas" drifted through the sliding screen door to the patio where Logan stood with Maria and Kayla on Saturday night.

All told, there were thirty or forty people in the fenced backyard of Kayla's mother's pale blue, one-story house. Almost all of them were related to Kayla.

"Thanks again for inviting us to crash your mom's party," Logan said. He'd been surprised when Maria accepted the invitation until he'd realized she could ask the guests about Mike. She had already flashed the age progression around the party.

Kayla waved a hand. "Think nothing of it. The more, the merrier. That's the Fryburger motto."

Everybody seemed to be having a good time. The fence and the palm trees in the backyard were decorated with the same tiny white lights that rimmed the house. The guests munched on Christmas cookies and hors d'oeuvres while sipping on eggnog and a spiked red punch.

"You don't seem particularly merry, Kayla," Maria observed. In her black hair, she was wearing one of the poinsettia blooms that Helene Fryburger had handed out when they'd arrived. Maria's dress, the same color as the flower, hugged her curvy figure. Logan's heart beat faster just looking at her.

"It's hard to get in the Christmas spirit when you couldn't stop somebody from putting devil horns on Santa," Kayla said. "I just can't believe I couldn't find anybody who saw it happen."

Earlier in the day, Maria had run her suspicions of Alex by Kayla. The apprentice P.I. had made the same observation as Logan, that an intelligent man wouldn't dress the statue in a shirt from his store. Then Kayla had given Maria and Logan a bare-bones rundown of her attempt to locate an eyewitness. She'd been so exhausted from staying up all night, however, that this was the first time they'd had a chance to go over details.

"Did you talk to anybody who was on the Conch Tour?" Maria asked.

"A bunch of people," Kayla said. "But the place where the tour makes a stop is actually about a half block from the intersection. Most of the shops in Truval Village don't face the statue."

"Too bad the person in the information booth didn't see anything," Maria mentioned.

"She said business is pretty steady all day long. She can't actually see the statue from where she sits, either." Kayla frowned. "After an hour or so of stopping people at random, I resigned myself to striking out."

"You handed out business cards, right?" Maria asked. Even in the midst of her personal crises, she was genuinely interested in helping Kayla. One more thing to admire about her, Logan thought.

"Sure did," Kayla said.

"Then don't give up," Maria advised. "Something still might happen."

"Yeah, Alex might fire me," Kayla said. "He was pretty steamed when I told him what went down. That's why I think it's crazy you suspected him of being the prankster."

"Well, I try not to rule out anybody or anything," Maria stated.

Smart words. Too bad Maria was having trouble following her own advice when it came to her brother.

"Did I tell you I was thinking about inviting Alex to the party, too?" Kayla asked. "I probably would have if the you-know-what hadn't hit the fan."

Logan exchanged a look with Maria. Without speaking, he knew she was also thinking about the brunette he'd seen Suarez with at the concert.

"You're so cute, Kayla," Maria said. "There must be other guys who are interested in you."

"James Smith asked me out," she admitted.

"The *Key West Sun* photographer?" When she nodded, Maria continued, "He seems like a nice guy, and he has that killer smile. You should have asked him to the party."

"You're forgetting James is the guy whose photo of Devil Santa is running in the newspaper tomorrow." Kayla shook her head. "I don't think so.… Hey, speaking of tomorrow, you two are going to be here, right? You're not leaving or anything?"

"I'm not leaving." Maria turned to look at Logan. "I'm not sure about you."

They'd had all day to talk about what would happen next, both in the investigation and their relationship. Yet after Maria had reiterated that there wasn't much they could do until a ransom demand was made, they hadn't discussed either subject.

Logan had seized the moment, persuading Maria to take a sightseeing tour of the island and to visit the Hemingway House. The day had been so pleasant that he hadn't even told her about the heated voice mail his boss had left in response to the news that Logan would be staying in Key West for a few more days.

"You'd better be back on Christmas Eve for that party at the Waldorf if career advancement is important to you," Logan's boss had warned.

Christmas Eve was two days away.

"I'll be here tomorrow." Logan imagined that Maria's body sagged with relief. But his observation, of course, could have been wishful thinking.

"Then could you two do me a favor?" Kayla rolled her eyes. "I mean another favor. I looked at the video to see if I'd notice anything out of the ordinary before somebody took the security camera out of commission. I didn't. It sure would help to have another couple pairs of eyes review it."

"We'd be happy to," Maria said. Logan thought it had to mean something that she'd included him in the response.

"Yeah," he said. "No problem."

He noticed that Maria's glass was empty and put out his hand. "If you like, I'll get you more punch."

"Thanks," she said, handing it to him.

"Kayla, how about you?"

"I'm good." She held up a bottle of water that was half-full. "Boring, but good."

He indicated her outfit with a sweep of his

hand. She was wearing a short, patterned dress with sky-high heels. "No way is a woman who dresses like you boring."

Kayla twirled around, lifting her hands over her head so her skirt fluttered. "Thanks."

He laughed, then went in search of the punch bowl. Refreshments were set up on the kitchen table just inside the door. Kayla's uncle Frank was already there, watching another man, who had his back to Logan, scoop the red liquid into his cup.

"Drink too much of that and you'll have to crawl home," Frank told him. "I added more booze when Helene wasn't looking."

"I can handle it." The man took a swig of the punch and Logan saw him in profile. It was Repeat, one of Frank's "cronies" from the poker game. The one who'd overheard the guy with the tattoo talking about naked photos.

"Can I get some of that punch, too?" Logan would warn Maria that it was liberally spiked. He hoped she would drink some, though. She was still far too tense.

"Hey, I know you," Frank said. "Logan, isn't it?"

"That's right," he said. "I remember your names, too. Frank and Repeat."

"It's actually Peter," the other man said. "I've decided not to go by Repeat anymore."

"Since when?" Frank asked.

"This afternoon," he said. "Gladys doesn't like the nickname."

"Do you listen to everything your wife says?" Frank demanded.

"Hell, yeah," Peter said. "Don't you?"

"Of course not!" Frank said.

A gray-haired woman appeared at the door of the kitchen. "Frank," she called, "you need to go out and buy more beer. Right away!"

"Coming," he said, then turned to Logan and Peter. "Excuse me. Duty calls."

"You mean Mariella called," Peter said, chuckling. "What were you saying about not doing whatever she tells you to?"

"Shut up, Repeat," Frank muttered.

"It's Peter," his friend called after him. He laughed and addressed Logan. "We like to give each other a hard time."

"I can see that," he answered.

Peter pointed at him. "Hey, did you find that guy with the serpent tattoo?"

"No, we didn't," Logan said.

"That's too bad. Your lady friend really seemed to think he was her brother."

That was what Maria desperately wanted to believe. "A lot of people have serpent tattoos," Logan stated.

"I wish I could remember more about this

guy. But like I said, I didn't see him real good."
Peter snapped his fingers. "Hey, did I mention
the tattoo was in color?"

Logan's heart felt as if it thudded to a stop as
he pictured the design that had been on Mike
DiMarco's arm. "No. You didn't mention that."

"Well, it was. That's probably why I noticed it
in the first place. I mean, how many guys have
a red snake tattooed on their arm?"

Logan knew of exactly one. Mike DiMarco
had gotten the tattoo in honor of the band whose
full name Logan just now remembered.

The Ruby Serpents.

CHAPTER TWELVE

MARIA STOOD IN THE BACK corner of Helene Fryburger's yard under a lit-up palm tree, holding her cell phone close to her ear in order to drown out the Christmas carols and the buzz of conversation coming from the other guests.

She was also cursing herself for answering the phone in the first place.

After Logan had gone in search of more punch and Kayla excused herself to use the bathroom, Maria got a call from her brother Jack, the DiMarco closest to her own age. When she didn't answer, he'd sent her a barrage of threatening texts.

Jack had vowed to keep phoning and texting until Maria returned his calls.

"I'm a big girl, Jack," Maria said. "You can stop worrying about me."

"Says the woman who called me daily last summer when I was rehabbing my shoulder," he retorted.

"That was different," Maria said. It was after multiple doctors had told Jack, a minor league baseball pitcher at the time, that he needed to accept the fact his pro baseball career was over. "You'd taken off to the Eastern Shore of Virginia. I wanted to be sure your head was on straight."

"You're in Key West looking for our dead brother," Jack blurted. "You need to worry about your own head."

Maria felt her spine stiffen. Her grip tightened on the phone. "I have good reason to believe Mike is alive."

"I wouldn't consider a few anonymous calls and letters and a man who spotted a tattoo of a snake on some guy's arm good reasons," Jack said.

Since Maria hadn't breathed a word of her investigation to Jack, Annalise must be filling him in on her progress. Maria had been avoiding calls from her sister, too, but she'd texted her an update yesterday.

"What would you have me do, Jack? Not pursue the leads?" Maria spotted Logan walking across the backyard carrying a beer in one hand and her glass of punch in the other. In dark slacks and a long-sleeved blue shirt open at the neck, he almost looked better in his clothes than out of them. Almost. She nearly groaned at the direction her thoughts had taken, especially because she needed to keep her wits about her or she'd never find Mike.

"I'd have you take the first plane back to Kentucky." Jack lived in Virginia, but he and his girlfriend were spending the holidays at the Di-Marco house in Lexington. Jack had obviously made it his mission to get Maria to leave Key West. "Mom and Dad are asking a lot of questions about what kind of case would take you away on Christmas week. You don't want them to find out, do you?"

"I want to bring Mike home to them," Maria said. "Can't you understand that?"

"Sure I can," Jack said. "He was my little brother, too. But sometimes wanting isn't enough."

Logan stopped a few paces from her. She held up a finger to let him know she'd be only a minute.

"Listen, Jack, I've gotta go," she said.

"I'll call you tomorrow," he promised.

She shook her head, but trying to dissuade him would be useless. "Tell Tara she might want to rethink dating such a stubborn son of a gun."

"Look who's talking," he retorted.

"Bye, Jack," she said and clicked off.

"Sorry it took a while," Logan said, extending the punch to her.

"Thanks." She took the glass, tipped it back and drained half the liquid in a single gulp.

"Whoa!" Logan said. "Go easy on that. Kayla's uncle warned me that was pretty strong stuff."

"I need something strong," Maria said. "Jack was giving me a hard time."

Logan shrugged his broad shoulders. "He's worried about you."

"I know." Maria sighed. Since Mike's death, the DiMarco siblings had kept close tabs on each other. She was the guiltiest party. Jack hadn't been exaggerating about the stretch last summer when she'd called him every day. "Annalise must have filled him in on what's going on in the investigation."

The back corner of the yard was fairly isolated but in full view of the festivities occurring closer to the house. Noise from the carols and the party guests filled what seemed to Maria like a pregnant pause.

"It wasn't Annalise," Logan finally admitted. "Jack called me earlier today when you wouldn't answer your phone."

Yet Logan had waited until this moment to inform her. "Why didn't you tell me that before?"

"Jack asked me not to," he said. "He thought I could get you to stop searching and come home. He must have given up on my powers of persuasion."

"Do you still think I should stop searching

for Mike?" She hadn't broached the subject in a few days.

Logan scratched his jaw. "I think we haven't moved off our conclusion that there isn't any more we can do until Caroline Webb gets a ransom demand."

It seemed to Maria that Logan was evading the question.

"You told Jack about the guy with the tattoo of a serpent on his arm," she said. "Don't you think that's a promising lead?"

Logan pressed his lips together, appearing deep in thought, as though he was debating something with himself. "There's something I need to tell you, something I just found out from Repeat."

"Repeat's here?" Maria scanned the party guests and caught sight of the older gentleman who'd provided the lead about the tattooed man. "What did he tell you?"

Logan shuffled his feet, then inhaled and exhaled. Even though he'd brought up the topic, he seemed reluctant to continue. "That tattoo Repeat saw... He remembered it was red."

The full name of Mike's favorite alternative rock band came to her in a flash: the Ruby Serpents.

"Mike's tattoo was red." Maria clutched at

Logan's arm, feeling excitement build in her. "That's further proof Mike is here in Key West."

"It's circumstantial evidence," Logan said. "It's not proof of anything."

She dropped her hand and shook her head. "Why do you find it so hard to believe?"

"Why do you find it so easy?" he countered.

Easy was the wrong word. Nothing about this quest to find out if her brother had really died on 9/11 was easy.

"Can't you at least entertain the notion that Mike might be alive?" Maria asked.

"If he's alive," Logan said slowly, "it would be a miracle."

"Christmas is the season of miracles," she countered.

Elvis Presley's distinctive voice drifted to where they stood at the edge of the yard. He was singing about how blue his Christmas would be without the woman in his life. On the back patio a few yards from them, some couples were slow dancing to the music.

Logan reached out a hand to her. "Dance with me?"

"Here?" she exclaimed. "In Kayla's mom's yard?"

He kept his hand outstretched. With the moon and the twinkling Christmas lights shining

down on his dark hair, he looked like temptation itself. "Why not?"

"The case." She chewed on her bottom lip.
"I feel like we're so close to solving it but so
far away."

"There's nothing we can do right now," he
pointed out.

But was that true? They'd pounded a lot of
pavement since arriving in Key West. They
could be out pounding more. Sometime in the
past few days, however, Maria had subcon-
sciously decided that canvassing Key West hoping to stumble across her brother or someone
who knew him was fruitless.

At the moment she wasn't sure whether she'd
arrived at the decision because it was the right
one or because so many things were getting in
the way of her investigation. Concern for Kayla.
The knowledge that her siblings wanted her to
suspend the search. But most of all, Logan.

"Come on," he cajoled. "Just one little dance."

"I'm not sure I can," she said. "I keep thinking I shouldn't be at a party enjoying myself
when Mike could be out there somewhere."

"If you like, I'll step on your toes while we're
dancing," Logan said. "Then you won't enjoy
it."

She tried to suppress the giggle she felt rising in her throat. It erupted, anyway, along with

a memory. "You stepped on my toes at senior prom without even trying."

"My mom's fault," Logan said. "I practiced with her for hours so you'd think I could dance."

"Really?" Maria hadn't known that. "Why was that important to you?"

"Are you kidding me?" He rolled his eyes. "I was a teenage boy in love with the most beautiful girl in school. I didn't want anything to ruin the night."

Yet the night had been ruined, not by Logan stepping on her toes but by Maria pressing for a decision about their future.

She'd known by then, of course, that he'd accepted his offer of admission from the University of Michigan. She'd been holding out hope that the prospect of living with her while attending art school in Louisville would be too much for Logan to resist. His love for her would win out and he'd withdraw his acceptance.

He'd told her on that long-ago prom night that he wasn't going to do that. She'd spent half the evening in the bathroom in tears.

They hadn't broken up that night but it had marked the beginning of the end.

"I've always wanted a do-over," he said, and she knew he was talking about much more than dancing. "Let me prove to you how much better I am now."

She simply wasn't strong enough to resist.

She placed her hand in his and he drew her close. The slight chill that had entered the air as the evening wore on immediately dissipated, replaced with an all-over warmth. Maria wasn't sure why, but the weight of disappointment she'd been carrying around over not finding Mike suddenly seemed lighter.

They swayed to the music, with Elvis still crooning about how blue his Christmas would be without the woman he loved.

"I shouldn't be trying to persuade you to go back to Kentucky," Logan whispered, his breath sending tiny shivers down her neck. "I get what Elvis is singing about."

Whenever they left Key West, they'd also be leaving each other. Maria would spend the holidays in Kentucky while Logan would be in New York City.

"You never told me what your boss said about you delaying your return," she said. "He couldn't have been happy."

"He wasn't," Logan confirmed, "but I'm happy right where I am."

He captured her lips and, at least for now, all her concerns melted away. She, too, was exactly where she wanted to be.

THE MEMBERS OF THE CHURCH choir raised their voices in song Sunday morning two days before Christmas, belting out a string of glorias in perfect harmony.

Kayla and her mother usually waited until the minister was all the way down the aisle before leaving church. Not today.

Her mom was home with a cold, something Kayla had discovered only when she swung by to pick her up. If she'd known earlier, Kayla would have skipped church so she could sleep and avoid embarrassment.

Throughout the service, she'd worried people would whisper that she was responsible for the photo in the newspaper of Devil Santa. Never mind that she'd arrived late and sat in the last row so she'd be less visible.

She'd failed in her attempt to save the merchants association from additional embarrassment, and today was the day she would suffer the consequences.

She darted out of the pew, for once wishing she'd worn flats instead of her signature high heels so she could move faster.

Nevertheless, she was one of the first people to leave the building. The church was only three or four blocks from home. She headed for the sidewalk, intent on making a quick getaway.

"Kayla! Wait up!"

The voice summoning her was male and familiar, although she couldn't quite place it. She slowed down, hid her grimace with a smile and turned to greet whoever was preventing her escape.

It was James Smith, the devil himself. She kept her forced smile, because that characterization wasn't fair. James had done nothing wrong. Kayla was the one who hadn't done her job satisfactorily.

"You sure got out of church fast," he said as he approached her. "I was sitting a few pews away and I almost didn't catch you."

He'd been seated near her? Kayla hadn't noticed him. She did now. He was dressed much the same as he'd been for his young cousin's play, in dress slacks and a lightweight shirt, with his hair combed back from his angular face. Jimbo aka James Smith was really quite something when he smiled, as he was doing now.

"I've been awake all night," Kayla said. "I need to go home and sleep."

"Still keeping watch on Santa?" he asked.

Kayla held up her smartphone, which she'd been checking at regular intervals throughout the service. "I haven't been fired. Yet, that is."

"James! Look what I drew!" A boy about six years old, with olive skin and dark hair, ran up to them. He thrust out a pamphlet that Kayla recognized as literature for children about the scriptures. On the back, the boy had drawn some sort of robot.

"It's a Transformer." He came close to James and pointed at the drawing. The boy's shirt had come untucked from his dress pants and one of his shoelaces was untied. "See how it has wings!"

"Cool," James said, "but should you have been drawing this in church?"

The boy thought for a moment. "Angels have wings, too. It can be a Transformer angel."

James laughed and ruffled the boy's hair. "Kayla, this is my cousin Manny. And those are his parents," he said, nodding at a young couple approaching them. Kayla had noticed them in church before. The woman, who had coloring similar to her son's, was long limbed and gorgeous. Her husband, several inches shorter than his wife, had a friendly, open face. "Silvana and Harry, this is Kayla."

"So nice to meet you!" Silvana exclaimed in a voice that was slightly accented. "James told us all about you."

He had? Kayla cast a glance at him. A faint red stain appeared on his cheeks. Was he blushing?

"We went to high school together." Kayla wasn't sure what else to say.

"James told us that," Harry said. "You'll have

to come over for dinner sometime, Kayla. Silvana is a wonderful cook."

"He's right," Silvana said with a laugh. "I'm not shy about admitting it, either."

The little boy suddenly took off, his destination unclear.

"Manny is done with grown-up talk," his mother said. "Gotta go. Nice meeting you, Kayla."

"Yes. Great to meet you," Harry said. "We look forward to seeing more of you."

The couple hustled off after their son. James grimaced, covered his face with his hands and peeked out at her. "Well, that sure was embarrassing."

She laughed. The church was emptying and people were having conversations all around them, but for some reason she couldn't take her eyes off James. He really was quite charming.

"I thought it was flattering," Kayla said.

He dropped his hands from his face. "You didn't mind?"

"No," she said, smiling at him. "I didn't mind."

"Hot damn!" he exclaimed, drawing some sharp looks from the people around him.

Trying not to laugh, Kayla put a finger to her lips. "Shhh. There are church children around."

"I'll try to do better," James said. "I can normally control what I say, unlike Silvana. She gives good advice, though. She's the one I asked about that photo of the Santa statue that ran in the newspaper today."

Kayla groaned and put up a hand. "Don't remind me."

His brows knit and his eyes narrowed. "Have you seen it?"

She released a heavy sigh. "I don't need to. I already know how Santa looks wearing devil horns."

"I really think you should take a look at it," James said. "I've got a copy of the paper in my car. Come on. I'll show you."

Kayla would have to look at the paper sooner or later. Grimacing, she followed James to a shady side street where he'd parallel parked his car, one of those eco-friendly hybrids. He unlocked the car remotely, pulled open the passenger door and took out a newspaper. He flipped to the second section and held it out to Kayla.

Just as she'd suspected, the statue of Santa was dressed in the tropical-print guayabera shirt with the sunglasses perched on his plaster nose.

However, he wasn't wearing devil horns.

Her eyes flew to James. She felt her mouth drop open. For a moment, she couldn't form words.

"I think Santa looks better in tropical wear," he said. "Don't you?"

She did, but that wasn't the issue. "I don't understand. Why didn't your editors run the other photo?"

"I didn't give them another photo," James said.

"Why not?"

He gave a low laugh. "Seriously? You think I'd blow my chance to get on your good side?"

She blinked at him as the depths of his feelings for her started to sink in.

"I know there's another guy in the picture," he said.

"Doesn't it bother you that I've got a thing for Alex?" she asked.

"Alex Suarez?"

Kayla almost clamped a hand over her mouth. Why had she blurted out his name like that? She was still working on getting the restaurant owner to think of her in a romantic light.

"Yes," Kayla said. Now that she'd brought it up, she could hardly backtrack.

"Alex Suarez is the guy you told me about?" James asked. "The one you said you had something going with?"

Kayla cleared her throat. "I might have exaggerated."

"You do know he's dating Vanessa King?"

Vanessa was the name of the woman who

was Alex's regular dart partner, the one Alex had claimed wasn't his girlfriend.

"How do you know that?" Kayla asked.

"I saw them together last night," James said. "And he brings her to our family get-togethers."

"You're related to Alex?"

"We're cousins. He and Silvana are brother and sister." James must have noted her puzzled expression. "You thought I was related to Harry, didn't you?"

Kayla nodded. "You don't look anything like Alex or Silvana."

"I should have said they're my stepcousins, although it's never felt that way. My parents got divorced when I was a kid. I use my real dad's name, but I was raised by my stepdad. He's Alex and Silvana's uncle."

The sun came out from behind a cloud and peeked through some trees, shining down with ferocious intensity. James took a pair of sunglasses from his shirt pocket and put them on. They had black frames and gray lenses, their aviator style reminiscent of the sunglasses Santa had been wearing. Only the ones the prankster had put on Santa had silver frames and black lenses, exactly like a pair Kayla had seen recently.

"Oh, my gosh," she exclaimed while suspicion dawned.

"What is it?" James asked.

"I think Maria was right about who's been messing with Santa."

THE SUNDAY MORNING SUN beat down on the park bench where Logan sat next to Maria in Mallory Square, illuminating the droop of her mouth and slope of her shoulders.

"I'd appreciate it if you didn't say I told you so," Maria said.

"Why would I do that?" Logan countered. "It was my suggestion to go back to those local breakfast spots."

They'd spent a fruitless morning popping in and out of restaurants, going table to table with the age-progression image of Mike and the new information that he had a tattoo of a ruby serpent on his left forearm. Logan had finally suggested they walk down to the harbor and take a break, which was how they'd ended up in Mallory Square. A fair number of people milled about, even though it was far less crowded than it was for the sunset celebrations.

"Yeah, but you didn't actually believe we'd hit pay dirt," she said. "You only suggested it because you know I need to be out doing something or I'll go crazy."

"Don't I get credit for figuring that out?" he asked.

"You'd get more credit if you actually believed we're going to find my brother." Her chin lifted and her voice gained confidence as she spoke. No matter what happened, Logan thought, she kept shaking off the disappointment and believing in the impossible.

Her fortitude was admirable, really. It was what had attracted him to her in the first place.

"Do you remember how we met?" he asked.

She seemed surprised by the question. "Certainly I remember. It was the summer before senior year when we were both counselors at that camp."

They'd gone to different high schools on opposite sides of Lexington, so it wasn't all that unusual that they hadn't run into each other before that point.

"Did I ever tell you when I fell for you?" he asked.

"It wasn't the first day of camp, I can tell you that much," she said. "I thought you were cute right off the bat. You didn't even notice me."

"Oh, I noticed you, all right," he said. "I just wasn't going to do anything about it."

"Why not?"

"Senior year was coming up, I was about to take the SATs and I was determined to get into a good business school," he said. "I couldn't let anything get in my way."

"What changed your mind?" she asked.

He smiled. "The Banana Olympics."

"I remember that," she said. "All the counselors had a team of kids who competed in these wacky relays. Holding a banana under their armpit and hopping on one foot down a field and back. Placing it between their knees and jumping."

"Yeah," Logan said. "That's right."

"But I don't get it," she said. "Why would the Banana Olympics change your mind about me?"

"Your kids were the least athletic," Logan said. "They came in last in every event by a mile. Yet you kept cheering them on, telling them they could get a win."

"They did get a win!" she said. "They won the last event. The banana roll!"

"Against all odds," he said. "You were jumping up and down and hugging all the kids. And that's when I stopped resisting you."

She tapped her knuckles against her lips. "I don't know what your point is, Logan."

"I'm not sure, either. The quality that lets you keep believing even when the odds are stacked against you drives me nuts sometimes, but it's what got to me in the first place." Something struck him that had never occurred to him before. "Maybe it's because I don't have that trait."

"You could develop it," she suggested.

She was right. Take the case of her brother, for example. Instead of continuing to insist Mike was dead, Logan could concede a chance existed that her brother had blown off work and seized the day to disappear.

He could entertain the possibility that Mike had sent Caroline Webb those nude photos, that Mike had made the telephone calls, that Mike was the man with the tattoo of the ruby serpent.

Who was Logan to tell Maria she was wrong to believe?

"The only way I could change," he said, "is if you were around to show me what's possible."

That was as close as he intended to come to the subject of the long-distance relationship. Her arguments of why it couldn't work made no sense to him. He hadn't given up on the idea, not by a long shot. His strategy was to show her that he could meet her halfway. That was the reason he'd suggested revisiting those breakfast spots.

He took it as a positive sign that Maria didn't discourage the inference of them being together after they left Key West.

Small steps, he thought.

"What do you want to do next?" He was all out of ideas.

"We need to get on a computer," she said. "Remember how we promised Kayla we'd look at the security camera recording from yesterday morning?"

With everything else that was going on, it had slipped his mind. "Should we go back to your hotel or mine?"

"Neither," she said. "There's an internet café a few blocks from here. We can rent a computer."

"Why would we do that when we both have laptops that work perfectly fine?"

"A couple of reasons," she said. "We need a bigger monitor so we can take in more detail on the screen."

"Makes sense," he said. "What's the other reason?"

"If we go back to a hotel room," she said with a wry twist of her mouth, "we'll probably end up in bed."

"I'm in favor of that," he said.

"I know you are." She should know. Making love to Maria after fantasizing about it since he was a teenager hadn't satisfied his craving for her. It had intensified it.

"What if I promise not to distract you?" he asked.

"You distract me by breathing," she said.

Logan took that as a good sign.

There was nothing distinctive about the internet café. Once inside, they could have been anywhere in the United States. Tables for patrons who'd brought their own computers were scattered throughout an open area. A young man with a shaved head and an earring in his nose stood behind a counter decorated with red bows and holly, selling coffee and snacks. Along the back wall was a row of six desktop computers. None of them were occupied.

After paying a fee and getting a password for internet access, Maria and Logan pulled up two chairs next to the computer with the largest monitor.

"Before we watch the surveillance recording, would you mind if I checked my email?" she asked. "I didn't get around to it this morning."

"Go ahead." He leaned back in his chair, intending to give her privacy while she read her messages.

"I've got an email from Caroline Webb," she exclaimed after a few seconds. She clicked through to it and was silent for a moment, presumably as she read. "Oh, my gosh!"

"What is it?" he asked.

"Listen to this." She read from the screen. "'If you find your brother, tell him to go to hell. I let Austin know about those photos. I'm no longer engaged.'"

"So Caroline's fiancé broke up with her because she'd be bad for his political career," Logan surmised.

"Looks that way," Maria said.

"If that news trickles back to whoever sent the photos, there won't be a ransom demand. There's no point anymore."

"Maybe Mike's already accomplished what he set out to." Maria sounded thoughtful. "He had it bad for Caroline, no matter how rotten she treated him. He might not have wanted anybody else to have her."

Logan remembered how heartbroken the teen had been when he'd arrived in New York. Logan had known his discontent was over a girl. He hadn't known how cruelly Caroline had treated Mike because he hadn't said a word against her. "That makes sense."

Maria started. "What? You mean you're willing to concede the person who contacted Caroline might have been Mike?"

"I think so," Logan said slowly.

She squeezed his hand, her expression tender. "Let's watch that surveillance video," she said. "Then maybe we can put our heads together and figure out how to get Mike to surface."

Maria explained how the security camera could transmit recorded surveillance material over the internet. Kayla had purchased a model with a higher image resolution, something that proved invaluable while they watched.

"This is great," Logan said. "I can see the faces of the people in each shot clearly. But what are we looking for, exactly?"

"I backed up the recording to about an hour before someone covered the camera," she said. "We're just supposed to look for anything out of the ordinary."

Even though Key West could be a wild place, it had been pretty tame that Friday morning. Most of the people who passed by the statue were nondescript except for a tourist wearing plaid shorts with a polka-dot shirt. He probably thought he matched, because both the shorts and the shirt were red and green, Christmas colors.

"Whoever covered the camera was probably careful not to come near the statue," Maria said. "I doubt we'll spot anything."

Not even a minute had passed when Maria stiffened, her entire body on alert. She leaned forward, putting her hand over the mouse. "I need to back up the recording."

She'd gone so white that Logan suspected the impossible had just become a reality. His heart hammered. She must have seen her brother passing by the statue.

Maria stopped the recording and then reversed it before letting it run forward again.

"There." She pressed a computer key that

froze the image. "Oh, my gosh. I was right. That is him."

Logan leaned forward to get a better look. A lean young man about six feet tall with brown hair was walking past Santa, his hands shoved in his pockets. Even though it had been years since he'd seen him, Logan recognized him, too.

"It's Billy Tillman." Maria supplied the name of Mike's best high school buddy, who she'd spoken to mere days ago. He evidently wasn't in California, as he'd claimed. "We need to have a talk with him."

"How will we find him?"

Maria pointed to the monitor. "See the monogram on the shirt he's wearing?"

Logan leaned closer to the computer until he could make out the stitching. "I'll be damned. Billy works at Alex Suarez's restaurant."

CHAPTER THIRTEEN

KAYLA PRESSED ON THE doorbell of the gorgeous two-story home on Stock Island, a pricey enclave within the city limits of Key West that boasted some of the area's only waterfront neighborhoods.

Evergreen wreaths with showy red bows hung from white balustrades, contrasting nicely with the house's pale yellow stucco. The landscaping was to die for, with colorful, fragrant flowers interspersed with green foliage.

Even the doorbell was fancy. It was shaped like a dolphin. Kayla pressed on it again and waited, tapping one of her feet. She was primed for a fight and now she might need to accept that nobody was home.

Except maybe that wasn't so. The showpiece of a house backed up to a quiet canal that led to both the Atlantic Ocean and the Gulf of Mexico. She'd bet anything there was a waterfront pool in the backyard and a private dock with a boat slip.

She circled around the house, navigating her

way through the lush landscaping. A gate separated the front yard from the back. It was unlocked. She swung open the gate and stepped through, finding exactly what she thought she would. The pool was tear-shaped and rimmed by lounge chairs with thick blue cushions. It was also empty.

The boat ramp wasn't.

Kayla squared her shoulders and walked determinedly on her high-heeled wedge sandals toward the man who was lifting a cooler onto a sleek motorboat that was at least twenty-four feet long.

Alex Suarez turned, straightened to his full height and watched her stride toward him. With his black hair, olive skin and long nose, he was undoubtedly a handsome man. Her heart gave one of those leaps it had been experiencing for the past two years whenever she spotted him.

"Stop it, heart," she muttered under her breath.

"Kayla," he called when she was close enough that he didn't have to shout. "What brings you here?"

She marched up to him and held out the sunglasses she'd taken off the Santa statue.

"I believe these belong to you," she said.

Alex made no move to take them. The sun overhead was bright, causing him to squint. Kayla own eyes were shaded by sunglasses.

"You must be mistaken." He sounded haughty, befitting their luxurious surroundings. The restaurant business had made him a wealthy man, she realized. Whatever she did, however, she couldn't let him intimidate her.

"I'm not wrong." She took a few steps closer to him and indicated the right lens of the glasses. "The pair you were wearing when you hired me had a scratch exactly like this."

"You sure about that?"

"Positive." She'd made some mistakes while learning the ropes of private investigation, but she was improving by the minute. She'd always been observant, a trait that would serve her well if her uncle Carl kept her on. "These are your sunglasses."

He said nothing, waiting for her to play her hand. It was time to go for broke, she thought. She raised herself to her full height.

"I know you're behind what's happening to Santa," she declared.

She heard him exhale before his neighbor a few docks down revved the engine of his boat. Two teenage girls ran to join him, their laughter and bright voices filling the silence. Kayla waited, refusing to lose the stare-down.

"Okay, you got me." He finally broke eye contact and the silence, his voice matter-of-fact. "But I'll deny it if anybody else accuses me."

Kayla caught her breath not because she was surprised but because she'd wanted to be wrong. The image she'd had of Alex for the past few years didn't jibe with what she now knew to be true.

"I don't understand," she said. "You're a member of the merchants association. Why would you pull those pranks?"

"You've seen the statue." He let out a short laugh. "It's commercialism at its worst, flying in the face of what Christmas is supposed to be about. I was trying to get the association to take it down."

"Couldn't you have just asked?"

Alex crossed his arms over his chest, stretching the material of his shirt. He had a surprisingly thin chest. James, who was several inches shorter, was built better. "I tried the diplomatic approach when we were discussing getting a statue commissioned. I even got another artist to present an alternative proposal. It didn't work."

Kayla remembered hearing that Alex had opposed the statue from the start. Heck, hadn't he told her that himself? She'd be more careful about checking all the angles in future. This case proved that sometimes the most obvious answer was the right one.

"You must have volunteered to handle things when the association decided to hire a private investigator," Kayla said, thinking aloud. "The better to throw suspicion off yourself."

He clapped three times. "Very good."

The wheels in Kayla's brain continued to turn. The Keys weren't teeming with private investigators, but every other P.I. she could think of had more experience than she did. A pelican was perched on a nearby post, seeming to listen in on their conversation. Even the pelican could have put this together.

"You knew my uncle Carl was out of town," she said with sudden insight. "You didn't think I could crack the case."

"Ah, I was hoping you wouldn't think of that," Alex said, seeming sheepish. "It doesn't sound good and I'm really not such a bad guy."

"You must have gotten worried when I called on Maria DiMarco for help," Kayla said.

"It turns out I should have been most worried about you. Was it only the sunglasses that gave me away?"

She shook her head. "I found out you and James Smith are cousins. You were tipping him off so he could get the photos. You even used a prepaid cell phone so the texts you sent him couldn't be tracked."

"Very good detective work," Alex said. "Like I said, it seems I underestimated you."

"Alex!" a melodic female voice called from

the direction of the house. Kayla turned to see a tall, stunning brunette walking toward them from the pool area. She wore short shorts that highlighted her long legs and a sleeveless top showcasing her large breasts. She stopped half-way down the dock. "Oh, sorry. I didn't mean to interrupt."

"Vanessa, this is Kayla," Alex said. "Kayla, Vanessa."

"Hi," Vanessa said with a friendly smile. "I thought I heard the doorbell when I was in the shower. Was that you?"

"That was me," Kayla verified.

"I just came out to say I need a few more minutes to get ready for our boat ride. Okay, Alex?" Vanessa asked.

"Take all the time you need," he told her with a smile.

"Thanks!" She blew him a kiss and hurried back toward the house. Her shorts were so brief they barely covered her rear end. Alex watched her go, a slight smile curving his lips.

"Vanessa is your girlfriend," Kayla stated.

Alex nodded. "That's right."

"Why did you tell me at the pub that she wasn't?"

"I did say that, didn't I?" Alex sucked in a breath. "I shouldn't have misled you. But I knew you had a little crush on me, and thought I might be able to use it to my advantage."

Kayla stifled a groan. How could she have been so stupid? "That's why you invited me to the pub."

"I was trying to figure out when you'd be watching Santa, so I knew when I could strike again," he said. "When you told me about the security camera, I had everything I needed to know. But first I emailed the merchants association about the camera so I wouldn't be the only suspect."

"You covered the camera," she stated.

"It was surprisingly simple to sneak upstairs at the souvenir shop," Alex said. "There were a lot of people inside and that clerk is easily distracted."

Kayla's stomach tightened. What Alex had done wasn't so awful in the great scheme of things. She even agreed with him about the tackiness of the Santa statue. However, if she couldn't get him to come clean, it would appear as though her investigation had failed.

"You'll really deny all this if I put it in a report?" Kayla asked.

"I really will." Alex smoothed an errant hair back from his handsome face. "I'll be sorry if your uncle doesn't keep you on. I like you, Kayla. I just like my position in Key West society more. One more thing. Under the circumstances, I'm sure you'll understand I have to fire you."

Kayla gave a short laugh.

"What's funny?" he asked.

"Remember that crush I had on you?" she asked.

He nodded.

"It's gone," she said before turning and leaving him on the dock.

It was nearly closing time when Maria and Logan got to the popular Cuban-American restaurant owned by Alex Suarez. Maria had wanted to confront Billy Tillman straight away, but Logan persuaded her it was best not to crash the kitchen when lunch hour was in full swing.

The wait had given Maria time to come up with a few possible scenarios.

"Billy could have known all along that Mike was alive," she said, speaking her leading theory aloud as they crossed the outdoor seating area. "He could be helping Mike get back at Caroline for the way she treated him."

"Let's not jump to conclusions," Logan said. "Let's just talk to Billy."

Maria nodded, knowing he was right. Since they'd spotted Mike's friend on the surveillance recording, Logan had been more clear-headed than her. He'd not only suggested waiting until the restaurant wasn't so busy, he'd verified that Billy Tillman was working today.

"I didn't even think about questioning the cooks about Mike the last time we were here," Maria mused.

"Why would you? Cooks don't usually come in contact with the customers," Logan said. "No way could you know Billy worked here."

"His mother doesn't even know. She told me he lived in California."

"Exactly." Logan squeezed her elbow gently as they reached the restaurant interior. "So stop beating yourself up over it. We'll know soon enough what's going on."

Logan was right. Maria could be minutes away from finding out what really happened to her brother on 9/11. She wiped her damp palms on the skirt of her sundress. A thousand butter-flies seemed to flutter in her stomach. Hope? Or dread?

As an investigator looking at the case from all sides, she'd been forced to concede that not all the possible scenarios had happy endings. She mentally stamped out the negative thoughts and chose to hope.

"Sorry, we're about to close." A smiling young waitress who hadn't been working the other day approached them.

"We're aware of that." Maria eyed a swinging door at the back of the place and pointed. "Your kitchen is through there, right?"

"Right." The waitress sounded perplexed.

"Thanks." Maria looked at Logan and indicated the kitchen with a jerk of her head. He nodded, receiving her silent message. When she headed straight for the kitchen door, he was with her.

"Hey, you can't go back there," the waitress called.

Maria ignored her, pushing the door open with an outstretched arm. The kitchen was spacious and modern, with stainless-steel appliances and gleaming white countertops. Three pairs of startled eyes flew to Maria and Logan. One of them belonged to Billy Tillman, who was beside the grill.

She read panic on his face before he dropped the spatula in his hand, turned and fled out the back door. Adrenaline surged in Maria like a tsunami. She gave chase, knocking aside a kitchen cart along the way. It clattered against a cabinet, a plate falling off and crashing to the floor.

"Hey! What's going on?" shouted a young kitchen worker in a hairnet.

Maria didn't take the time to explain. She followed Billy out the door and found herself in an alley. She looked left, then right, spotting him maybe twenty yards from the back of the restaurant.

"Hey! Stop!" she yelled.

Billy kept running. Maria dashed after him, her heart pounding at an even faster tempo than her feet.

"I just want to talk, Billy." She could barely get the words out as she ran. This was crazy. She knew he worked at the Daybreak Café so she could eventually track him down. Surely she could say something that would make him listen to reason. "I know where to find you."

Billy slowed noticeably, then came to a stop between a row of palm trees lining the fence of someone's backyard and the rear of a pale pink building that housed a retail shop. He bent over at the waist, gulping in air. She stopped, too. Within moments, Logan was upon them.

"Why did you run like that?" Maria demanded. She was breathing fast, too, but more from the adrenaline still coursing through her system than exertion.

Billy gazed up at her, trying to catch his breath. "I dunno. It was dumb, I guess. I wasn't thinking." His eyes shifted to Logan. "Logan? What are you doing here?"

"He's helping me," Maria answered for him. "We want to talk to you about Mike."

"Aw, hell," Billy exclaimed, standing up straighter and scrubbing a hand over his face. "This isn't the way I wanted things to go. I never thought Caroline would involve you."

Maria frowned. "So you know about the phone calls and the blackmail note?"

"Blackmail note? Hold up!" He put up a hand. "I wouldn't have asked for money. Not after I found out you were in town. You've gotta believe me."

"I'm not the police, Billy," Maria said. "All I'm interested in is the truth."

"Okay." His features contorted. "Here it is. The bitch doesn't deserve to marry a rich guy and live the high life, not after what she did to Mike."

Maria wanted to yell at Billy to skip ahead. She didn't care about Caroline. Her only concern was Mike. If Billy told the story at his own pace, however, she'd have a better understanding of the events of the past few weeks. She forced herself to decipher his comments.

"You were trying to stop the wedding," she observed.

"Hell, yeah," Billy said with gusto. "Caroline was the reason Mike dropped out of high school and went to New York. Why should she be happy?"

Maria had thought the same thing when Caroline stopped by her Lexington office and set the search for Mike in motion. "Caroline isn't happy. Her fiancé broke up with her after she told him about the photos."

"Great," Billy said. "That's all I wanted. I swear it."

A cold hand seemed to grip Maria's heart. Billy kept saying *I* instead of *we*. If Mike were alive, wouldn't he and Billy be in on this scheme together? They had to be collaborating, though. Maria still believed that Mike wouldn't have passed on those nude photos of Caroline. Not when he'd been angrier at Maria for interfering than at Caroline for breaking up with him.

"Where did you get those pictures, Billy?" Logan voiced the question that had stuck in Maria's throat.

Billy hugged himself and rubbed his upper arms, as though he was cold even though the temperature was in the low seventies. A chill swept through Maria as she waited for his answer.

"I found them in Mike's stuff." Billy looked at her with sad eyes. "Remember? I volunteered to help go through it."

In the dim recesses of her memory, Maria could picture Billy in the house when her family had undertaken the heartbreaking task of sorting through Mike's belongings. Her throat felt like it was closing up.

"I knew Mike had naked pictures of Caroline," Billy continued. "Your folks had been through enough. I didn't want them to find the photos and think less of him."

Logan edged closer to Maria and put an arm around her shoulders. She leaned into him, trying to prepare herself for the blow that was coming. Her throat was so clogged with emotion she didn't trust herself to speak.

"Do you have a tattoo on your left forearm, Billy?" Logan asked.

"Yeah." He seemed surprised by the question. He rolled up the sleeve of his shirt to reveal a ruby serpent. "Me and Mike got them together, for our favorite band."

Repeat had overheard Billy talking about the naked photos, not Mike. Billy, who must have known that Caroline sometimes called his friend by the hated nickname Mickey. The nickname was another reason Maria had convinced herself there was hope. She felt sick to her stomach.

"Mike wasn't in on this with you, was he?" Logan asked Billy. The question was barely audible above the traffic noises coming from the nearby street.

Billy shook his head, his eyes bleak. "I pretended to be Mike to fool Caroline. I didn't want to hurt Mike's family. I wouldn't have done it if I'd known it would go this far."

A sob caught in Maria's throat. The terrible truth was that Mike was truly gone. He'd died on 9/11 in the tragedy that had rocked not only the DiMarco family but the nation.

"This wasn't cool, Billy," Logan said, flint in his voice. "Your little stunt caused the wrong people a lot of pain."

"I didn't mean to," he said. "I should have come clean when Maria and I talked on the phone, but I was afraid."

Maria could barely see past the tears that had gathered in her eyes. Her knees felt as if they were giving way. Logan's arm tightened around her.

"So afraid you didn't even tell your mother you were in Key West so nobody could figure out you were behind the blackmail?" Logan countered.

"Hey, that's not the way it was," Billy protested. "My mom thinks I move around too much. And I mailed the second note about an hour before I talked to Maria on the phone. After that, I was done with all of it. I never wanted to hurt anyone. Especially you, Maria."

She could barely hold her tears at bay. Now she'd never get the chance to apologize to her brother and tell him how much she loved him. She'd have to live the rest of her life knowing that Mike had died resenting her.

But wait a minute. What had Billy just said? She cleared her throat and forced herself to ask for an explanation. "Why especially me?"

"Mike was close to his brother and both his sisters," Billy said. "But he told me all the time you were his favorite."

Maybe at one time she'd been Mike's favorite sibling. That hadn't been so at the time of his death. She shook her head.

"It's true," Billy said in response to her silent denial. "He even said you were right about Caroline."

Maria couldn't imagine how that could be so. The last time she'd seen her brother, before he'd stormed out of the house and went to New York, he'd vowed he'd never forgive her for wrecking his relationship.

"It was when I called him in New York," Billy continued. "He felt real bad about the things he said to you. He was gonna phone you and apologize."

The tears that Maria had been battling trickled down her face. Within moments, great gulping sobs racked her body. Logan immediately drew her into his arms, cradling her face against his chest.

"Just go," he told Billy.

Or at least that was what Maria thought Logan said. She couldn't hear past the roaring in her ears, the pain in her heart and the comfort she'd found in Billy's words.

Mike had died knowing she loved him.

Her brother had forgiven her.

CHAPTER FOURTEEN

KAYLA ROLLED BACK IN HER uncle Carl's comfortable desk chair and locked her hands behind her head. She'd spent the better part of an hour typing up a report on the investigation, and now she wasn't sure what to do with it.

Presenting the report to Alex Suarez was out. Even if he didn't tear it up, what kind of credibility would Kayla have with the rest of the merchants association? She hadn't only been fired, she was a rookie P.I. Not even a rookie, an apprentice.

She unhooked her hands and sat up straighter in the chair. Yeah, she was an apprentice. But she'd cracked the case and that had to count for something.

She rolled the chair back to the computer, saved her report in a word document and hit the print button. When she heard the soft whir of the printer waking up, she logged on to the internet.

She discovered the president of the merchants

association was Max Pinney, who owned a water excursion company on Key West Bight. Those places did big business on weekends, so chances were good that Max was working today. He might not listen to her, but by gosh she was going to talk. She could really blab, too. That was one of her talents.

One of her *many* talents.

She hopped out of the chair, grabbed the report from the printer and heard the chiming of the silver bells she'd attached to the front door. She must have forgotten to lock it.

"We're closed!" she called, coming around the corner to the front room.

A large, grizzled man in shorts, a Hawaiian shirt and sandals was crossing the office.

"Uncle Carl! What are you doing here?" Kayla had been under the impression he and his girlfriend would be gone until after Christmas.

"I was homesick for God's country," he said.

"That's the only reason you came home early?" Kayla ventured, careful not to say too much. "Because you missed Key West?"

"What? You think I had another reason?" He rubbed the side of his nose. "Like that my niece was working a case she didn't tell me about?"

The bottom seemed to drop out of Kayla's stomach. "How did you find out?"

"Doesn't matter who told me," he said. "What matters is why didn't you?"

"I can explain," she said in a rush. "I thought it was my chance to prove myself. I would have called you if I needed help but I had everything under control."

Barely stopping to take breaths, she told him the whole story, from enlisting Maria DiMarco's help, to setting up the security camera to getting a confession.

"The problem is Alex says he'll deny it." Kayla tapped the report she was holding. "I was about to go have a talk with Max Pinney. He's president of the association."

"Let's go." Uncle Carl rose. "I've been sitting around eating Christmas cookies and staring out the window at snow for days. I need some excitement."

Exciting wasn't a bad word choice for the Bight Marina. People strolled about, most of them either returning from a water excursion or embarking on one. The Bight was the place to rent a sailboat, take a boat tour or book a snorkeling or scuba trip. A person could do all of those and more at Wet and Wonderful, the business owned by Max Pinney.

"Carl Dexter, you son of a gun," Max called when they entered the small shop. He was probably in his mid-forties, with a deep tan that made his skin seem leathery. His T-shirt and baseball cap were both imprinted with the name of his shop. "You're not here investigatin' anything, are you?"

"I'm not," Carl said. "My niece Kayla is."

"Hey, Kayla," Max said. "I thought you sold bottle art."

"I'm giving private investigation a go." Kayla marched up to the cash register, digging deep for the confidence solving the case had given her. "Alex Suarez hired me on behalf of your association. He also fired me."

"I know," Max said.

"This is my report." Kayla laid the pages on the counter in front of Max with a resounding slap. "Alex was behind everything. He volunteered to hire an investigator precisely to deflect suspicion from himself."

"I know," Max repeated.

"He used inside information from the investigation to..." Kayla abruptly stopped talking when his replies registered. "You know?"

"That's right. I know what Alex has been doing to that Santa Claus. Can you believe his rationale? He didn't like the message Santa was sending." Max emitted a short, harsh laugh. "Give me a break. We're merchants. We're in the business of selling things. It's what we do!"

Kayla supposed he had a point, although the Christmas season was about so much more than material things.

"Alex was adamant that he'd deny everything," Kayla said. "I can't believe he told you what he did."

"He didn't tell me," Max said. "That newspaper photographer did."

Kayla gasped. "James Smith?"

"Yeah, that's his name. Nice guy. Just moved back to the area."

"What exactly did James tell you?" Kayla had called James after leaving his cousin's waterfront house to tell him Alex was the culprit.

"He said not to believe Alex if he denied responsibility, that Alex tipped him off whenever there was a photo op with Santa," Max said. "He was pretty insistent that you get credit for solving the case."

James had put her needs above those of his own cousin? Something softened inside her, but she couldn't bear it if she was responsible for driving a wedge between the relatives. She had to convince Max there were no villains in this scenario.

"Alex really isn't such a bad guy." Kayla repeated what the man himself had told her. Despite everything, she believed that. "What will happen to him?"

"He'll get a great big pat on the back," Max said. "I know it wasn't his intention, but the publicity has been wonderful!"

Kayla was seldom speechless. She was now.

"Tell me how much the merchants association owes for your services and I'll see that you're paid," Max said. "And if we're ever in need of a private eye again, we'll come to you."

"I appreciate that." Kayla cleared her throat. "Except I've been working on a trial basis. I'm not sure I still have a job."

"You bet you do!" Uncle Carl's voice filled the small shop. Until that moment, he'd been hanging back and letting her handle things. "I couldn't have done a better job myself."

Kayla squealed and crossed the shop to him, standing on tiptoe in an attempt to kiss his cheek. She was so short her lips didn't even reach his chin. She blew him a kiss instead.

"Whoa there, Kayla," Uncle Carl said. "I'm not the one you should be thanking."

She stepped back, not even trying to suppress the happiness bubbling inside her. "Oh, no? Who should I thank then?"

"James Smith," her uncle said. "He called me, too."

THE PIER AT HIGGS BEACH was a wooden structure that stretched perhaps one hundred yards into the sparkling blue water of the Atlantic Ocean. Maria wondered what she was doing, walking the length of it with Logan.

She'd been operating on autopilot since Billy Tillman's confession. Finally, after all this time, she'd been forced to face up to the fact that Mike was truly gone. The knowledge had slammed into her with such force that even her body felt battered. Behind her sunglasses, her eyes still felt sore and puffy.

"I need to call Caroline Webb and let her know the threat is over," Maria said, thinking aloud.

"Will you tell her who was behind it?" Logan asked.

She needed to think about that only for a few seconds to reach a decision. "I don't see what good that would do, especially since Billy didn't actually go through with the blackmail."

"There is that," Logan said. "You should let him stew a little over what kind of action you might take. He didn't break any laws, although he did wreck Caroline's relationship with her fiancé."

"I wish I could be more sympathetic toward Caroline. I mean, I don't believe adults should be judged on their actions in high school. And yet I don't feel very sorry for her." Maria shook her head. "What kind of a person does that make me?"

He put his hand on her shoulder and squeezed. "It makes you human."

She blinked back tears at his understanding.

"You okay?" Logan asked gently. He'd been nothing but kind since the events of the afternoon had unfolded. Whereas she probably would have gone back to her hotel room, he'd suggested taking a walk.

"I don't know yet if I'm okay," Maria said. "I'm still trying to process it all."

"I thought the fresh air would help. What better place to think than at the beach?"

He gestured to the shore. She stopped walking and looked where he indicated. Even though the setting was picturesque, with a fair number of people sunbathing and snorkeling, tourists didn't come to Key West for its beaches. Higgs Beach, for example, was a narrow strip with sharp rocks and washed-up seaweed near the shoreline.

It was undoubtedly pretty, though. The perfect backdrop for a romantic photo, like the one a young man and woman were posing for not far from the pier. He had his arms hooked at her waist and she was leaning against his chest while a photographer snapped away.

"Isn't that James Smith taking photos of that couple?" Maria squinted to get a better look. "Why, yes. It is James."

"He must do some freelance work on the side," Logan said.

The young woman turned in the man's arms to gaze up at him, appearing as though she was about to kiss him. James rose from his crouched position and repositioned the camera, then turned his head away from the couple as though something had distracted him. A petite blonde in bright clothing was rushing toward him across the sand.

"That's Kayla," Maria exclaimed.

Kayla paused a few feet from James, appearing to say something to him. Then she launched herself into his arms and kissed him.

"Well, I'll be damned," Logan drawled. "Didn't you tell me Kayla had a crush on Alex Suarez?"

"I have a feeling we've missed something." Maria approved of the latest development, though. Alex Suarez was much too suave and smooth for Kayla, who was the most genuine person Maria had ever met. The down-to-earth James was a much better match for her new friend.

"Whatever we missed, I think it was good,"

Logan said, echoing her thoughts. He indicated the rest of the pier with a sweep of his hand. "Shall we keep going?"

Maria nodded and strolled on, feeling some of the ice inside her—ice that had encased her heart since learning her brother was dead—begin to melt. Life went on, she thought. Yes, it was full of disappointment and heartache. But there was great potential for joy.

Only a few other people walked the pier. When she and Logan reached the end, where somebody had hung a Christmas wreath decorated with tropical flowers, they were alone. Beyond the structure, pelicans, seagulls and cormorants perched on top of wooden pilings left over from a previous incarnation of the pier. Much farther on, at the horizon, the blue of the sky collided with the deeper blue of the water.

The day and the setting couldn't have been more beautiful.

They both gazed out at the scene for long moments, listening to the calls of the seabirds, the song of the wind and the distant shouts of children back on shore.

"I'm sorry you didn't get your miracle," Logan finally said.

Was that true, though? Maria had spent so

many years harboring the mistaken belief that Mike had gone to his grave resenting her. With a single sentence, Billy had refuted that.

"Maybe I did get my miracle," she said. "You heard Billy. Mike knew right up to the end how much I loved him."

Her voice broke on the last words. Logan put an arm around her, pulling her close. She drew strength from his embrace. Suddenly, she couldn't bear it if guilt was eating away at him the way it had torn at her.

"Please tell me you're not still blaming yourself for convincing Mike to go to work that day," she said. "There was no way you could have predicted what would happen. None of us know what's around the corner."

"I understand that now, thanks to you," he said, kissing the top of her head. "You helped me to figure it out when we talked about it."

A warm feeling swept through her, so unexpected it took a while to figure out the healing process had begun.

"You know what?" she asked, twisting in his arms to gaze into his face. "Remember what you asked me before, about whether I was okay? I think I am."

"That's great," he said.

"Maybe it's because we're surrounded by so much beauty," Maria continued, "but I feel like I can think clearly for the first time in weeks."

"What are you thinking?" he prodded.

"That all we have is the here and now. My brother's life—and the lives of almost three thousand others—was cut short in an instant." She thought about Kayla, running up to James and flinging her arms around him. "The lesson we need to take from that is to live life to the fullest."

"How do you propose we do that?" Logan was staring at her, waiting for her to continue.

"We can't take the people we care about for granted," she said. "The connection between you and me, it's still strong. Time and distance couldn't weaken it."

"What are you saying?" he asked.

The realization burst inside her, so strong it must have been lying dormant for years.

"I love you!" she blurted out. "Oh, my gosh. I still love you."

"That's a very good thing," he said, his voice thick with emotion, "because I've never stopped loving you."

Emulating what Kayla had done to James on the beach, Maria threw her arms around Logan's neck and kissed him, laughing when their sunglasses bumped. He flipped hers back from her face and then raised his own, leaving the two of them free to explore each other's mouths.

The certainty of how she felt about him soared through Maria. She loved Logan Collier, completely and irrevocably.

Minutes later, she leaned back in his arms. "Let's not go to Kentucky or New York tomorrow morning. Let's fly to Vegas!"

"Vegas? Really?"

"We'll get a marriage license at one of those chapels," she said. "We can be married by Christmas."

Logan didn't answer immediately. A warning bell sounded in her head, but she ignored it. Things between her and Logan would be different this time. She'd make sure of it.

"What's the hurry?" he finally asked.

"If we get married right away," she said, "nothing will prevent us from being together, like it did the last time."

Logan's mouth opened, then closed. He stared at her and shook his head.

Her stomach dropped. It felt as if someone were gripping her heart and had started to squeeze.

Here we go again, she thought.

LOGAN WAS AFRAID that what he had to say wouldn't go over well. Maria had flipped her

sunglasses back down to cut the glare of the
sun shining on the water, but her body language
screamed at him to tread lightly. She looked as
if she were preparing herself for another blow.

He took both her hands in his. It was most
important that she know how he felt about her.

"I realized days ago that I loved you. Now I
know I never stopped." He hesitated, thinking
about how to express himself so she'd understand.

"But?" she pressed.

"But I have obligations in New York." He'd
already put the promotion he'd worked so hard
for in jeopardy by delaying his return to the city.
It was imperative that he be at the Christmas
Eve party at the Waldorf tomorrow. "I can't run
off to Las Vegas and get married."

"Okay. Maybe I was a little rash," she said.
He started to relax, relieved that she was willing
to listen to reason. The younger Maria hadn't
been as rational. "We don't have to go to Vegas
tonight or tomorrow. Anytime in the next month
would be good."

He was wrong. Maria hadn't changed. They
were having a variation of the same argument
that had broken them up.

"I think we should take things slower than
that," he ventured. "What's wrong with giving
a long-distance relationship a try?"

She yanked her hands out of his and took a step back from him.

"A try?" Her voice was so much louder than before that the seabirds on the closest posts flew off into the blue sky. She seemed to gather herself, because her next words were softer. "That sounds like you're hedging your bets in case things don't work out."

"C'mon, Maria," he said. "You know what kind of person I am. I don't jump into things."

"We were apart for fifteen years! How is that jumping into anything?" She shook her head, the movement pronounced. "If you really loved me, you'd take a chance on us."

"If you really loved *me,*" he countered, "you'd accept me for who I am instead of getting some crazy idea into your head and refusing to let it go."

She straightened her spine. "That's what you think I'm doing?"

"It's what you've always done," he said. "It's the same thing as with that art school in Louisville. I never understood why you thought that me deciding against that school meant I was deciding against you."

"Because you wouldn't take a chance!" Maria cried. "Because you can't open yourself to possibilities. Look how hard it was for you to even consider that Mike might be alive."

"Oh, but I did consider it," he said. "For a day or so, I let your optimism rub off on me. But he's not alive. Because there are no miracles. Not even at Christmas."

"Then how do you explain what Billy said? About Mike not blaming me?" Maria asked.

"I'm glad you got closure, Maria," Logan told her. "I understand how hard it was to know your last words to Mike were angry ones. But just because a brother and sister argue, it doesn't mean the love goes away. Of course Mike knew you loved him."

"Well, I think it was a miracle," Maria refuted. "The Christmas season is full of them."

"You also think you'll get what you want by wishing on a shooting star," Logan said, then could have kicked himself for not keeping that to himself. He had no doubt she'd wished for Mike to be alive. "I wanted you to have your miracle, Maria. But if you were a bit more practical, you wouldn't get hurt so much."

"How's this for practical?" Her voice was strong, but her lips were trembling. "I've accepted things will never work out with us."

She whirled, turning away from the beautiful vista of sea and sky and walking blindly back toward shore. Water slapped against the pier and a bird cried overhead, the sound plaintive.

Logan opened his mouth to call her back. He could try to convince her that everything would work out between them if she compromised just a little, that he wanted to be with her forever.

In the end, though, he let her go. She'd had an emotional day. He needed to give her time to calm down so she was more apt to listen to logic.

Logan stood alone on the pier, watching the distance between himself and Maria grow with every step she took.

"I CAN'T BELIEVE YOU'RE leaving," Kayla exclaimed with all the fervor Maria had come to expect from her. The younger P.I. had expressed the same sentiment a half dozen times on the drive from Maria's hotel to the airport.

Maria had gotten a call on her cell from Kayla minutes after discovering she could fly out of Key West at six that night. The last-minute flight cost more, but she was so eager to leave that she'd booked it immediately. Since she'd turned in her rental car days ago, she readily accepted Kayla's offer to drive her to the airport and fill her in on what had happened with her case.

"There's no more reason for me to stay," Maria said. "I told you how Billy Tillman was pretending to be Mike."

They were inside the terminal between the airline counter, where Maria had checked her baggage, and the security checkpoint. People passed them on both sides, most toting carry-on baggage. Nobody seemed to be in a rush, as though the easygoing Key West spirit had spread to the airport.

"What about Mr. Tall, Dark and Dishy?" Kayla covered her mouth with a hand and looked over at James Smith. Maria wasn't terribly surprised that her friend had shown up to drive her to the airport with James in tow, considering the kiss she'd witnessed on the beach.

"Sorry, Jimmy," Kayla said. "Nothing to worry about, though. Logan and Maria have something hot and heavy going on."

"I'm not worried." James slung an arm around Kayla, who grinned up at him. His answering smile transformed him from average-looking to something special in a heartbeat. Then he dipped his head and kissed her sweetly on the lips.

James was perfect for Kayla, Maria thought. Their relationship was in its infancy, but she could already tell it would be a lasting one. Unlike her own with Logan. She blinked back the sudden moisture in her eyes.

"Logan and I don't have anything going on.

Not anymore." She had to choke out the words. "It's over between us."

"Are you sure?" Kayla's big, guileless eyes got even larger. "Did you even tell him you're leaving?"

"No."

"Why not?" Kayla asked. "You know he wouldn't let you go!"

Maria thought of her long walk down the pier and back to the hotel earlier that afternoon. She'd waited in vain for Logan to come after her and say that of course he was willing to take a chance on them, that their love was worth every risk.

"You're wrong," she said. "He wouldn't try to stop me."

"I don't believe that for a second," Kayla insisted. Her denial was to be expected. She was in a brand-new relationship brimming with promise. It was perfectly natural that she would believe in the all-consuming power of love.

"Can we drop the subject?" Maria's smile felt tight. "I only have a few minutes before I need to go."

She had been advised by the ticket agent to arrive at the airport early for additional screening, because she'd purchased a one-way ticket, an extra security measure that stemmed from 9/11. Strangely, though, Maria was not a nervous flyer. What had happened on 9/11 was an anomaly, the likes of which she had to believe would never be repeated.

"You haven't even finished telling me about what happened with the case," Maria pointed out.

Kayla had already filled her in about why she'd kissed James at the beach. Not only had the photographer gone to bat for Kayla with the president of the merchants association, he'd also called her uncle. James had made sure both men knew they should believe Kayla over Alex, his own cousin.

"You know how I told you Alex has a girl-friend?" Kayla asked.

"Vanessa, right?"

"Yes. She's an absolute sweetheart," Kayla said. "Turns out she thinks one of her employees is stealing from the beauty salon she owns. She called a short while ago and hired me to look into it."

"Alex recommended Kayla," James said, his voice full of what sounded like pride. "He knows the stunt he tried to pull on Kayla was bogus. Dude is already trying to make amends."

"Vanessa wants me to go undercover!" Kayla added. "Isn't that cool?"

"Very cool," Maria said, "but can you cut hair?"

"No, but I can wash hair. I'm going to be the shampoo girl!" Kayla grinned. "A very well-paid shampoo girl."

"If you need someone to bounce ideas off when you're working the case, you have my number," Maria said.

"Thanks! You're the greatest."

"You're not so bad, either," Maria said. "Just remember to believe in yourself."

Kayla nodded, blinking rapidly. "Oh, Maria! We have to keep in touch! I'm going to miss you so much." Kayla hugged her, holding tight for several minutes.

Maria hugged her back, realizing that she was going to miss her young friend, too. They both were blinking back tears when they drew apart.

"I wish you were staying, too." James came forward and also hugged Maria, though briefly. "Any friend of Kayla's is a friend of mine."

James really was one of the good guys, Maria thought.

"Promise you'll come back and visit," Kayla insisted. "You and Logan could even make it a Christmas tradition."

"I told you, Kayla," Maria said. "There is no more Logan and me."

Kayla pursed her lips, claimed the arm of her new boyfriend and said, "We'll see."

If Kayla truly believed things would work

out between Maria and Logan, it seemed the younger woman was another one who believed in miracles.

Too bad the man Maria loved—the man she was afraid she'd always love—didn't.

CHAPTER FIFTEEN

MARIA HAD CHECKED OUT of the hotel.

Logan stood at the front desk of the Blue Tropics, angry at himself for missing her. He'd returned to his hotel room after their heated talk on the pier and made the mistake of catching up on email. How could he have overlooked the possibility that Maria would leave Key West sooner rather than later?

He'd suspected Maria was gone after getting no answer either on her cell phone or at her hotel room door. The front desk clerk had just confirmed it.

"Anything else I can help you with?" The clerk had prematurely gray hair he wore loose to his shoulders. He flipped it back. "We've got some rooms available if that's what you're wanting."

"No, thanks." Logan shook himself out of his stupor. "That's all I needed."

"Okay, then." The man smiled. "You have yourself a happy holiday."

"You, too," Logan said.

A happy holiday? Was that even possible? he wondered as he turned away. He'd be in New York City for Christmas, while the woman he loved would be seven hundred miles away, in Kentucky.

The lobby door swung open and Kayla breezed through, infusing the lobby with a mix of energy and purpose.

Logan looked behind her, hoping Maria was with her. Nobody else came through the door.

"Logan!" Kayla hurried over to him. He'd noticed she didn't do anything at half speed. "What are you doing here?"

"Looking for Maria," he said. "Have you—"

"I knew it! I told that girl you'd try to stop her from leaving Key West. But would she listen to me? No."

Logan focused on the key point in her torrent of words. "Can I still catch her?"

"Her plane left probably an hour ago," answered Kayla. "I can't even imagine how much her ticket cost, booking it at the last minute like that. She was in a real hurry to get out of town."

To get away from him, Logan thought.

Kayla held up one of the large, old-fashioned keys the hotel issued its guests. "She took the key by mistake and asked me to run it by the hotel. Can you believe this place still uses these things? Wait till I text her and tell her I ran into you. Then she'll know I was right."

Logan tried to keep up with Kayla's lightning-fast change of subjects. "You mean you were right about me trying to stop her from leaving?"

"Yes! That's what you would have done, isn't it?" Kayla gestured at him with the big key. "I knew things weren't over between you and her."

"She said things were over?" Logan asked.

"She most certainly did," Kayla declared.

That wasn't good. Logan wasn't ready to give up on Maria. Maybe he never would be. He'd have to come up with some strong arguments to persuade her why a long-distance relationship was infinitely preferable to going their separate ways.

"She hardly listened to my suggestion about you and her coming to Key West every year in Christmas week," Kayla said. "That might be getting ahead of things, though. You've got some work to do to get Maria to understand where you're coming from."

"I do," he agreed.

"Good," she said with a sharp nod of her head. "So are you headed to the airport?"

He might as well go there. If he could get a flight out today, he'd definitely arrive in time for that party at the Waldorf. The thought was depressing.

He'd spend Christmas Eve with clients instead of the woman he loved.

"I sure hope it works out between you two." Kayla held up the key again. "I've gotta return this. James is waiting in the car. We're going to his cousin's house for dinner."

That sounded nice. Logan's own parents would have loved to spend the holidays with him and the woman he loved, but they were cruising the Caribbean. Not because they needed to take expensive trips to be happy, but because Logan had insisted.

He'd never heard his parents complain about not making enough money to enjoy the finer things in life, the things that Logan had been working so hard to afford these past eleven years.

All his parents had ever needed, he realized, was each other. And possibly him.

"Merry Christmas, Logan," Kayla said, oblivious to the thoughts that were crowding his head.

"Merry Christmas, Kayla."

She walked to the counter, her step even bouncier than usual. Because it was Christmas and she was in love.

Logan was in love, too.

The question was, what was he going to do about it?

MARIA BARELY CALLED OUT a greeting and shrugged off her coat before Jack barreled into the living room and wrapped her in a bear hug.

"You're back!" her brother said, lifting her clear off the floor.

"Put me down!" she ordered. For the first time in more than twenty-four hours, however, she cracked a smile.

"Not until you say, 'Jack knows best,'" he retorted, just as she'd known he would. Never mind that they were both in their early thirties. He'd been greeting her this way since she'd told him—okay, nagged him—not to aggravate his shoulder by lifting heavy things.

"No way am I saying that," she teased.

He spun her around once. The rat knew going in circles made her dizzy. He started to do it a second time.

"Okay! Okay!" she said. "Jack knows best."

He put her down, gave her the full wattage of the grin that made him look as handsome as sin, and punched her lightly on the arm.

"Seriously, sis. I'm glad you're here." His statement carried an air of sincerity. She'd already filled him in over the phone about Billy Tillman posing as Mike.

She nodded, not quite able to respond that she was glad to be here. Her emotions were too jumbled, although she supposed it didn't make sense for her to be anywhere else. Her family spent every Christmas Eve and Christmas Day together.

Maria spotted Jack's girlfriend behind him. Her brother had fallen in love with Tara Greer last summer, when he'd been recuperating from his shoulder injury on the Eastern Shore of Virginia. They'd met, ironically, because Maria had asked Jack to run down a lead on a missing person's case she'd been working.

"Tara," Maria said by way of greeting. "I've asked you this before and I'll ask it again. Are you sure you're willing to keep putting up with my little brother?"

"Positive." Tara laughed and came forward to give her a hug. "I'm glad you're home, too."

"Where's Logan?" Jack asked. "I thought he'd be with you."

"You thought wrong." Maria ignored the pang in her heart and changed the subject. "Let me guess. Annalise and her family are in the game room. And Mom and Dad are in the kitchen."

Jack crossed his arms over his chest. "I take it you're not going to tell us what happened with you and Logan?"

"There is no me and Logan." Maria pointed to the kitchen. "I'm going to say hi to Mom and Dad."

"You do that," Jack said, apparently giving up on the topic of Logan. "Just know that you enter at your own risk."

Maria didn't need to ask what he meant. Their parents prepared an extravagant Christmas Eve meal every year and kept the menu a surprise.

"Want us to put those under the tree for you?" Tara gestured at the bag of presents Maria had brought with her. She'd picked up most of them at airport gift shops.

"That would be great. Thanks." She followed the delicious scent of what she guessed was a seafood dish into her parents' spacious kitchen. They both were at the stove with their backs to her, working away.

"Merry Christmas, Mom and Dad." Maria made her lips curve into a smile she knew wasn't reflected in her eyes.

They turned from the stove in unison, blocking her sight of the burners with their bodies. Her father wore the same red-and-green-checked sweater he put on every Christmas Eve. Her mother was dressed head to toe in red. Even her cheeks were flushed.

"Welcome home, darling!" she intoned. With her slim build, thick brown hair and virtually unlined face, she looked a decade younger than her fifty-five years. "Did everything go okay with your case?"

"What kind of case is so important you had to go out of town at Christmas?" Her dad was a few years older than her mom but just as fit. He had the same black hair and blue eyes as Maria. He also had a tendency to grumble.

"You heard Annalise," her mother told him in a slightly scolding tone. "Maria can't talk about the case. Her client demanded discretion."

So that was how Annalise had explained her absence in order to shield them from the knowledge that Maria was looking for Mike. Maria was grateful to her sister for not resurrecting their pain.

"What's important is that you're here now." Her mother craned her neck to see past her. "Is Logan with you? Annalise said he was helping you on your case."

Maria closed her eyes briefly. First Jack, now her mother. Annalise, it seemed, hadn't been entirely discreet with the information she'd relayed.

"No, Logan isn't with me," Maria said. "I'm pretty sure he's back in New York by now."

Her mom frowned. "Then you two aren't getting back together?"

"Celeste…!" Now her father sounded chastising. "You said you wouldn't bombard her with questions."

"I can't help it," her mother said. "I was so hoping they'd work things out."

"Hey, Maria. How about you scram?" Her dad made a shooing motion with his hand. She got the impression he wanted to cut off her mother's nosy questions as much as he wanted her out of the kitchen. "We're cooking up a surprise in here."

She went willingly, following the raucous sound of what was decidedly not Christmas music to the basement game room. Annalise's husband and two sons were gathered around a television displaying a video game. The older of Maria's nephews, fifteen-year-old Ryan, strummed a plastic guitar. His younger brother, Bart, pounded a set of drums that were a cross between a toy and the real thing. Scott, Maria's brother-in-law, was singing.

"Hey, Aunt Maria!" Ryan called to her over the amateur band music. "Isn't it cool that we can play rock band? We got an early Christmas present."

Scott turned to Maria, belting out a line from a rock song—was it a Van Halen tune?—in perfect disharmony.

Annalise stood off to the side, watching her family. She covered her ears and made a face, then gestured for Maria to accompany her to the opposite side of the room.

When they were away from the worst of the noise, Annalise hugged Maria. She held on tight the way she used to when they were kids and Maria was upset about something. Maria clung to her big sister.

"You looked like you needed that," Annalise said when they drew apart. "You barely cracked a smile at Scott's horrible singing."

"I guess I've had a tough couple days," Maria said.

Annalise nodded. "I'm glad Logan was in Key West with you. Is he upstairs?"

"Why does everybody think we're together?" Maria glowered at her. "And by the way, thanks so much for telling Mom he was with me in Florida."

"Hey, there are only so many secrets I can keep," Annalise retorted. "Besides, Mom and I have been hoping for years that you and Logan would get back together."

"Not gonna happen." Maria tried to sound flippant. Instead, her voice shook. She cleared her throat. "If I seem sad, it's because of what I found out about Mike."

Even as Maria uttered the sentence, she knew it wasn't entirely accurate. Yes, it hurt to know her younger brother was irrevocably gone. But it also hurt to know Logan was in New York when he could have chosen to spend Christmas with her.

"You really thought Mike might be alive?" Annalise asked.

Maria nodded. "I really did."

"I didn't. Not even for a second." Annalise looked over to where the males in her family were attempting to perform another rock song, then back at Maria. "When the North Tower fell, it was like I could feel Mike's spirit leave. I've had years to come to terms with his death."

Maria reached for her sister's hand and squeezed it. "Why did you never tell me that before?"

Annalise shrugged. "I guess because I was afraid you might think it sounded silly."

"No sillier than believing the wishes I made on shooting stars would come true," Maria said wryly.

"That's what Mom always claims," Annalise said. "But I didn't know you'd seen a shooting star."

"Two of them," Maria told her. "The first outside my office and the second when I was in Key West with Logan."

"And you wished the same thing both times?" Maria nodded.

"Let me guess." Annalise's voice was so quiet

Maria could barely hear it over the rock song. "You wished for Mike to be alive."

That made sense. Maria had spotted the first shooting star shortly after Caroline Webb had visited her office and told her about the strange phone calls and letter.

Except Maria hadn't wished for Mike to be alive. Not exactly. She'd formulated her wish in much broader terms.

Maria had believed it hadn't come true when the search for Mike ended badly.

But maybe it had.

The band played on, the beat of the drums reverberating inside Maria. Her mother often said all things happened for a reason. Maybe there had been a compelling reason for Maria to be drawn into the drama with Caroline Webb and Billy Tillman.

"What are you thinking about?" her sister asked gently.

"About Logan." Maria figured she might as well confide in Annalise. Her sister would get the information out of her eventually, anyway. "I wanted to run away to Vegas and get married. He wanted a long-distance relationship."

"Then why did you say things were over between you?"

"Because I told Logan they were," Maria said. "I was angry that he wouldn't take a chance on us, just like he wouldn't the first time we broke up."

"Oh, really? Logan wouldn't take a chance?" Annalise put emphasis on his name.

Understanding dawned on Maria like a Key West sunrise. "I wouldn't take a chance, either. I could have offered to move to New York to be with him."

"You could have," Annalise agreed.

"Oh, my gosh. How could I have let him go a second time?" Maria brought both hands to her cheeks.

Her mind raced. If she got a flight out tonight, she could spend Christmas with Logan. That is, if he forgave her for being bullheaded. She would max out her credit card paying for another last-minute flight, but that didn't matter. All that mattered was Logan. "I've gotta go."

She dashed away from her sister and past her brother-in-law and nephews. Then she grabbed the handrail and pounded up the steps.

"Who's running on the stairs?" her father shouted. "It sounds like an earthquake."

Maria kept moving. Her parents' computer was upstairs in their office. A doorbell rang. She headed for the staircase to the second floor and started climbing, vaguely aware that somebody, probably Jack, had answered the door.

It was strange to get a visitor on Christmas Eve. At another time, Maria would be curious as to who it was. Not tonight. Her entire focus was on getting to a computer to check airline flights.

She'd reached the halfway point when she heard the visitor greet Jack. She froze.

It was Logan.

MARIA KEPT PERFECTLY still in the stairwell, straining to hear what Logan might say next. Why was he here in Lexington instead of in New York City? Dare she hope he'd come for her?

The rush of blood in her ears was so loud, Maria was afraid she might miss his next words.

"Forget this," she muttered, dashing down the steps and hurrying to the entryway.

Logan was in the process of following Jack and Tara into the living room.

"Logan!" she called.

He turned, his eyes crinkling in a smile. A burgundy sweater that made his brown hair appear burnished peeked out from the collar of his black jacket. He did look tall, dark and dishy.

Above his head, in the archway between the foyer and the living room, dangled a sprig of mistletoe. Perfect!

Maria closed the distance between them, threw her arms around his neck and kissed him.

The feeling that swept through her was electric, as though somebody had switched on an entire bank of Christmas lights. She'd kissed Logan mere days ago, yet it felt as though it had been years, maybe because she'd feared she would never be this close to him again. His arms came around her and his mouth captured hers until she felt as dizzy as when Jack had spun her around.

Finally, Logan lifted his head and smiled into her eyes. "What was that for?"

"I was taking a chance," she said.

"Oh, no." Logan shook his head. He smelled great. "You're always taking chances. It's my turn."

"What are you talking about?" she asked.

"You'll see." He stepped back and turned her toward the front door. "But first we're gonna have to go outside."

Logan stopped at the closet to pull out her coat and chose the right one on the first try. While helping her into her black pea coat, he said, "We'll be back in a bit."

It took Maria a moment to realize he was talking to Jack and Tara, who'd witnessed their embrace. Maria had completely forgotten about them.

"And here I thought there was nothing going on between you and Logan," Jack quipped.

Maria was so focused on what Logan might say she didn't even have the presence of mind to reply to her brother.

The temperature outside was probably in the low forties, but it felt frosty after the tropical weather in Key West. The moon shone down on the neighborhood, adding more light to the houses decorated for Christmas. Stars sparkled in the night sky.

Logan kept hold of her hand, walking with her halfway down the sidewalk before stopping.

"Are you going to tell me what's going on?" she asked breathlessly. Her pulse was skittering, she wasn't sure whether from being near him or from anticipation over what he might say or do.

"I'm going to do something I should have done in Key West." He gave a little laugh. "No, way before that. I should have done this years and years ago."

He reached into the pocket of his jacket, pulled out a black velvet box and snapped it open. Inside was a pear-shaped diamond nestled between two light green gemstones in a white-gold setting.

Maria gasped and covered her mouth with her hands, her heart beating triple time.

"I've loved you for a very long time, Maria

DiMarco," he said, looking deeply into her eyes. "Will you marry me?"

Her eyes filled with tears and her throat clogged with emotion. His proposal was so unexpected she literally couldn't speak. Long moments passed with neither of them saying a word.

"This wouldn't be a long-distance marriage," Logan said hurriedly, his forehead wrinkling in consternation. "I already gave notice at my job. I'm moving back to Kentucky. I'm even going to start painting again. I can be the man you've always wanted me to be. I—"

Maria placed three fingers against his lips, stopping the spate of words.

"Yes!" She forced the reply from her throat, the word coming out louder than she'd intended. She punctuated her acceptance with a nod. "Yes! I'll marry you."

The lines on his forehead smoothed. He grinned and swept her up in a kiss every bit as fervent as the one they'd shared inside the house. When they came up for air, he took the ring from the black velvet box and slid it onto her finger. His hands weren't entirely steady, which Maria found endearing.

"I wanted to get you something with a Key West feel, since that's where we fell in love again," he said. "Those green stones are the color of key lime. They're called peridot."

"I love the ring." She held out her hand to gaze at the diamond set off by the lime-colored gemstones. Blinking back happy tears, she lifted her gaze to his face. "Don't take this the wrong way, but can you get your job back?"

"Why would I want my job back?"

"Because I can move to New York City," she answered. Oh, man. She really would move away from her beloved Kentucky. For Logan.

"I love you for making the offer," Logan said, "but it's better if I move home. I'll even have a job. A friend of mine has been trying to get me to work at his financial firm for years."

"Were you considering it before now?"

He shook his head. "I didn't think it stacked up to my job in New York. But you know what? Until these last few weeks, I had my priorities all wrong. I should have taken a page from my parents' book. Life away from work is what's important. And you're the most important thing in my life."

Maria lifted a hand and traced his cheek. "I won't let you forget that."

His hold on her tightened. "Believe me, I won't. In fact, if you still want to go to Vegas and get married, I'm game."

She needed to think about that only for an instant. "I've changed my mind. I'd like to wait, so our friends and family can see us get married."

"You mean, like they've seen us get engaged?" He nodded toward her parents' house.

Crowded around the two windows in the living room was Maria's entire family. She even picked out her two teenage nephews. Annalise and Jack were giving her a thumbs-up, her mother's smile was ear to ear and her father seemed to be whistling.

Suddenly embarrassed, Maria buried her face against Logan's shoulder. He laughed.

"It's okay with me if we wait to get married," Logan said. "Your wish is my command. That's why I wanted to propose out here. I thought we might see another shooting star."

"I thought you didn't believe in things like miracles and wishes coming true," she said.

"With you in my arms, I could be persuaded into changing my way of thinking," he said. "But I'm sorry the wish you made on those shooting stars didn't come true."

"Oh, but it did."

"What?" His brows lifted toward his hairline. "Didn't you wish that you'd find Mike?"

"Not exactly," Maria said. "I wished for a second chance. And that's what I got. With you."

"A second chance. I like the sound of that." He lowered his head to hers, with her family still watching, and the stars and the Christmas lights sparkling all around them, as bright as their future promised to be.

* * * * *

The series you love are now available in

LARGER PRINT!

The books are complete and unabridged—
printed in a larger type size to make it
easier on your eyes.

❖ Harlequin® *Romance*

From the Heart, For the Heart

❖ Harlequin®
INTRIGUE
BREATHTAKING ROMANTIC SUSPENSE

❖ Harlequin® *Presents®*

Seduction and Passion Guaranteed!

❖ Harlequin® *Super Romance®*

Exciting, emotional, unexpected!

Try **LARGER PRINT** today!

Visit: www.ReaderService.com
Call: 1-800-873-8635

❖ Harlequin®

 A *Romance* FOR EVERY MOOD™

www.ReaderService.com

HLPDIR11

FAMOUS FAMILIES

YES! Please send me the *Famous Families* collection featuring the Fortunes, the Bravos, the McCabes and the Cavanaughs. This collection will begin with 3 FREE BOOKS and 2 FREE GIFTS in my very first shipment— and more valuable free gifts will follow! My books will arrive in 8 monthly shipments until I have the entire 51-book *Famous Families* collection. I will receive 2-3 free books in each shipment and I will pay just $4.49 U.S./$5.39 CDN for each of the other 4 books in each shipment, plus $2.99 for shipping and handling.* If I decide to keep the entire collection, I'll only have paid for 32 books because 19 books are free. I understand that accepting the 3 free books and gifts places me under no obligation to buy anything. I can always return a shipment and cancel at any time. My free books and gifts are mine to keep no matter what I decide.

268 HCN 0387   468 HCN 0387

Name	(PLEASE PRINT)	
Address		Apt. #
City	State/Prov.	Zip/Postal Code

Signature (if under 18, a parent or guardian must sign)

Mail to the **Reader Service**:
IN U.S.A.: P.O. Box 1867, Buffalo, NY 14240-1867
IN CANADA: P.O. Box 609, Fort Erie, Ontario L2A 5X3

* Terms and prices subject to change without notice. Prices do not include applicable taxes. Sales tax applicable in N.Y. Canadian residents will be charged applicable taxes. This offer is limited to one order per household. All orders subject to approval. Credit or debit balances in a customer's account(s) may be offset by any other outstanding balance owed by or to the customer. Please allow 4 to 6 weeks for delivery. Offer available while quantities last. Offer not available to Quebec residents.

Your Privacy— The Reader Service is committed to protecting your privacy. Our Privacy Policy is available online at www.ReaderService.com or upon request from the Reader Service.
We make a portion of our mailing list available to reputable third parties that offer products we believe may interest you. If you prefer that we not exchange your name with third parties, or if you wish to clarify or modify your communication preferences, please visit us at www.ReaderService.com/consumerschoice or write to us at Reader Service Preference Service, P.O. Box 9062, Buffalo, NY 14269. Include your complete name and address.

ReaderService.com

Manage your account online!

- Review your order history
- Manage your payments
- Update your address

*We've designed
the Reader Service website
just for you.*

Enjoy all the features!

- Reader excerpts from any series
- Respond to mailings and special monthly offers
- Discover new series available to you
- Browse the Bonus Bucks catalogue
- Share your feedback

Visit us at:

ReaderService.com